HENDERSON
MANOR

EMMA L.
CLAPPERTON

*This book is dedicated to Alexander Clapperton
and Elaine Clapperton.*

Just a quick thank you to those who have once again helped me with Henderson Manor. Chris, your patience is amazing. Lee Brook for your technical support. Noelle Holten and Mark Harkin for your kind but thorough and honest advice. Casey Kelleher, Denzil Meyrick, Stephen Edger, Mel Sherratt and other fellow authors who have offered advice and help along the way. Mum, Dad, Gran and everyone else who has supported me in my work as an author. Just because your name is not here doesn't mean you have been forgotten about.

Thank you all.

CONTENTS

PROLOGUE
(3RD MAY 1950)

George Henderson stood by the grave and watched as his father's coffin was lowered into the ground. He couldn't believe that he was here again just seven months after he had buried his mother.

George's wife, Anna Henderson, wept softly as she watched the man she loved so dearly, fight for composure. No matter what age you were, it was never easy saying goodbye to a parent. Anna knew that this time around was going to be the hardest for George, for they had only just buried Ava, shortly before Walter's passing.

Ada and Walter Henderson were George's late parents and a fine job they had made of it. Their son was a complete gentleman and was a credit to his parents. Having been brought up in a house

1

that had been big enough to house an army, George was not at all spoiled or selfish. He would give his last penny to anyone who was in desperate need of it. Walter had taught him about the value of money and how the hard-working man should always bring the family together around the dinner table. George had always lived his life by that rule and it had never let him down. Walter had shown George the importance of the women in their lives and how without them, nothing would be worth working towards. Men like this were rare as far as Ava had been concerned and she was immensely proud that her only son had turned out like his father.

Anna too, was entirely proud to say that she was married to a wonderful man who had come from a wonderful family. The Henderson men came from a long line of hard working families and nothing was ever taken for granted. This was the way that Walter Henderson had lived his life and he always made sure that his boy had understood this.

Walter Henderson had inherited the family home from his own father and he was unsure as to how long the family home had actually been in the family. It could've gone back several generations and he would never know. What he had known was that his own Grandfather had been successful in the whisky business and it had been part of the family since the early 1800s. Walter had been raised with the thought that he would inherit the business and the family home when he turned twenty one years old. And that is exactly what had happened. Walter had started at the bottom of the barrel, so to speak, when he had begun working in the distillery. He had learned everything there was to learn about the Scotch Whisky business and he had loved every minute of it. He loved the smell of the distillery and the grounds around the building and would spend hours just wondering what it would be like when he eventually was able to hand it over to his own son. That time had come around so quickly and he was able to watch George learn the trade and know that when his time on earth was over, he would leave knowing that his family would be financially comfortable and able to bring up the next generation of Hendersons.

George watched his family and friends around him as they grieved for his father. He had been a well-respected man, one who had made many friends and acquaintances over the years. He felt his wife squeeze his hand and it brought back the harsh reality that he would never hear Walter's voice again, never see his gentle smile or hear his larger than life laugh.

"It'll be ok you know. He's in a better place," whispered Anna.

George nodded. "I know he is. It just doesn't seem right. How am I supposed to go on, knowing that he won't be there if I need him. Or if I have a question about the business; he won't be there to answer me."

Anna's heart ached. "You will have all of the answers darling, you will. All you have to do is think of him and they will come to you."

George wasn't so sure. He felt completely lost without Walter, he was George's guidance in life.

"We commit Walter's body to the ground, ashes to ashes, dust to dust," the priest spoke. Someone offered a box with dirt inside for George to throw the first handful in. He grabbed a fistful and squeezed as hard as he could, for some reason he didn't want to let go.

"Go on, George," he heard Anna prompt.

"I can't."

"You can, you're a Henderson."

George took a deep breath, desperately trying to keep the tears at bay, before he released his fist and let the dirt fall gently on top of Walter's coffin.

He was briefly aware that Anna was repeating the process, along with a few other family members, before collapsing to his knees in despair.

The piper began to play 'Amazing Grace' as the crowd made their way back into the house. George stayed down, on his knees as everyone gave him the space that he needed. Anna stayed by his side, allowing him to expel his anguish.

The spring time breeze was barely warm and the air carried a dampness which matched the circumstances of the day. Anna placed her hand upon George's shoulder to let him know she was still there but he did not respond. "I'll give you a moment, dear."

He held his breath as he listened to breeze, hoping to hear his father's voice, but of course all he heard was the breeze brushing through the tall fir trees around the grounds of Henderson Manor.

"What am I supposed to do with all of this without you?" George said out loud. He waited for an answer, willing for a sign to come and reassure him. Nothing came.

George stood up and brushed himself off. He gathered up his emotions, displayed composure once more and made his way back towards the house.

Henderson Manor was an extremely large house that some would say could pass for a hotel. It had belonged to the Henderson family of many generations and housed not only George, Anna and their son James along with his wife Helen, but it also housed many memories that would be embedded in the foundations of the manor. "If only these walls could talk," Walter used to joke.

George looked in through the kitchen door and could see Anna busying herself with trays of glasses for the people who had come to pay their respects. Of course, the family had hired help for the occasion, it was just Anna's way of coping with the situation. He made his way into the large kitchen, expecting Anna to begin fussing around him, like she always did. However, this time she just smiled at him and carried on with what she was doing. She was in and out of the kitchen like a woman possessed, although she carried herself like a calm breeze. She had such a gentle manner about her that even when she was angry about something, she was as polite as one could be when angry. "Take as much time out as you need, dear," she said as she poured a large brandy for him.

"Actually, would you mind pouring a whisky? If I am going to celebrate my father's life, I may as well do it with his very own brand."

Anna smiled but it didn't reach her eyes. "How silly of me, of course."

George led Anna by the hand, out to the back grounds of the house where the family plot had just received its second member. He put his arm around Anna's shoulder and raised the other hand, holding a glass of Henderson Whisky.

"Here's to you, Dad. I hope you find Mum and your broken heart is finally mended. Cheers." George threw the whisky down his throat and placed the glass down, next to the many wreaths and flowers that people had left in respect. The plot was still to be filled in.

"Let's go inside darling," George said.

"Are you ready to face everyone? You don't need more time?"

"I have everything I need inside that house. Let's go."

CHAPTER ONE

PRESENT DAY

Glasgow Royal Concert Hall was packed out for the third night in a row and Sam Leonard felt excited at the success but relief that it was finally over. He had worked on his performance for months on end and now that the show had come to a close he felt like he could finally relax. It was his first stage play where he played the lead role and he had been so nervous just thinking about it. The venue could hold 1200 people and as he stood on the stage he could see not one empty seat on any of the three nights.

His role in the play was a husband struggling with alcoholism and a failing marriage to a woman with cancer. Sam had hesitated when offered the part at first, not sure if his experience as an actor would be enough to fulfil the role. His agent had encouraged him that he was perfect for the part and so after some persuasion he signed the contract and began rehearsing.

It all seemed to go by in the blink of an eye and as the curtain rose for the final bow, Sam focused on the back of the audience. Lights flashed from the thousands of cameras in the audience and his ears buzzed from the sounds of cheers and applause.

The curtain was lowered and the rest of the cast applauded one another for their hard work and commitment to the play.

"Well done Sam, you were fantastic yet again," said his agent, Miles.

"Thanks, I am overwhelmed by the response!" he replied.

"You should be. They bloody love you out there."

"Oh I don't know about that," Sam felt a little embarrassed.

"Are you kidding? This play is going to make you huge!" Miles patted him on the shoulder.

"Cheers Miles. I'm going to get changed, you joining us for dinner and drinks?" he said, motioning a glance to the other cast members.

"Need you ask?" Miles replied with a bright wide grin.

Sam made his way back to his dressing room and went in to the shower. He turned the switch to power mode and stood under the head, allowing the water to beat down on his neck and shoulders. He hadn't realised it but in the last three nights his neck and shoulder muscles had been so tense that as soon as the curtain fell for the last time on that show, he felt the pounding headache set in.

He finished showering, stepped out of the cubicle and reached for his sports bag. Sam pulled out the paracetamol and swallowed two with a large glass of water.

As he pulled on his jeans and a shirt he heard a knock at the dressing room door.

"Come in!"

"You ready yet, Mr Diva?" Miles laughed.

Sam rolled his eyes and smiled "Diva? As if mate."

They made their way down Sauchiehall Street and were the last to arrive out of the cast and crew from the play. They had hired out three booths in a bar called 'Lounge' and had pre-ordered food and drinks.

A few hours passed and the Lounge bar was beginning to get busy. Sam had relaxed and his headache had subsided. He stood at the bar waiting to order a drink and couldn't help feel eyes on him. He turned to see a young woman standing behind him. She smiled and he returned the smile.

"Hi," she said, her voice was soft.

"Hi," Sam replied.

"You're Sam Leonard aren't you?"

"That's me, and your name is?"

Her smile widened. "It's Deborah."

Deborah Bell stood talking to Sam and her entire body felt like one huge thudding heart. She tried to control the quiver in her voice and she didn't have to strain to hear the blood rushing through her ears.

Deborah Bell was twenty five years old and her blond hair sat on her shoulders. Sam was almost a whole head and shoulders taller than she was and this made her feel even more nervous. She was Sam's biggest fan and she found it difficult to keep that information under control.

"Would you like a drink?" Sam asked.

"Thanks, I'll have a vodka with lime please."

As Sam turned to order the drinks, Deborah stood behind him and tried to compose herself. She had never had the guts to actually approach him before now but her determination to meet him just once pushed her to do it tonight. She just wished that her heart would calm down as it was banging so hard against her chest now and she was sure that if in a quiet room even he would hear it.

She had watched Sam for a long time on television and had been to all of the plays he had appeared in. She always knew what his next job was and where he would be appearing. She admired his work, followed his acting career and most of all thought that he was the most beautiful man ever to have been created.

She reminded herself to play cool, if he learned just how much she knew of him, just what she had gone through to be near him, it might scare him off. But all she wanted right now was to have a drink with him.

He turned to face her, passing her the glass as he did so. "So, what are you up to tonight?" he asked.

Shit! I didn't think this question through.

She searched her brain for a quick answer. "My friends are upstairs. I wanted a drink but the bar upstairs is too busy so I thought I would chance using this one. Oh, thanks by the way," she held up the drink.

Nice one.

"Oh, am I keeping you?" he asked.

"Not at all, most of their boyfriends are here, so to be honest you're keeping me from feeling like a bit of a spare part."

Sam smiled. She seemed nice; she was quite

pretty and not, as far as he could tell, like the rest of the girls who had approached him in the past. They all instantly turned out to be crazy and all they could talk about was him and how much they watched him on television, read all about him in magazines, or how in the latest interview they found out his favourite colour and how much they fancied him. Sam wasn't looking for a woman who thought she already knew him inside out. He wanted the normal first date where a couple actually talked and got to know one another by asking questions, not by watching him on television or reading about him in the newspaper.

"Oh right, your boyfriend not here tonight then?" he asked.

Deborah's stomach flipped and she had to contain the giggle that crept up from her throat. "I don't have one actually."

"No? Well, you'll be able to join me for more drinks then." It wasn't a question.

"Why not?" she replied trying not to sound too excited.

Instead of going back to the table where the rest of the cast were drinking and celebrating the last night of the show, Sam took Deborah's hand and led her to another booth that was catered for two people.

Deborah's heart raced and the more time she spent with him the more she became attracted to him. "You don't want to join your friends?" she asked.

"Not really, I have spent the last eight months with them day in and day out. A few hours without them won't kill me," he smiled.

Sam allowed Deborah to slide in to the booth first and she thought that he would sit opposite her but instead he sat next to her.

I don't know how much faster my heart can beat before it explodes.

"So, tell me about yourself," Sam said.

Deborah felt lost for words and she couldn't suppress the smile that was beginning to make her cheeks ache. "I'm actually at university."

"What are you studying?"

"I am studying for a degree in Journalism," she replied.

"Cool. Are you nearly finished?"

"Actually I am doing a placement at the moment," she said. She questioned whether or not she should reveal where the placement was and that she had asked her lecturer if she could go to that particular venue.

"Where is your placement?" he asked, oblivious to her nerves.

14

She decided not to tell him just yet. "I am in a local newspaper office. It's just small, nothing exciting happens really."

He was nodding as she spoke; enjoying the conversation. There were a few moments where he stared into her eyes. Again her heart raced and now all she wanted was to kiss him.

"So you're an actor?" she broke the silence, maintaining her self-control.

"That I am. Have you seen any of my stuff?" he asked, hoping that she wasn't going to turn out a fanatical fan.

"Just the play tonight," she lied. She was aware of everything he had worked on. Television adverts, television dramas, newspaper articles, magazine interviews, radio interviews. She had even followed him to the venues where he worked on all of those things, thankfully he had never come across her. If he had, they wouldn't be sitting here tonight.

"Oh, you were in the theatre? What did you think?" his eyes lit up.

"You were very good. You play a good drunk," she said with a smile.

What she really wanted to say was that she thought that he was amazing and that if love at first sight was real then she was very much in love with him. Deborah knew that what she was feeling for Sam Leonard was not normal, but the lust to have him and the uncontrollable desire within to keep him near her right now was becoming unbearable.

"So, what do you say we go somewhere quieter?" he leaned in close to her face. He could feel the lust to. But that was all it was for him. For Deborah, the desire to have him had grown so strong for all of the time she had followed his success that at times it physically hurt.

"Where do you have in mind?" she asked. She wanted to tell him exactly how she felt but she knew that it could destroy any chance she had of being with him.

There's no need to tell him. You have him right now and that is all you have ever wanted. Just take what is here and enjoy it, she thought to herself.

"What about going back to my place?" he asked.

"Sounds like a good idea to me."

They slid out of the booth and Sam took her hand and led her down to the street. It was cold outside and Sam could see that Deborah had goose bumps on her arms. The little blond hairs stood on end and she trembled in the November breeze.

"Here, you can have my jacket," Sam said wrapping it around her. As his fingers gently brushed off her shoulder she felt the urge to kiss him but she fought it off. She couldn't believe that she was going to spend the night in Sam Leonard's flat.

A taxi pulled up outside the Lounge bar and Sam opened the door to let Deborah in. As it pulled away, she could feel every pulse in her body thumping and she could hear the blood rushing in her ears. She knew she should have had another vodka to stay calm but when he had offered to take her back to his flat she just wanted to get out of the bar and into a taxi as fast as her legs would carry her.

"So do you live far?" she asked, trying to take her mind off what was about to happen between them.

"I'm only in Merchant City and not far in either. We will be there in about five minutes," he replied.

The taxi pulled up outside a set of new build flats and Deborah didn't have time to look around the street as she was gently but quickly being led up the four flights of stairs to Sam's flat.

"Do you live by yourself?" she asked.

"No I have a flat-mate but they're out till tomorrow," he replied as he put his key in the door.

He allowed Deborah to go in first and as she

looked around she couldn't quite believe that she was in Sam Leonard's home. It was so clean and tidy with photographs on the wall of friends and maybe family, she wasn't entirely sure. He guided her into the kitchen and she sat down on a bar stool.

"Drink?" Sam asked as he opened the fridge and pulled out a bottle of wine.

"Yes please," Deborah replied, noticing a gentle quiver in her voice.

He poured a large glass and handed it to her, again his fingers brushed her hand as she received the glass. She felt like an electrical charge ran through her fingers at the feeling of his touch. As he turned to get himself a glass she gulped the large glass of Rosé wine down and felt it burn in her chest.

He turned and walked towards her and she felt her body begin to tingle. "So, how long have you lived here then?"

"About a year," he replied.

Now their faces were close together, she could feel his breath on her face and it smelled good.

"You smell great," he said as their noses brushed together.

"Thank you, so do you." She noticed that she was whispering.

He took a sip of wine from his glass.

"I don't normally do this you know," Deborah said with a gentle smile.

"What's that?"

"Come back to a guy's flat who I've only just met."

"How does it make you feel?" he asked pushing his lips to meet hers but ensuring that there were still a few millimeters between them.

"It feels good," she whispered again.

She couldn't be sure who started the kiss but at this point in time she did not care. It was gentle at first, tender in fact. But as the kiss lasted she felt Sam push hard on her lips and his tongue very gently searched for hers.

If lust could create electricity then Deborah would have enough to generate power to Sam's flat for a week. She felt weak under the passion in his kiss and he began to take control of her.

He slid his hand under her thighs and lifted her from the bar stool. She closed her eyes and allowed him to carry her to another room, she assumed the bedroom.

He laid her down on his bed and gently pushed down on top of her. He was heavy but she liked the feeling of him on her. He pulled his shirt over his head with one hand and with the other gently unbuttoned her blouse. He opened it wide and she slid her arms out.

Deborah pulled at Sam's belt and slid his jeans down as he slid his thumb through the space between her skin and underwear.

Deborah relished every second with Sam, taking in every part of his body as they spent the night together.

As Sam slept, Deborah familiarized herself with his home, looking at photographs on the walls and memorizing everything around her.

There was nothing that she could not know about Sam Leonard.

CHAPTER TWO

Jenny Lawson was sitting at the breakfast bar in the flat which she shared with Sam. She skimmed through the newspaper as she sipped at her mug of black tea. She had heard Sam getting up earlier and he had been in the shower for around thirty minutes. As he entered the kitchen he saw the large grin that Jenny had on her face.

"What are you so smiley about this morning?" he asked her as he pulled a box of cereal out from the cupboard.

"Shouldn't I be asking you that question?" She pointed to the small black handbag that was sitting on the counter. "So, she didn't fancy staying all night?"

"I guess not. When I woke up she was gone but to be honest I am glad. I can't be bothered with the small talk once the alcohol has worn off and the sex has been had," he said smugly.

"Oh, you dirty stop out!" Jenny laughed. "Well, she may have left but she clearly wants to see you again, she left a note with her number on it."

Jenny and Sam had been best friends since they were in high school and had never been anything more. A lot of people had asked them if they had ever kissed, or wanted to try it. Their answer had always been the same. "Would you kiss your best friend if you didn't fancy them?"

They had decided to live together when they were at college and the setup was still working so they had decided to keep living together until one day one of them was ready to move on to somewhere else.

"What do you think I should do?" Sam asked her, holding up the handbag.

"If I was her, I would want you to phone me," Jenny replied.

"Really?"

"Yep, the way I see it is she gets her bag back and you will know if you want to see her again."

"How do you work that one out?" Sam asked confused.

"Well, you will see her for the first time sober and you will know if she is as good looking as you thought she was last night."

Sam smiled and gave Jenny a pat on the head. "You know me so well Jenny."

"Yes, I do," she replied with a smile.

Sam made some breakfast before deciding to phone Deborah and arrange to meet to return her bag. He could remember clearly what she looked like and could remember how much he had genuinely liked her.

Swallowing the last mouthful of cereal and placing the bowl into the dishwasher, Sam patted Jenny on the shoulder as he made his way to the front door of their flat.

"See you sometime this afternoon? Maybe we could meet up for a drink and lunch?"

"Sounds like a plan. Text me when you decide where we're going and I'll meet you there," Jenny replied as she got up to put a tablet in the dishwasher.

Sam was already out the door. "Will do," he called back before closing it behind him.

Jenny pressed the button that was labelled 'Intense wash' and left the kitchen to go and get ready for the day.

On her way passed Sam's bedroom she paused when she saw that the door was open. He had actually managed to make the bed. *Jeez, he must be in a good mood,* Jenny thought to herself as she closed the door.

The flat was always quiet when Sam was not around. She did not like being on her own, the place gave her shivers but she never really understood why. The flats in Merchant City were relatively new so there wasn't much chance that it was haunted, if you believe in that sort of thing of course.

Jenny and Sam's flat was decorated according to each of their individual tastes. It was modern and fresh with white and slate grey painted walls and wooden flooring. There were photo frames on the walls all around the flat and there were also frames that included photographs of Sam's achievements, like the cast on the last night of a sell-out show. There were also posters of his shows and appearances up on the walls of his bedroom.

Perhaps this made Sam look a little vain, although apart from the frames, Sam never came across as such. He kept himself to himself generally and tried not to be noticed when out on his daily business. He was quite well known in Scotland and not a day went by where someone did *not* notice him.

***

Sam listened to the ring after punching Deborah's number into the keypad on his mobile phone. It rang for a few seconds before it connected.

"Hello?"

"Hello, Deborah? It's Sam here."

"Oh, hello again," she bit her bottom lip, stunned that he had actually called and so soon after she had left.

Sam smiled. "You left your bag here last night."

"Oh really? I thought I'd left it in the taxi that dropped me home."

"Well, would you like it back?" His voice teased her, knowing fine well that she would.

Deborah hesitated, she really was pleased to hear from him but she was not at all prepared for the call to have come so soon. "Yes I would like it back," she replied trying to sound as equally teasing as Sam had.

Sam heard the smile in her voice and he was amazed at how right Jenny had been when she said he would know if he would want to see her again. He knew right then that he did.

"So, should we meet up and I'll bring your bag?" Sam asked.

"Yes, that would be good."

Is he asking me on a date or does he just want to hand my bag back?

Sam knew what he was doing to her and he was

enjoying it, he had no intention of hurting her though. "Let me take you out again, properly this time."

Deborah tried to control her breathing but felt it impossible. "Ok, where do you want to go?"

God even his voice is beautiful. Is this really happening?

"I'll take you somewhere special." He was speaking so low it was almost a whisper. "A romantic dinner, wine and maybe back to mine for after's?"

"Sounds good." Her throat had become as dry as the Sahara desert. She found herself, clinging to the phone as though it were the most precious thing she owned.

"Great, I'll pick you up at seven tonight then."

Deborah's heart fluttered and she panicked. "No, we can meet in town."

"You don't want me to pick you up?" Sam asked.

"No, I'll meet you. You could be an axe murderer for all I know, I don't want you knowing where I live."

He heard the playfulness in her tone and he laughed. "Good move Miss Bell, I'll meet you at seven at the new Italian restaurant on Argyll Street."

"Ok, sounds great. See you tonight, Mr Leonard."

They hung up and Deborah noticed that she had backed herself onto the wall in her bedroom as she spoke to Sam. She peeled herself off the wall and made her way into the bathroom.

As she thought about the man of her dreams, she wondered if seeing him was such a good idea. She couldn't pretend to know nothing about him, could she? Obviously being a fan and then becoming the date wouldn't be easy to do, but she was living her dream, so why not?

She knew she had to, but her big secret wasn't far from the back of her mind. She had followed Sam's career for the last three years and watched him become a Scottish star.

Deborah knew everything that there was to know about Sam Leonard; his career to date, the shows, the television appearances, radio interviews, past girlfriends, everything. It was her knowledge on his previous relationship that she had to keep quiet.

If she was going to go on this date, it may turn into something serious. She asked herself if she was prepared to deal with a serious relationship with such a high profile man. She may become high profile herself and if she did, she would have so much explaining to do, to a lot of people.

Deborah put that thought to the back of her mind and decided to enjoy the moments that were to come.

CHAPTER THREE

Sam walked into the café and if he wasn't hungry before then he was now. He loved the smell of fresh bread and coffee and that was the scent that was invading his nostrils as soon as he was inside the door. He looked for a table and sat down just as a waitress approached him. "You're Sam Leonard aren't you?"

Oh, here we go, he sighed inwardly. "Yes, that's me."

The girl blushed a shade of crimson and handed Sam the lunch menu. "Uh, erm if you need anything at all just ask; my name is Claire."

"Thanks Claire." He took the menu from her, careful not to make skin to skin contact, worried that it may tip the girl over the edge. "I'll decide what I am having once my friend arrives."

Claire, the waitress scurried back to the counter just as Jenny walked through the door.

The sound of teacups clinking on saucers and coffee machines hissing made Sam feel relaxed. The cafe was empty except for the waitress, which he was glad for. The surroundings were decorated a mocha colour with leather couches at the waiting area next to the door. There were picture frames all around the place with fifties style photographs inside them.

"Sorry I'm late, I got sidetracked," Jenny said as she sat down, fighting with shopping bags which refused to go under the table.

"By a shoe sale no doubt?" Sam replied.

"Ha, you know me so well. Fifty percent off, so I bought two pairs."

Sam rolled his eyes and raised his hand to alert the waitress. She was at the table in an instant and had an expectant smile across her face. "Yes Sam, what can I get you?"

Jenny looked at her, then to Sam with a confused expression across her face.

"I'll have a chocolate cappuccino and Jenny will have..."

Jenny was still confused. "Erm, I'll have a black tea please."

Claire didn't make eye contact with Jenny as she

spoke. She only watched Sam, unaware of his discomfort. She continued to stand at the table after they had given their order, almost in a trance like state.

"That'll be all," Jenny said with a little force.

Claire snapped back from her trance and blushed a shade of crimson again. "Oh, yes sorry. I'll be right with you."

Sam laughed quietly and shook his head as Claire walked away from their table.

"Do you know her?" Jenny asked.

"No," Sam was still laughing gently.

"So, how?"

"A fan most likely, I don't know. She asked me if I was Sam Leonard and when I said yes she went all weird on me."

Jenny began laughing. "We can't take you anywhere. So how did it go with, Deborah is it?"

"Actually, I asked her out again," Sam replied, aware that he was being watched from the counter by the star struck waitress.

Jenny followed Sam's gaze. Jenny caught Claire's eye and again, her skin became red and blotchy through a mixture of embarrassment and excitement.

"What is *with* her? You'd think that she'd never met a famous person before."

Sam frowned. "I'm hardly famous Jenny."

"Well she seems to see it that way, I mean look at her. She can't take her eyes off you!" Jenny raised her tone, knowing Claire would hear her.

Sam cringed. "What are you doing?"

"What? She needs to tone it down and stop making you uncomfortable."

Sam wasn't sure how to take this one. He knew that Jenny was just looking out for him, but for Christ sake she didn't have to do it like this.

"Jenny, it's fine, honestly. She's just a little shy. Wouldn't you be if you were in the presence of someone famous?" He said using his fingers to make inverted commas.

Jenny sat back in her seat and took a silent, deep breath. Sam looked up at Claire, who had turned her back to their table.

Sam knew that Jenny was protective of him, especially since the incident from the beginning of a few months ago. "Jenny, it's ok. We're just having lunch, it's all cool, nothing's wrong here."

"I know. I just don't want, you know what, to happen again."

Sam smiled gently. Jenny had been his rock when it had all gone wrong. He knew in his mind that it was unlikely to happen again and Jenny probably did too, but sometimes when it crossed his mind, he couldn't help but worry about it.

"Hey, as long as you're around, I don't think I have anything to worry about. And don't you go getting all worried for me. I'm a big boy Jenny, I can handle things on my own."

Jenny seemed to relax at his comment. "I know you can. You know what I'm like, I just couldn't bear to see you go through that again."

"And I won't. I ended it for a reason and I haven't heard from her since. It's all fine now, she's gone."

A few silent moments passed before Claire returned to the table with their order. She smiled gently at Jenny, who returned the smile but only briefly.

"I'm sorry if I made you uncomfortable Mr Leonard. I didn't mean to," Claire said quietly.

"You didn't. Thanks," he replied. He felt sorry for the waitress. The poor girl was only doing her job. He didn't want Jenny thinking of every female the way she thought about *her*.

'Her,' was an ex, sort of. Sam had gone on a few dates with her and they had become an item. Sarah was her name, and a nice girl she was too; at first.

Sarah had learned about Sam's fame (Sam didn't believe that he was famous, just that he was successful in his work as an actor) after the first date. He had chosen to tell her, knowing that the new relationship could go one of two ways, intense or on course as normal.

At first it seemed to flow as a new relationship would. They went on dates, talked and dined, all the normal stuff. After a few weeks, Sam was really beginning to like Sarah and decided that he wanted to make them an official couple.

That was when things started to go wrong. Sarah changed, she hated that fact that he lived with Jenny, even though she would never admit it. He did tell her that there was nothing to worry about and that he and Jenny were just friends but Sarah would always go quiet around Jenny. Sam couldn't cope with the fact that his best friend and his girlfriend didn't get on well, so he made a decision. He would only see Sarah out-with Jenny's company, just for a while, to see how it worked.

It didn't work well. Sam began receiving threatening notes through his door, which said things like Jenny would be harmed if she didn't stay away from Sam. He and Jenny would receive threatening text messages from an unknown number and creepy silent phone calls, all of course when Sarah wasn't with Sam.

Sam never could be one hundred percent sure but his instinct told him that his every move was being watched, followed and listened too. He had the prickling feeling on his back whenever he was alone and as the weeks drew on, he decided to confront her who he believed to be behind it all; Sarah.

Sam had distanced himself from her in the time that the threats and stalker-like behaviour had begun. He hadn't bothered to tell her why, he was pretty sure that she would know the reason behind his choice. But she still incessantly called and turned up to the flat. He was glad that Jenny had been there to help him, she was able to put sympathy into her tone and make it look as though she understood that she missed Sam but gently tell her that he was no longer interested.

Sam had thought that Jenny's words had done the trick, but he still felt uneasy. He still received disturbing letters which threatened violence and his phone rang out for the majority of the day and into the night. The threats on Jenny became more violent and intense.

Enough is enough, Sam had thought to himself. He had decided to turn up at her house, unannounced. If he was going to find out about her unnecessary behaviour towards him then he didn't want to do it with warning. He also wanted to scare her shitless so that she would just leave him and Jenny alone.

As he had approached Sarah's house, he wondered why it had come to this so suddenly. She had been lovely to begin with and then taken an instant dislike to Jenny. In fact, dislike was too kind a word to use. Hatred would be more fitting, even though Jenny had done nothing to cause it. You could hardly say that being a friend of Sam's was an excuse.

Maybe it was due to them living together and Sarah had become intensely jealous. It was the only explanation Sam could think of. Whatever the reason, Sam had to find out why and tell her to back off. He walked up the gravel driveway with his jacket slung over his shoulder as he did so. He was surprised to see Sarah had open the door before he'd even thought about knocking on it.

"Didn't expect to see you here," she said with a timid voice.

"No? Well I didn't expect you to turn out psychotic, but we learn something new everyday don't we?" Sam's reply was nastier than he had first anticipated.

She stood firmly in the door way, not granting access to the hallway. "You want to talk?"

"You're damn right I do, although I'll be doing the talking and you'll be doing the listening."

36

Sarah nodded and stood back, allowing Sam to enter. He hesitated at first, unsure of how she would react when he was inside. "You're not going to go all possessive and lock me in, are you?"

Sarah's expression was sad, with a deep sense of loss reflecting in her eyes. "Of course not, I would ever hurt anyone Sam, let alone you."

Sam watched as Sarah closed the door on the world outside and he genuinely wondered if he would ever see the other side of it again.

She led them into the sitting room, where she gestured for him to sit down. A large rocking chair sat in the corner next to the bay window and an old grandfather clock stood in the opposite corner. The decor was of an older time and Sam remembered that this house did not belong to Sarah. She must have felt lonely in the house, it was huge and she lived here all by herself. It was big enough to house a family of ten and there would still be plenty of room left over.

"Sarah, are you lonely in this house?"

"Meeting you made my life feel fuller than it actually is."

Sam was beginning to feel guilty for being so brash on his arrival and was beginning to forget why he had made the trip to see her. It quickly came back to him. "Sarah, you have to stop all of this behaviour."

Sarah frowned in confusion. "*I* have to stop this behaviour?"

"Yes."

"If you didn't want to see me anymore then you could have just said so instead of completely blanking me. I have tried to contact you and you have cut me off!"

Sam was speechless, how could she just sit there and blatantly lie to his face? He was beginning to think that she had completely gone off the rails. Maybe living in the house on her own after the recent death of her only remaining family member had caused it. Sam pushed his feelings of guilt to one side again and tried to remain firm. "Cut you off? I wish Sarah, I can't breathe without you knowing about it. I tried to work my time around you and Jenny but it just wasn't working. You can't accept Jenny being in my life then we can't be together."

Sarah smirked, "Jenny. She has some hold on you."

"What do you mean by that?" Now Sam was the one who was confused.

"She hates me, because of you."

"You're deluded. Me and Jenny..." Sam couldn't finish his sentence, Sarah had gotten up from her seat and was already shouting.

"Just get out Sam, if you can't see what is going on here then this conversation is already over!"

Sam stood up and walked slowly over to the door, where Sarah was waiting for his exit. He shook his head, in sadness and frustration. "This could have really gone somewhere Sarah, but you have ruined it before it even had a chance."

"I didn't ruin this Sam," she had tears in her eyes. "Jenny, she just can't stay out of our business. You need to know the things that she has been saying, about you, about us."

"No!" Sam lost his temper. "You need to know that you are out of order, you're right, this conversation is over." Sam proceeded to leave however, Sarah blocked his way. She grabbed his shoulders and would not allow him to move any closer to the front door.

Sam felt a rush of anger flood his veins and he instinctively pushed Sarah away from him, who was now crying. "Get off me Sarah, let me out!" he shouted.

"No," she sobbed. "This isn't right, I am not crazy."

"Of course you're not. Sarah, just forget us."

Sam couldn't understand why Sarah had gotten so mad, they hadn't been together that long. And nothing had ever happened between him and Jenny for her to become so jealous of. What on earth had happened to her?

He watched Sarah as she slid down the wall in a flood of uncontrollable tears, and Sam's conscience set in. He approached her slowly, bending down to her level. He saw something in her eyes, something that wasn't right. It scared him. "I'm sorry if I have hurt you. It wasn't meant to be this way."

Sam got up and tried to block out the sounds of her sobs as he closed the front door behind him. He could hear her, shouting something about Jenny harassing her and saying she had been sleeping with Sam behind Sarah's back. He couldn't believe she would say such a thing just to try to keep them together. He ignored the words behind the sobs and continued to walk away. Sam wasn't a bad person, although closing the door on a crying girl made him feel pretty heartless. He really wondered why she had changed so much. Was she really feeling that threatened by Jenny. Jenny had been nothing but nice to her and she had to go and make up lies about her. Jenny would never do anything like what Sarah had said.

Sam had to stop himself from turning back, he knew that as the genuinely caring person that he was known for, he should. But then he thought of the phone calls, the threatening letters and the general crazy behaviour, and that what he had just witnessed would have all been an act. She would want him to turn around and go back.

He decided to go for a drink, by himself to clear his head before heading back to the flat. As much as Jenny was his best friend and he loved her dearly, he just didn't want to face her questions when he told her what had happened between him and Sarah.

As he sat at a table at the back of a small pub, he felt beside himself. A range of emotions had taken over and he didn't know how to deal with them. He sipped on a whisky and in his mind he had convinced himself that he had done the right thing. As much as it pained him to walk away from a woman whom he had begun to fall for, he knew that for her sanity, his safety and his friendship with Jenny that it was best all round that he walked away.

He took his time with the whisky. He enjoyed the feeling of it warming his blood. The pub where he consumed his nerve-calmer was not the usual type of pub he would choose. It was what may be described as an old man's pub and that was why Sam had picked it. No one would think to look for him here. He nursed the same whisky for around two hours before having the mental strength to get up and go back to the flat.

He walked home, taking in the autumnal views around him. The leaves were beginning to turn beautiful shades of red and orange and the pavement was littered with them. They crunched as he placed his feet upon them. He heard his steps repeated behind him, although when he turned, an empty space was where he expected to see Sarah. He expected that the house wouldn't be the last place that he would see her. She wasn't going to give up without a fight. Sam just wanted the end of their relationship, if you can even call it that, to be exactly that, the end. Could it be that simple?

**

The feet stepped over the body as it lay on the floor of the house with the old style decor. It lay perfectly still at the bottom of the stairs on the worn carpet and it looked unnatural. It was plain to see that bones were broken.

Sarah had not known of her intruder, not at first anyway. The intruder had followed Sam to the house, went around to the back door and snuck inside as they had argued. The back door was in the kitchen, at the end of the hallway and with the sitting room at the front of the house, neither Sam nor Sarah had heard them.

As the figure crouched down over Sarah's body, a hand encased in black leather fell over the eyes to close them. As the figure stood up to leave, they were unaware of the soul which rose with them. The soul itself was disorientated and unaware of what had just happened as it watched the human figure walk out of the house through the back door.

A few hours passed before reality checked in. Sarah stood over her own lifeless body and wondered helplessly what would happen next.

CHAPTER FOUR

"So you're going on a date with her then?" Jenny asked as she sipped at her black tea after realising she was being a little irrational towards Claire.

Sam smiled, glad that Jenny had calmed down and was engaging in conversation again. "Yes, I am going to take her to the new Italian restaurant in town then maybe just on to a bar."

Jenny smiled, "It's good to see you happy and confident enough to date again."

"Please don't bring it up again, it tires me out just thinking about it."

"I am not bringing up anything. God, I am just saying that it is nice to see you smile and not worry about..."

Sam cut her off. "Yes, I know. Sorry, I just want to forget about Sarah and what happened. Not every girl will be like that, I just want to move on and enjoy myself."

Claire had distanced herself from the table, allowing the unwanted attention from Jenny to ease off. She kept her ears on the conversation and her mind on pouring coffees.

I cannot believe that he is actually here, at my place of work, Claire thought to herself, almost scolding her wrist with boiling water due to excitement. *I mean, he is actually here, it's insane.*

She listened to the exchanging words between Sam and Jenny and wondered who they were discussing. It became apparent that it was an ex-girlfriend that Jenny seriously didn't like.

"There is no reason for you not to enjoy yourself, however all I am asking is that you are wary of *who* you enjoy yourself with. It was bad enough the first time, you don't want to let your guard down and have it happen again!" Jenny sipped at the tea once more.

Sam sighed, "I know you're right. I just hate to think about it."

Jenny *was* right and she was the only person who knew how he really felt about the whole situation. She was the only one that he ever really opened up to about personal things.

"Why don't you just take things slowly with Deborah first off and see how it plays out. If you

45

keep her at arm's length then maybe things will develop well alongside your trust?"

What on earth happened? Claire thought as she listened intently, careful of her mannerism.

Sam nodded, accepting this to be the best scenario for future relations with other females. He understood that Jenny's worries were justified considering the hell he had been through with Sarah and how she had been so offended by his relationship with Jenny.

"Is there anything else I can get for you both?" Claire was suddenly at the table.

Jenny smiled, trying hard to keep the irritation from her tone and expression, "No, we're fine thank you."

Sam looked up at Claire, who was now staring into his eyes again. He relaxed under her gaze, "Thank you."

Claire nodded and returned to the counter. *He's so beautiful.*

Sam sighed deeply, then the light came back to his eyes and the charm to his smile, "Ok, enough with this dreary reminiscing session. Let's get out of here and go back to the flat and open that bottle of wine that's in the fridge."

"I love that idea," Jenny replied.

They stood up and proceeded to approach the

counter where Claire pretended not to notice his presence.

"Could we pay please?" He asked.

Claire spun round to face Sam, disappointed to see Jenny stood next to him, "Of course."

Jenny linked her arm through Sam's and was unaware of Claire's jealousy. She watched Jenny out from the corner of her eye as Sam punched his pin number into the card machine to pay their bill. She was stunning, with a figure to die for.

Bitch! Claire thought. Her thoughts were halted when Claire reached over to hand the receipt to Sam and her skin connected with his. She felt her hand begin to tingle and her heart leapt. On connection, she raised her head and saw that he had already pulled his hand away, proceeding to put his card back into his wallet.

"Was service to your satisfaction today?" Claire's voice quivered.

"Everything was fine thank you." At his reply, she felt the heat rise from her neck and once again, her face changed from pale to crimson in a second flat.

For God's sake, Jenny thought, rolling her eyes.

As they left, Claire watched as she tried to control her breathing. She couldn't get her head around the fact that she had just served Sam

Leonard. The one time she finally got to see the man whom she had followed from play to play through most of his acting career and she was in her work attire.

Nice! I'm dressed in the worst possible apron with coffee stains on it and this is when the universe decides to put him in my path.

Just at that, Jenny appeared back in the cafe, looking for something under the table where she and Sam had been sitting moments before.

"Have you lost something?" Claire called over.

"I left a bag in here," Jenny replied.

Claire walked over to the table and pulled one of the chairs out to help Jenny look for her missing item.

"I can do it myself," Jenny snapped.

Claire took a step back in shock. She hadn't expected to have her head bitten off when she was trying to help. "Alright, I'm only trying to help!"

"Well, you've done enough!"

Claire frowned at the comment. "What's that supposed to mean?"

Jenny retrieved the bag and stood up, pushing the hair away from her face. It shone beautifully in the sunlight flowing through the windows, a lovely autumn red colour.

"Just do as you're told and stay away."

"What?"

"You heard, stay away!"

Claire could see venom in the eyes of the girl who stood in front of her. She felt as though the venom had been injected into her blood stream and she could feel it trickling through the veins inside her, burning as it did so.

"What the hell is your problem?" Claire stood her ground.

Jenny turned her back on Claire and made her way to the door of the cafe. Before leaving, she turned to Claire and smiled. "Have a nice day," she replied sweetly as if the last thirty seconds hadn't happened.

The bell on the door rang as Jenny walked out and left Claire, standing in bewilderment in the middle of the cafe.

"Are you ok?" a voice came from a corner table.

"Yes, thank you. Just an angry customer I think," Claire replied to the girl who was sitting with her back to the window.

Claire felt a little shaken. *What the hell was that? Did I do something wrong?*

After a few moments of being rooted to the spot in disbelief, the cafe came to life with fashion students from the local University. Claire instantly snapped back to reality when her ear canals were flooded with the sound of girly giggles and shoe chat.

She was about to turn to the counter once more before realising that the girl who had been sitting in the corner was gone. She had been the only one in the cafe when Jenny and Sam had left. Claire hadn't seen her leave.

Come to think of it, she hadn't seen her enter either.

CHAPTER FIVE

Deborah looked in the mirror one last time before finally deciding on the dress she had tried on the first time. It had taken her almost two hours to decide on what she was going to wear. She was so nervous about finally getting a date with the man of her dreams that she wanted to look more perfect than perfect itself.

Obviously she had already been on a date with Sam, if you can call it that. But this time was going to be the first *proper* date.

Hopefully he will melt when he sees me in this, she thought as she applied her lipstick.

On arrival at the Italian restaurant where Sam had arranged to meet her, she felt as though her stomach had fallen out in the taxi on the way and her heart was going to burst out of her chest. She saw him waiting in the seated area by the door and her heart did a little dance.

"Hi," he stood to greet her. He walked over to the door where she was stood and kissed her on the cheek.

The restaurant was decorated with warm colours, oranges and reds. The walls were mirrored in places and the floors were made up of black and red ceramic tiles. There was a bustle of chat, clinking of glasses and a low hum of music which played in the background.

"Hello," Deborah replied.

Sam walked around to her back and slid her coat off her shoulders. She almost crumbled.

"So, have you eaten here before?" Sam asked.

"No, but I'm open to new things," she smiled; her eyes twinkling.

"Well, in that case let's get seated and we can sample some of this fine food."

A waiter approached them and led them to a table in the back of the restaurant where Sam had requested flowers and candles to be laid out. Deborah was impressed that Sam had thought about the fine detail, she had a feeling it was going to be a good night.

The waiter took their drinks order and moved away from the table. Sam motioned for Deborah to sit down before he did.

He's such a gentleman.

Deborah wanted to hide her face behind the menu to cover up the fact that she was blushing. She couldn't understand why she was so nervous; she had already gone further than this, why so coy now?

"Are you ok?" Sam asked.

"Yes, to be honest I'm a little nervous."

Sam smiled. "No need to be nervous. Just relax, I don't bite."

Deborah laughed. She knew he was right but she just couldn't believe that she was spending a second night with Sam Leonard, the famous Scottish theatre actor, among other things.

As the night went on, Deborah did relax and was beginning to enjoy Sam's company. He had such wonderful charm and it was working its magic on her. The food was delicious and the drinks were flowing, all courtesy of Sam.

"So, what do you do for a living then Deborah, outside of university obviously?"

"I work in a little off license," she replied.

"You must see all walks of life going in and out of there every day."

"Sam," she laughed. "It's an off license, not Hollywood. The majority of people who come in are either still drunk from the night before or about

53

to get drunk."

Sam laughed. "Nice."

Deborah smiled. She really had fallen for his charm, even before she had met him. She was, as far as she was concerned, his biggest fan. She didn't dare tell him that though in case it scared him away. She had even asked her lecturer that she do her university placement at the theatre where Sam's recent show had been running for two months. She specifically made sure that she was in the same place as he was whenever she could. It scared her sometimes, how much she thought about him, how much she wanted to be around him; what she would do to make that happen.

She would never do anything to jeopardize her opportunity to meet with him again in the future, and if that meant keeping everything to herself about her need for his presence then that's what she would do.

"Shall we get the bill and move on to a bar?" Sam asked as he poured the last of his beer down his throat.

Yes, he wants to stay out, this couldn't get any better, she thought.

Deborah nodded as Sam gestured for the waiter to bring them the bill. A few moments passed before the bill arrived at the table.

"Here is your bill Sir," said the girl who brought it to the table.

"Claire?" Sam said in a surprised tone.

The waitress looked down at him; it was Claire from the cafe. "Hi Sam. How are you?"

"I'm great. What are you doing here?"

Deborah looked on at them, not at all happy that another female had interrupted the attention she had been receiving from Sam.

"I work here," she said, looking around the restaurant.

"*And* the café?" Sam asked.

"Yes, and the cafe."

Claire seemed wary, and now she found a new pair of eyes burning into her like a fire raging out of control.

"I'm sorry, I'm disturbing you. I'll leave you two alone."

Sam stood up. "No, you're not disturbing us."

Deborah could feel the frustration building in her as every word was exchanged between Sam and this woman.

Sam could see the worry on Claire's face. "She's not here."

Claire smiled. "Am I that obvious? She was really pissed off the last time I was talking to you."

Sam sighed. "She's just over protective, sorry

about that. She didn't mean any harm."

"Could've fooled me!"

"Why do you say that?"

Deborah felt as though she had been forgotten about and like *she* was the one interrupting a date. Who the hell were they talking about anyway, and who was this girl so rudely interrupting her date? She struggled to keep her frustration from showing.

"She came back into the cafe just after you both left," Claire went on.

"Yes, she left a bag under the table."

Claire wondered if she should tell him the rest, then she figured that she would probably never see Jenny again, so there really was no reason why she shouldn't. "She was really aggressive and told me to stay away from you!"

Sam seemed shocked by this. "What exactly happened?"

Deborah cleared her throat, allowing Sam to realise that he had forgotten to introduce the girls to one another, but he just smiled at Deborah and said, "Just a minute, sorry about this."

Deborah was in shock, where had his charm gone? And she had a sneaky suspicion that this conversation would lead to the outcome she was not willing to think about. It made her sick to think that he had a girlfriend and this is what the conversation with this Claire character was all about. She kept quiet and decided to listen to the rest of the conversation between her date and the stranger who had brought the bill to the table.

"When she came back into the cafe a few minutes after you'd left, she was fishing around under the table you were sitting at. I asked if there was something I could help her with and she went crazy, telling me to stay away from you. When I asked what the hell she was on about she just turned to me and said, *'Have a nice day'* as if nothing had happened!"

Sam frowned. "Are you ok?"

"Why did she behave like that?" Claire ignored his question.

"I don't know. I just think that she probably didn't mean it the way she said it."

Claire shook her head and proceeded to walk away, much to Deborah's relief, until Sam called her back.

"Claire, wait! I'm sorry that she made you feel like that. She's just... protective of me."

"Is she your mother or something?" Claire replied with sarcasm.

Sam shook his head, not wanting the situation to become an argument, "She's just a friend who's been there for me when I needed it most."

"Anyway, I need to get on, don't want my boss thinking I'm lazing around."

Sam took her hand and leaned in to kiss her on the cheek, "Sorry for the hassle."

Claire smiled, how could she be angry at him when his eyes sparkled like that? "It's ok, just make sure if you see me in the street and she's with you that you give me a wide berth. I can't be bothered having to deal with that again."

Sam nodded, unsure if she was kidding or not. "You have my word."

As Claire walked away from the table and Sam sat down, he looked up to see that Deborah's eyes were no longer relaxed and happy. They had an anger in them that he realised was justified.

"Oh my God, I am so sorry about that. I didn't even introduce you to her."

"No you didn't. Who was she, and more to the point, who is the other one you were talking about that bit her head off?"

"It's a long story; you really don't want to hear it, especially on our first date."

Deborah didn't want to ask too many questions in the fear that he would end up telling her to get lost. She decided on just one more question before changing the subject and forgetting the last five minutes had ever happened. "Are you involved with any of those women?"

"Not at all, I promise you. I'm a one woman kind of guy. Claire is a waitress who served me and a friend today, and the woman who she was referring to is my best friend who, as you may have gathered, is a little on the protective side when it comes to me," he held her hand as he explained.

Deborah accepted this, for now. She didn't want to rock the boat after what had just happened. But then she started to think, if this woman was so protective of Sam and had a go at a complete stranger in a cafe, then what would she think of her?

Sam must have seen the look on her face. "Don't worry, Jenny will love you. She's excited to meet you."

Deborah smiled. "Ok. I'd like to meet her too. She seems very important to you."

"She's like a sister to me."

Sam helped Deborah on with her coat and he led her out of the restaurant onto the busy street. It was cold and the street was dazzling with car headlights and street lamps. Deborah wrapped her coat around herself and hugged it close. Sam led her into a bar which was quiet and cosy with a real log fire burning at the back of the room. The decor was designed like a living room in someone's home. There were brown leather sofas dotted around with little tables in front of them and the walls were teal blue and mocha coloured. Above the fireplace was a large flat screen television and the windows were dressed with thick lined mocha coloured curtains.

"Wow, it's like a house in here," Deborah said.

"That's the idea. What would you like to drink?"

"I'll have a white wine please."

Sam left Deborah to make herself feel comfortable as she positioned herself on one of the large sofas. She looked around and couldn't help but wonder if yet another female would appear during her date, after the lengths that Deborah had gone to so she could be with Sam; it wouldn't surprise her at all.

"Hi, you're Deborah aren't you?" A voice interrupted her thoughts.

She looked up to see a red head standing at the end of the sofa. Deborah knew exactly who she was but wouldn't dream of allowing it to be known. "Yes, and you are?"

"Jenny, Sam's best friend," Jenny held out her hand to greet Deborah.

CHAPTER SIX

The flat was dark and empty. The windows were closed but that didn't stop the cold air creeping in from the autumnal evening.

The bedroom doors were closed and everything was in its original place. Sam's bedroom was in pristine condition with a bed that looked like it had been ironed and the window was dressed beautifully with the curtains symmetrically placed. The bottles of aftershave were also placed symmetrically on his dresser.

Her presence was not reflected in the mirror of the dresser, which was good. She didn't really want to look at herself as a dead girl, especially after the way she had died.

She moved from Sam's room to Jenny's room, not sure how she was going to commence her plan. She couldn't get her head around what had happened to her and she certainly was not ready to pass over to the other place. No, there was work still to do before she would be able to go anywhere.

It had been over a month since she had died and she hadn't exactly wrapped things up before passing. Things could've gone so much better for everyone involved, unfortunately that's not the way things had turned out.

Sam hadn't listened to anything that she had had to say and Sarah had decided that it was time to give up and accept the fact that things were over between them

How could he honestly think that she would do such things to him? She had begun to fall in love with him, why would she do anything to jeopardize that?

From the day she died, it had taken her three weeks to learn how to apply a physical presence to her spirit. She had almost given up trying, but then remembered that she had given up on something important to her once before and look where it had gotten her. So she journeyed through it and eventually she had managed to succeed. She had finally learned how to move things using her mind, make things happen that would seem impossible to the human eye. Sarah had to make Sam see sense, she had thought that what she had said to him as he walked away from her the last time he saw her that he would have turned around and really listened to what she had said about Jenny. Of course, Sarah understood that Sam would never believe that Jenny was capable of such a thing and now that Sarah knew the whole truth, she had to make sure that Sam knew before it ruined his life.

Sarah looked around, in drawers, behind the wardrobes, under the bed. But she didn't find what she was looking for. She was looking for *anything* that she could use to show Sam what had really been happening and why things had gone so wrong.

She moved again, around the flat from room to room, looking to see what she could move in order to make Sam notice that things were not right. Sarah had two choices, to be subtle or frighteningly obvious. She had decided to go with subtle to start, as much as she wanted to tear the place apart, she still cared deeply for Sam, even though she was dead. She didn't want to hurt him anymore than he had been. Sarah knew she had plenty of time to get the message across, she just didn't want it to take too long.

***

"Nice to meet you," Deborah replied, all the while blazing inside her was the urge to get up and walk out.

Jenny happily plonked herself next to Deborah on the couch as Sam waited for his order at the bar. Deborah didn't want to speak, in fear of saying something catty, or worse, but she needn't have worried as Jenny did most of the talking.

"So, Deborah," Jenny said. "What are you and Sam doing tonight?"

Deborah looked through Jenny, the way she had said her name... she couldn't quite work it out. Was it sincerity in her tone, or down right sarcasm? "Well, we actually haven't had much time to talk, people keep interrupting us!"

She knew it was a slight bend in the truth but she couldn't help herself, she was so angry.

"Oh?"

"It's ok though, we'll arrange another evening to really become acquainted."

Jenny flashed her bright white smile, sensing that Deborah was feeling threatened by her presence. Jenny placed a hand on her shoulder. "There's no need to worry Debs, I'm just his friend, more like his sister in fact."

Deborah smiled. "I know that, he's told me all about you."

Where the hell did she get off calling her Debs? The tension was about to reach breaking point just as Sam appeared at the table. "All good here I hope?"

Jenny smiled. "As always. I was just introducing myself."

Deborah also smiled but inside she was screaming. This was not what she had had planned for her night at all and Sam could sense what was going on. He could tell that Deborah wasn't happy.

"So, it was nice meeting you Debs, but I am going to get off, got a long day ahead of me tomorrow at work and I don't want to be tired," Jenny said.

Sam gave an hidden sigh of relief. He was happy that Jenny was there, but at the same time he was glad that she was leaving, he didn't want to make Deborah anymore uncomfortable than she already was.

"Nice to meet you too," Deborah replied, a little too chirpy.

Jenny kissed Sam on the cheek. "See you back at the flat."

As she walked away, Sam could feel eyes burning into the back of his head. He turned to see Deborah smiling. "What?"

Deborah shook her head. There was nothing she could say, all she could do was smile, enjoy the rest of the evening and hope there were no more interruptions. "Nothing at all. So, where were we?"

***

Jenny put her key in the door and as it turned in the lock, she froze. Intuition told her something wasn't right but she didn't know what it was. She wasn't sure if she should go any further or go back to the bar and wait with Sam.

Jenny knew she was probably being stupid, besides, she didn't want to be the spare part at the table and she could already tell that Deborah wasn't keen on her. She wasn't sure why exactly but she could guess that it was something to do with the fact that she was Sam's best friend. They were all the same, the girlfriends, always jealous.

Her mind was back in the present time and she decided that she would investigate what had stopped her in her tracks. Jenny was nervous as the tension built on opening the front door. The darkness in the hallway was deep and uninviting as she entered; she could feel it closing in on her. She felt suffocated by it and began to panic as she reached for the light switch to her left. She flicked it and as she did, the bulb made a popping sound before it flew out of the light on the ceiling and landed on the floor. Jenny screamed out at the sudden power surge and she had to steady herself. She fished for her mobile phone in her coat pocket and fumbled with the touch screen for the light setting. She shone the light from her phone down the hallway to see if anything untoward was inside as she slowly stepped further into the flat.

She made her way down the hallway toward the kitchen where she thought she would be able to turn the light on and have it shine out. As she crept slowly, terrified to turn and face the open doors of the bedrooms in case a face met her gaze, she looked straight ahead until she reached her safe haven, the kitchen. She flipped the switch and the light came on, much to her relief. It shone out of the kitchen and into the hall, where she instantly saw what had been making her feel uncomfortable.

As she faced her bedroom, horror was written in her expression at the message on the door of her wardrobe. She couldn't move, frozen in anticipation of what might come next. She read the message over and over, not sure what it meant or who had put it there.

Do not trust her!

The words alone were strange enough, but the medium used to put it there was what freaked her out. Her red lipstick laid on the floor next the bedroom door and she could tell that force was used to write the strange message as it was completely crushed out of its proper shape.

She was scared but also a little pissed off. Who, for a start would break into her home and secondly why would they write such a message with lipstick? Then it dawned on her, could it be Sarah? Surely she wouldn't be so desperate as to break into Sam's flat and try to scare them?

"Stupid bitch," Jenny muttered as she bent down to pick up the lipstick. When her hand connected with the tube, it felt cold, unusually cold. Freezing in fact, she couldn't lift it as it stung her hand at the very touch, like lifting an ice cube and holding it for too long.

"Jesus!" She exclaimed, pulling her hand away.

She stood back up and as she did, felt a breath on the back of her neck. She twirled around to see who was there so quickly that she almost lost her balance. No one stood in the place she had expected to find her intruder. The hairs on her arms stood on end, like on a cold day when the bitter wind bites and rain drops fall onto your skin.

"Who's there?" She called out, fully aware that the person wasn't going to reply with an introduction of themselves.

There was no sound, which scared her to the depths of her soul. It was too silent, until she heard the drawn out rasp which chilled her blood.

Jenny...

She didn't know where to look, what to say. She didn't want to breathe.

Jenny...

Again, the long, drawn out rasp came and this time, Jenny decided in a split second that she was leaving, regardless of who or what was in her home.

She forced her feet to leave the floor, allowing her to escape whatever it was that was tormenting her. She moved quickly out of her bedroom and down the hall towards the front door, without looking back. Already in her head were unpleasant images of what could be approaching her from behind, she didn't dare look round to have her thoughts confirmed. She finally reached the door and moved out to the landing. The silence was still intense, almost like she had gone deaf.

"Now what?" She found herself saying aloud.

She moved down the stairway to the bottom of the building and to her relief, she saw Sam approaching the main door. He was alone and could see that Jenny had gone pale. He put his key in the door before she could open it and she fell into his arms.

"Oh my God, what is it? What happened?" He asked in terror at the sight of his friend.

Jenny felt a wave of calm wash over her the

minute that Sam spoke. "There's something in our flat," she said quietly.

"What do you mean *something*?" Sam held her away so that he could look into her eyes. He saw terror, even though the now steadying calmness that had begun to take over her.

"I mean *something*, as in I don't think it was human!" She exclaimed.

"Ok, stay calm. I'll check it out, you wait here."

Jenny shook her head vigorously, becoming panicked again. "No, don't go in there."

Sam gripped Jenny's arms tightly to support her. He was a little frightened at how much she was beginning to shake. "We have to go back in at some point, we live here."

Jenny knew he was right. But she didn't want him to go back in, not because of what was in there, but in case of what he might see. The message written in lipstick, if it really was Sarah who had left it, then how would Sam react? He had only just got back to normal after their break up. She didn't want Sarah coming back into his life and attempting to ruin their friendship. However, the chilling voice was something that tampered with her rational explanation.

***

Sarah watched as Sam came quietly through the

front door of the flat. She knew that he was thinking that Jenny was being a little irrational when she said that she didn't think the presence in the flat was human.

Of course, Jenny was wrong. The presence *was* human, or at least used to be. Sarah wasn't sure what to class herself as, now that she was dead.

She could feel herself beginning to ache at the sight of Sam approaching her as he walked strongly and firmly towards her down the hallway. She still loved him with everything she had, and could still feel it in her heart (even though she no longer had a physical form) when she saw him that he was and would be the only one for her. She would wait for him for as long as it would take.

"Hello?" He called out as he threw open the doors of the rooms in the flat. "If you're in here, I strongly advise you leave within the next five seconds before you get hurt!"

Sarah knew that her time was up, for the moment. She wanted to let him know that she was with him, ready to protect him at any expense. She passed him by and made her way to the front door, ready to leave. But before she did, she gathered her energy into her mind and once she had enough, she lifted her hand and knocked a photo frame from the wall.

She watched him turn to face the direction of where the noise had come from. When he noticed the frame on the floor, he called out. "Jenny, was that you?"

"I'm still downstairs. Are you alright?" Her voice was strong again.

Sam moved closer to the frame which now lay on the floor. He wondered to himself how it had managed to fall from its hook. It had been up there for a long time, why would it fall now?

"Yes, I'm ok. You can come up now, there's nothing in here," he said as he cautiously picked the frame up from the floor and placed it back on the hook.

"Are you sure?"

Sam looked at the frame as it was back on the wall and then he turned to face the rest of his flat. He failed to mask the doubt in his voice. "Yeah, I am sure."

Jenny reluctantly made her way back up to their front door to see Sam staring at the photo frame that he had just hung back up on the wall. "What are you doing?"

"It fell off the wall, I'm hanging it back up," Sam replied with little expression in his tone.

"It *fell* off the wall?"

Sam nodded and turned to face Jenny, who was

now inside the flat, closing the door. She watched him as he regarded her, unsure of what he was about to say next. She was nervous, had he found something that he shouldn't have.

"Are you ok? You seem... weird," she asked quietly.

"What exactly happened in here? Something doesn't feel right, I feel, invaded."

"Invaded?" She almost laughed.

Sam frowned. "It's not funny, I really don't feel right."

Jenny took his hands in her own and gripped them tight. "I told you, I thought there was someone in here, but obviously I was wrong."

"But you were so sure, you were scared when I found you downstairs. What's changed?"

Sam's head began to ache and he wasn't entirely sure if what he had just experienced was real or not.

"Nothing's changed, I must have gotten it wrong," she said, even though she knew that someone or something *had* been inside. She had seen the lipstick message on the wardrobe door. She had heard her name in her ear, just thinking about it made her shudder. But she couldn't show her fear, not now after seeing Sam like this. He seemed genuinely spooked by something. And how did that frame just happen to fall off the wall?

"I need a coffee. You want one?" His tone suddenly changed, he seemed less tense.

"Erm, yeah I'll have one."

Jenny watched Sam walk to the kitchen and heard him fill the kettle. She ushered herself into her bedroom and closed the door. She turned to face the wardrobe, seeing the message on the door made her feel sick. Someone had been in here and left it for her to see. They had gone through her things, looking for something to write the message with.

Do not trust her.

She wracked her brain, trying to think of who could have been in her home and who the message was about. She definitely wasn't about to let Sam see it, he'd been through enough crap. Jenny was quite sure this was down to Sarah and if she was proven to be correct, she wouldn't be held accountable for her actions. Jenny would kill Sarah for this if she caught up with her. Jenny took out her mobile phone and took a photograph of the message before wiping it away. She decided that she wouldn't go to Sarah's house to confront her, which is what Sarah would want them to do. Jenny would wait to see if anything else would happen. Then and only then she would deal with the situation by herself. Sam didn't need to know about this.

***

Sarah had left, allowing Sam to calm down. She could see how distressed he had become after she had knocked the frame from the wall. Sam had meant and still did mean everything to her so she didn't want to be the one who caused him to freak out.

Sarah watched Jenny in her bedroom, studying the picture on her phone of the little message that had been left for her. There was anger in Jenny's eyes as she read it over and over. Sarah couldn't hear her thoughts but she knew what Jenny was thinking.

Sarah knew that her work for the moment was done, so she left Jenny and Sam to have a peaceful night. But she wasn't going to be gone for long and she would make sure that everyone knew the truth. Sarah was already dead, so she had nothing else to lose.

CHAPTER SEVEN

Deborah took the wipe across her face, removing the make-up that she had carefully applied to impress Sam. She looked deep into her own reflection in the mirror and wondered what had happened. She knew that Sam had a female friend, she understood that they were close and that it was nothing else other than friendship but she just couldn't get it out of her head. She just couldn't help but think that there was something else between them. She had felt it, in the air as they all sat together.

Sam had seemed oblivious to her thoughts as did Jenny. Deborah didn't want her imagination to ring true, but she just couldn't shake it off. Something had or was going to happen between Sam and Jenny. She didn't know what that something was but she knew that it was going to be big, something that would change things for all them all.

She wiped her eye, leaving a smear of black mascara across her cheek. Deborah could feel the tears begin to sting her eyes and even though she knew that she shouldn't, she couldn't help but allow them to fall.

Get a grip, she thought to herself as she dabbed at her face with the wipe. She looked into the mirror once more and continued to remove the make-up.

The mirror resembled that of a dressing room mirror backstage at the theatre, oval in shape with small light bulbs all around the frame allowing the person sitting in front of it to see the whole face. Deborah loved the theatre, she loved plays and productions.

That is how she had come to know of Sam. He was the biggest Scottish theatre actor there ever was and he had also come to appear in some small time television dramas. Everyone knew who Sam Leonard was, especially in Glasgow.

Deborah had specifically asked her university lecturer if she could do her placement in Glasgow Royal Concert Hall. It just so happened that Sam's current project was showing there at the time her placement was ready to commence; at least that's what she told herself. She had impressed the concert hall staff, offering to stay on and help out when the big productions were about to start. She would show people to their seats and ensure the audience were comfortable and had everything they needed. Of course, all free of charge. The purpose of her placement was to observe and learn how to write reviews but the more she was in Sam's company and breathing the same air as him, she couldn't bring herself to leave, knowing that he was still there. She needed to be near him, feel him around her and most of all she wanted to introduce herself to him, however every time that she tried to do that, something would stop her, like rehearsals or just plain old nerves getting the better of her. What if he rejected her? What if he laughed in her face?

Deborah had decided that she didn't want to face rejection during her placement there and mess up her degree, so she waited. She waited until the final show, the final curtain call. She wanted to be able to meet Sam for the first time without being tied to the concert hall and it just so happened that the final night of the show was her final day of placement.

She had listened in on a conversation between cast members about a celebratory drink in a bar in town after the show had finished and Deborah had decided to go along to the same bar and try to bump into Sam.

Her plan had worked and had worked well. She didn't mention her involvement in the concert hall, or the fact that she had become a little obsessed and followed his work. She had made sure that she knew everything about his work, where his schedule would take him, what his next project would be. All she had mentioned was that she had seen his play that final night. He had seemed to like the fact that she knew of him, little did he know just how much.

She had scanned his home that night, as he slept beside her. She had taken in every photograph, every object. She had even gotten up to go to the bathroom and noticed that there had been another room next to Sam's. The door had been slightly ajar and Deborah could see that there was a girl sleeping in there.

Deborah had found herself standing over this girl, Jenny, as she slept soundly in her bed. She instantly found this girl irritating, even though she hadn't had a conversation with her. She didn't know anything about her and maybe that was the problem. She knew everything that there was to know about Sam, so maybe she would feel better if she knew more about Jenny. But how would she find out the things that she needed to know without looking suspicious to Sam?

She decided that she would start by making it look as though she knew that all Sam wanted was a one night stand. She would trick him into thinking that that was all she had wanted too.

Deborah crept back into Sam's bedroom to retrieve her clothes, with every intention of keeping Sam's t-shirt which she had pulled on once she had decided to have a look around.

She had dressed herself quietly and made her way to the kitchen to get her handbag. Then she thought better of it. If she *left* her handbag, he'd find it and bring it to her, surely?

Deborah did one final scan of the flat, making sure she took everything in, just in case her plan didn't work and she might not find herself in the flat or his company ever again. As she crept past Sam's bedroom, all she wanted was to climb back into that bed and snuggle into him. But she knew this was the crucial time to leave if she wanted to find out if he really liked her. Waking up beside him in the morning wouldn't give her a true reaction. If he didn't like her, he would have to pretend, giving her a false impression. If she left at the moment she had intended then she would know for sure. He would either ignore the fact that she had left her bag in the flat and she would never see him again or he would bring it to her and she would know for sure if he wanted another night with her.

Deborah admitted to herself that it was a long shot but if it worked, everything would be amazing. She had smiled as she continued her way down the hall with her thoughts, stopping one last time outside Jenny's bedroom. She watched Jenny sleep, wondering what would come of Sam living with another female if he got into a serious relationship. Jenny began to stir, so Deborah made a quick and quiet exit.

Of course, her plan had worked as Sam had phoned her the very next day and asked her out on the date.

She continued to wipe her face, all the while thinking of the disastrous date and how Jenny turning up had thrown a spanner in the works. Sam had a history that Deborah didn't know about, with other females that she didn't know anything about. She began to worry as she looked at herself in the mirror.

She viewed her reflection and wondered what she was turning into. Deborah used to be strong, independent and full of drive towards a happy life with a good career. Now all she could think about was Sam Leonard. It wasn't that she wanted him, she needed him and she knew that it wasn't healthy. She wanted to stop her obsession, but it had taken her over. She could feel it in her bones and hear it in her heart beat.

Deborah wanted Sam and it scared her that she would stop at nothing to get him.

***

Deborah had been staring at her reflection for over an hour now, completely unaware of the time and the fact that the room was bitterly cold. She snapped out of her trance and got up to close the window, only to find that it was already closed.

"Where is that breeze coming from?" Deborah found herself saying out loud. She looked around her bedroom, confused by the breeze that had crept its way in without an open entrance.

Things had gone eerily quiet and she didn't like it. She traced her movements after coming home. She had locked the door, closed the window in the kitchen, and turned all the lights out. So where was it coming from?

Just as the question came she heard a thumping sound coming from the other side of her bedroom door. She was frozen in fear.

"Who's there?" She called out.

There was no reply. The breeze had stopped and so had the thumping.

"Hello?"

Deborah watched as the tiny hairs on her arm stood on end and she felt them rise on the back of her neck too. What the hell was going on?

Deborah refused to leave her bedroom, instead she turned on the television and climbed into bed. She refused to let the thought of ghosts enter her mind, she couldn't think of anything else that could have made that sound. She was too scared to leave the room to check. The fear of the unknown held her there, in her bed. She wanted to do something to take her mind off what had just happened.

As she flicked through her recordings on the Sky plus box she found the drama which starred Sam Leonard. It had been on her box for almost one year now and she listened to his voice as she drifted off, completely unaware of the entity still lurking in her home.

Being surrounded by the sound of his voice comforted Deborah but she knew that she needed more than just his voice. She wanted Sam Leonard to belong to her and only her. She had already stopped at nothing to get what she wanted and she was beginning to realise that she didn't care who got hurt in the process, so long as it wasn't her.

CHAPTER EIGHT

"Are you kidding?" He asked furiously.

Jenny couldn't believe that he was so angry, he never normally acted this way when she did something that she thought was right by him.

"I'm asking you a question Jenny!" He raised his voice again.

"No, I'm not kidding. Why are you so pissed off?"

Sam couldn't believe how calm she was. She had threatened a complete stranger and she thought it was ok. "Why am I so pissed off? I'll tell you why Jenny. The girl was serving us *lunch*, not trying to rob us. What the hell is wrong with you?"

Jenny felt a knot in the pit of her stomach.

"Well?" Sam persisted.

Jenny shook her head. "Look, I was just looking out for you. You know, after all the Sarah stuff I thought you would appreciate it."

Sam sighed. "I do appreciate it. But that was a little different Jenny, Sarah was my girlfriend."

"Psycho girlfriend," she rolled her eyes.

"She wasn't well in the head."

She could see how angry he felt about it and it killed her to see him like this. She felt her heart wrench and instantly regretted what she had said to Claire. "Come here," she said as she wrapped her arms around him.

"I'm sorry to shout. I just don't see why you had to threaten her, she hadn't done anything wrong."

Jenny gritted her teeth but relaxed before she replied. "I know. I just, I don't know. I suppose I'm just protective of you after everything that's happened. Is that such a crime?" She pulled away to see his face. His eyes were sad after speaking about Sarah.

"It will be if you keep threatening people. I'm going to meet someone eventually Jenny and she won't be crazy. She will be like anyone else, and you will have to learn to trust her."

Jenny nodded. "I know," was all she could manage. She hated seeing him like this, and she certainly didn't want to be the one to make him feel this way.

"And anyway, I may have met her already."

Jenny let go of him and walked over to the kitchen sink, "Really?"

"Yep; Deborah. She really is something else."

Jenny managed a smile. "You think she's something special?"

Sam shrugged his shoulders. "Who knows? But I would be happy to continue to find out. Although after last night I'm not so sure that she'll want to see me again.

"Why didn't you ask me about Claire last night at the bar, or when we got back here?"

Sam looked out of the window, remembering the disastrous date with multiple interruptions and then the strange happenings in the flat when he had come home. "Wasn't the right time to discuss it."

"Are we ok?" Jenny asked apprehensively.

Sam smiled. "I can't stay angry at you. But just tone it down Jenny, not every girl I see or even just talk to is going to turn out crazy."

Jenny smiled again, knowing that he was right but not willing to admit it. "So, Deborah wasn't too keen on me appearing last night, was she?"

"Well considering Claire had turned up at our table discussing your antics I'm not surprised. But don't worry, once you meet her properly you will be able to show her how nice you really are," Sam flashed his charming grin. "Listen, I have to get going to see what the reviews are saying about the final night of the play. I'll see you later. If anything weird happens in here again, let me know straight away, ok?"

Jenny nodded. She worried that Sarah wouldn't stop her harassments. The lipstick message was easy to hide from Sam and yes; since he had ended things, the letters and the phone calls had ceased. But what if the lipstick message was the beginning of it all again? Girls didn't treat Sam like a normal guy. They were all giggly and stupid around him and Sarah had been so head over heels with him that she had tried to drive a wedge between him and Jenny. What if she kept coming back? Jenny pondered with the idea that she should tell Sam about the message but decided against it. He had found Deborah and seemed happier than he had been in a while. Jenny didn't want to be the one to spoil that.

CHAPTER NINE

There was a strong stench of death and decay as DS Paul Preston entered the manor house he and DC Jim Lang had been called to earlier. It lingered in the air and soon would begin to linger in their nostrils and cling to their clothing. The forensics had been there for an hour or so before their arrival and the area around the house had been taped off by the uniformed officers, who were now standing guard at the bottom of the drive.

"Oh dear, this doesn't look good," Lang said as he examined the entrance hall to the property. He looked at the body on the floor at the bottom of the stairs and grimaced at the angle of the left leg. "Well, I think that this leg is broken."

"You think?" Preston replied. Being used to Lang's sarcasm, he brushed it off.

The forensic team busied themselves around the

two men as they continued to look around the house. It was a large property; a manor house in its day, now just one of the many large houses in the Glasgow area. Over the years its decor had tired and was in good need of some renovation work but its current state was liveable. The manor emanated years of life where people came and went, lived and died and spent many happy years. There were picture frames all over the walls and each one was a family picture, with many different faces. The body that lay on the floor looked to be the youngest in the photographs.

The forensic team were dusting surfaces for fingerprints as Preston retrieved a pair of gloves from one of the younger members of the forensic team. Preston had worked in the force for years but it never got any easier seeing a dead body, especially if it had been a possible murder. The face was not recognizable due to the length of time the body had been there and the colour of the corpse suggested that time of death had been around four weeks previous to their arrival. Preston was no coroner but after years of experience he was becoming more aware of time scales in death. It still sickened him a little but the smell was the worst thing about it. He sometimes struggled to remind himself that a corpse that had laid for this long had once been a person; it was hard to imagine, what with the colour and change in appearance. His thoughts were interrupted by his colleague's voice.

"Do you think she was pushed?"

Preston shook his head, unsure of the answer. "I'm not sure. It's a fifty-fifty chance at the moment since we've only just found her. What did the informant say exactly?" He gestured for them to leave and allow the forensics team to get on with their jobs.

Lang sighed. "Not much to be honest, apparently a local florist who delivers flowers here on a monthly basis hadn't received payment and had tried to phone to see if everything was all right. When she couldn't get through, she decided to drop by to check in person. She knocked on the door a few times and when no one answered, she looked through the letterbox and saw the deceased lying on the floor."

"Do we have a name?" Preston asked, crossing the threshold and savoring the fresh air that now filled his lungs.

"Yep," Lang checked his notebook from his breast pocket. "Sarah Henderson."

Preston pulled his gloves off. He looked back into the house and at the girl, now known as Sarah and shook his head. "Ok, we need to speak to this florist, see if she noticed anything unusual about the house when she came to check on her; anything which may have been out of place."

Lang agreed. "Yes, we also need to check her phone records; see who she's been in contact with. Maybe there's a boyfriend or someone we can talk to who might've been close to her."

"Aye, you get on that and I'll question the florist, let's see what we can come up with. You never know, it could've been a genuine accident."

"Here's hoping, a house this size; someone could've been after her money."

Preston nodded. "The world's not short of a greedy bugger, right enough."

As Preston and Lang headed to their car, they could hear the forensic team busying themselves around the house and the grounds, searching the property for any kind of clue which would explain Sarah's death.

"If anything crops up, no matter how small, contact either myself or Lang at the station right away. Got it?" Preston called out. The team stopped in their tracks and there were muffled replies of agreement before they continued with the search.

The gravel crunched under the officers' shoes as

they made their way back to the car. The driveway was extensively large and they had parked just at the entrance. The weather matched their mood with grey clouds hanging over Glasgow's West End. Clouds always seemed to hang over the city, especially if there was a death to deal with. Preston had seen enough dead bodies in his time and so some would suggest that he would be used to it by now, but it never did get easier. Perhaps it was the father in him, knowing that someone's child was the victim always got to him. His family meant everything to him and he was never fully relaxed knowing that there were crazy people out there, willing to kill- sometimes for no other reason than because they could. He had come to accept the fact that since the day he had welcomed his first daughter into the world he never would feel relaxed again. He was definitely a soft touch when it came to his girls, but if anyone ever tried to mess with them, God help them. When Ross Turner had been on the rampage, Preston's heart was in his throat the whole time. Ross had targeted young women like his beautiful girls and Preston had been quietly terrified that his girls would fall prey to his sadistic way of thinking. Thankfully, they hadn't and Preston was grateful for that but still sorry that someone else had to deal with their daughter's murder. He remembered Mrs Noble, the mother of Angela Noble and the state that she was in when they had gone to see her with Patrick. He had remained professional, but remembered thinking that he never wanted to feel her pain.

"You alright there, Paul?" Lang asked, noticing how distant he was.

"Aye, let's get back to the station and get stuck into this. The sooner we know what happened to the girl the better."

They reached the car and climbed in. Lang brought the engine to life and slowly eased out of the driveway. "Some size of house isn't it? I mean, why was a girl like her living here by herself?"

Preston shook his head. "Maybe been left to her in a will, we'll find out more about her when we speak to the florist, who by the way seems to be the only person to have brought attention to this death."

"Aye, that's a bit strange. Suppose we'll just have to see what her phone records say. We'll be able to get a feel for who she was in contact with, see if any of her friends know if anything has happened which could have led up to her death. How long do you think she had been lying there?"

"I'd say around four weeks Jim, the stench was unbelievable and her face was pretty much gone.

But we'll wait for the coroner to get an accurate time of death. You never know, she may not have died immediately, she could have been alive and then died later. Either way, I'm not sure."

"Poor kid, what a waste," Lang said, pulling up to a set of traffic lights. Preston looked up, realising they were on South Street and wondering how Patrick was getting on since deciding not to work with them after the Turner case. "What do you think Mr McLaughlin has been doing since we last saw him?"

"Ghost hunting most likely," Lang said; his sarcastic attitude never far away when the subject of psychics was brought to the table.

"Ghost hunting?" Preston raised one eyebrow and smiled.

"I don't know, conjuring up spirits, or whatever it is that he does."

"Still not convinced then?" Preston laughed.

"Never will be, no matter what happens in front of me. That Turner case was all coincidental as far as I'm concerned. The guy turned out to be his bloody brother for God's sake."

Preston knew that Lang would never accept Patrick fully and it was fair enough. "If you say so, Jim."

"I do say so, Paul. I did come to like Patrick in

the end but no one on this earth could change my mind about death and the afterlife. In my opinion, when you're dead, you're dead and that's the end of it. I don't know, maybe he's just good at guessing." They both laughed. Lang may not have ever said it out loud but Preston knew fine well that even if psychics were proven to be one hundred percent legit, Lang would never back down. He had been secretly glad that Patrick had turned down the offer; he didn't want to be known to anyone as the officer who relied on the word of a psychic. Patrick had told Lang particular things that he couldn't have known about when they were investigating the Turner case, and at first Lang had begun to loosen up about the whole psychic thing, but not long after that he was back to his old skeptical self.

The discussion came to a close when they pulled up to the station in Pitt street. The weather had gone from dull and grey, to rain pelting down from the heavens and as Preston and Lang got out of the car they ran to the entrance, trying to save their suits from looking like they'd just been in the washing machine.

"Come on Jim, we've a lot to get through."

As they made their way down the corridor, Lang stopped at the coffee machine. "Fuel for the mountains of paperwork we're bound to have to go through?"

"Aye, better make it a strong one. I'll get in contact with the florist." Preston replied. Whether Sarah Henderson was murdered or died by accident, Preston had a feeling that this case was going to cause him a serious headache.

CHAPTER TEN

Lang had trailed through endless amounts of Sarah Henderson's phone records, looking for anything that he could use to find out what actually happened to her. He had written down a few numbers and found out who the servers were, allowing him to match names to the phone numbers. There were a lot of call records, made and received and they spanned over a number of weeks leading up to Sarah's death. He sat back on his chair, running his hand over his head and then pinching the bridge of his nose. He wasn't so sure how he was going to explain to Preston that he recognised two of the names on the records. Of course, Glasgow was a big city and there were likely to be several hundred people with the same name so surely this had to be coincidental. He watched as Preston entered the office, coffee in one hand and a stack of papers in the other. "How you getting on with those phone records, Jim?"

Lang sighed, "There are a handful of numbers on here spanning over a few weeks, it seems like Sarah Henderson only had a handful of contacts."

"Ok, so where are we headed to first?" Preston blew into the plastic cup allowing the steam to float up around his face.

"Paul, you'd better come and sit down. There is something I need to ask you about these records."

Preston frowned, not fully understanding the meaning behind Lang's words. "What's wrong?" He sat down on the seat next to Lang.

"Well, I've been going through these records and the same numbers have been cropping up from calls made and received, apart from the odd call centre number. So I got in touch with the providers and got the names of the accounts linked to the numbers." He stopped, not sure where to take it next.

Preston gestured, moving his hand in circular motions telling Lang to continue, "And?"

Lang slid the records across to Preston, allowing him to look for himself. Preston lifted the paper and his eyes scanned over it. Lang watched as he read each name and as he expected, Preston's eyes stopped over the two names that he knew would catch his attention. He looked up at Lang and simply said, "Shit!"

Lang nodded. "Do you recognise the number next to the names?"

Preston pulled his phone out of his pocket and scanned through the names in his contacts list. "I don't memorize numbers Jim, that's what these things are for. I need to check the number against my contacts."

A few moments passed where Preston stared at the phone then the paper. "Aye, they match."

Lang sighed heavily. "It's nothing to worry about Paul, we'll sort it."

"Sort it? My daughters' names are on Sarah Henderson's phone records and if you hadn't already guessed it, Sarah Henderson is dead. Whether it was murder or not, I have to go and tell them that a friend of theirs has been found dead."

"Do you know that she was a friend of theirs?" Lang asked, trying not to sound too accusing.

"Well, she's not family, so I can't see any other way that they would know her."

Lang nodded, he knew fine well that Preston's daughter's involvement with Sarah would be innocent but he had to go down every avenue of scrutiny until they were sure Sarah's death was accidental. "We'll both go to see them, but I think I should do the talking. You're the father after all; you have to have some separation."

"Aye, I know. Let's just go and get this over with."

***

The journey to the Preston household was quiet. He never liked to allow work and home life to come together but with this he didn't see that he had much choice. The weather had turned nasty and the rain battered off the wind screen as the wipers fought to keep it clear. With the rain came the dip in temperature and this followed the dip in Preston's mood. "Why did I pick this as my career?"

"Because, you love to catch the baddies Paul, you've always been good at it." Lang didn't dare take his eyes off the road; he could barely see it as it was with the rain lashing over the car.

"Is there a baddie to catch in this though, Jim? I mean, my daughters are university students who still live at home. Could there be something dark in this or am I just being paranoid because Lisa and Jane are involved in this somehow?"

Lang wasn't sure how to respond, he couldn't imagine how he would be feeling if it were his daughter involved. "Let's just wait and see what

100

they say first."

As they pulled up to the house, the rain didn't do them any favors, in fact it seemed to get heavier. Preston and Lang got out of the car and ran the ten yards to the front door. Preston turned to Lang who was behind him and said, "Wipe your feet; my Janet will go mental if you get mud on the floor."

"That's what you're worried about now?" Lang shook his head. It was clear to him that Preston was nervous about telling his daughters about Sarah and it was also clear that he was nervous about their involvement in her life. Lang wasn't stupid, he's seen enough dead bodies in his time to recognise a murder when he saw one but he was never one for jumping to conclusions.

Janet Preston came out from the large kitchen at the back of the house with an apron around her and oven gloves on. "Oh, hi dear, what are you doing here at this time of the day? Hi Jim, would you like a drink?"

Lang nodded, "Tea would be great Jan, thanks."

"I have to speak to the girls, are they home?" Preston asked. Janet picked up on his nervous tone.

"What's wrong Paul?" Now she sounded nervous. Janet Preston was a proper house wife and stay-at-home mum, even though their two daughters were in their twenties and at university.

Her physical health had deteriorated in the last few years, having slipped a disc in her neck when making the bed one Saturday morning, Paul insisted she give up her job in hairdressing. She had loved it dearly but with it being such a demanding job and causing her to be on her feet all of the time, it was best that she gave it up. Janet still coloured and styled Lisa and Jane's hair and cut Preston's when the sides became wispy but that was about as far as it went. She did miss her job, the social side and the constant development of hair styling but she would never go back to it. Her body wouldn't allow it, she struggled to do the weekly food shop and couldn't carry more than two full bags without her neck becoming unbearably painful. Now, she lived for her family, cooking meals for her and Paul every night, making sure that the girls were well equipped for their university course and her weekly book club. Janet was happy with her life and wouldn't change it now.

"Something has happened to someone that the girls know and we need to ask them a few questions," Lang answered for him.

Janet couldn't hide the worry in her expression, especially since Lang had answered the question. "I'll go upstairs and bring them down, they're studying."

Janet climbed the stairs, her feet barely making a sound on the wooden slats that lined the floor. She was a petite woman, with a small frame and very slim face. Her hair was of shoulder length and light brown in colour and her eyes were a clear blue. Preston often thought of the ocean on the sunniest of days when he looked into her eyes- it was one of the many reasons as to why he fell in love with her.

"Are you going to be ok with this Paul?" Lang asked.

"They're my girls Jim, its better if this comes from me. So long as there is nothing sinister in it, which I whole-heartedly believe there isn't."

They heard foot-steps above them, approaching the top of the stairs and the muffled voices of Lisa and Jane Preston as they descended them, completely unaware of the knot in their dad's stomach. Lisa Preston was a twenty six year old student teacher at Glasgow University and on her second year and Jane Preston was twenty four years old and a drama and dance student at the Royal Scottish Academy of Music and Drama. Both girls led very different lives and were quite close. They shared the same group of friends and went out together as often as their busy university schedules would allow them to. The girls adored their dad and were often referred to as 'daddy's girls' by their mum.

They entered the living area with beaming smiles and hugged their dad as if they hadn't seen him in a week. "Hi dad, what's up?" Jane asked.

"Hi Jim," Lisa added as Janet hurried by them to make the tea she had offered him on his arrival.

"Girls, have a seat. I have a few things that I want to ask you." Preston sat down on the single recliner in front of the window. He noticed that the rain had stopped.

The girls sat down on the sofa next to the door. Lisa noticed that there was something not right with her dad and it bothered her. She lowered her cheery tone, "What is it, dad?"

Preston took a breath. "Are you girls friends with a female named Sarah Henderson?"

Both girls gave their full attention at Sarah's name. "Yes, she's our friend. She's in my course at uni, although she has been on placement so I haven't seen her for a few weeks," said Lisa.

"She's lovely but I think she is a bit lonely. She has this *massive* house that was left to her in a family will. Don't think she wants it to be honest but I can't see why, it would be an amazing party house," Jane added, still unaware that Lisa had noticed something untoward with their dad.

"What's happened to her?" Lisa asked. "You wouldn't sit us down and ask about a random friend if everything was ok."

Preston could see that Lisa was worried; Jane on the other hand was a little slow at picking up on where the conversation was headed. "Something has happened to her, we're not sure what yet. But she was found dead this morning."

Jane's expression changed then, from pure oblivion to utter devastation. "Dead? Are you sure dad?"

Lisa's eyes had filled with tears and her bottom lip quivered. "What do you mean she was *found* dead? Where?"

"At the bottom of the staircase in her house," Lang cut in before Preston. This was becoming too personal. He wanted to take over until the girls calmed down. "We're not sure if she fell or was…"

"Pushed?" Lisa finished his sentence for him.

"We are going to be looking at all lines of enquiry. But we need your help. We need to know more about Sarah, who she was friends with, where she went out, who she was seeing- that sort of thing."

Jane got up and went into the kitchen to get a tissue for herself and Lisa when Janet suddenly encased her in her arms. "Oh darling, I am sorry.

Are you alright?"

"Yeah, I'm just in shock."

"Come on darling, let's go into the living room and face this together."

Jane nodded and allowed her mum to lead her back through to the living room. They sat down on the couch and Janet placed herself in between her two daughters and held their hands. "Ok Paul. Tell the girls what you need to know."

Preston felt a mixture of emotions as he watched his wife take control of the situation. She was the family rock who everyone leaned on when times were tough and for such a little woman, she sure as hell knew how to put a brave face on a tough situation. "Yes, so like Jim said, we're not one hundred percent sure yet if Sarah's death was accidental and we need more information about her and her life which will help us to determine that."

Lisa's mind had gone into overdrive. "How did you find out she's our friend?"

"We tracked down her phone records, there were only a handful of numbers on it and your numbers were in amongst them," Lang answered.

Lisa nodded. "Ok. So what can we do to help?"

Lisa Preston displayed a hardened exterior but on the inside in times like this she would often

106

breakdown. She was a private person when it came to her feelings and she would often hide how much she was hurting.

"We would like a list of names; friends, boyfriends, that sort of thing." Lang had taken control of the discussion; he could remain impartial and at some point in the investigation Paul would be able to distance himself from Lisa and Jane's involvement once they had done their bit.

"Let me get my phone and a notepad and pen and I will write everything down that I know." Lisa got up and went upstairs to her bedroom, Jane followed her.

"Can you believe this?" Lisa said as she rummaged in her bedside table for her notepad. She could feel the tears sting the corners of her eyes but fought against them.

"That our friend may have been murdered; no, I can't believe it!" Jane's hands trembled as she took her phone off the charger dock. "How can you be so calm?"

Lisa took a deep breath. "It's not without difficulty. Come on, Sarah was our friend and she would want us to help her. Let's get this over with."

Lisa took Jane's hand and together they faced their friend's death.

CHAPTER ELEVEN

It didn't take long for the girls to give Preston and Lang the information they needed to take their enquiries further. It seemed that Sarah Henderson hadn't had that many friends and she had been the last remaining member of her family- according to Lisa.

"Why was she living in that huge house by herself?" Preston had asked.

Lisa was struggling to keep her emotions at a level of control but she was determined to answer as many questions as she could to help her friend. "She was the last Henderson in her family; she said that the house had been in her family for over a century and that it would remain in the family until they died out; if they ever did. She was a private girl but I do remember her saying that she wanted to have a big family so that she could carry on the blood line- she wanted to keep her own name so that the house would always remain 'Henderson Manor'. It's so sad that will never happen now."

Lang was scribbling everything down in his notepad and Preston was nodding along as Lisa spoke. "She thought that she would marry Sam but it wasn't going too well."

Lang stopped writing. "What do you mean?"

"They kept arguing apparently," Jane added, wiping a tear from her cheek.

"What would they argue about?" Preston went on to ask.

Lisa shook her head, as though she were gathering her information before she spoke. "Like I said, she was pretty private. She mentioned that they argued about stuff to do with his best friend but she never really elaborated on it."

Lang looked out of the window; the sun had broken through the clouds and the wet ground glistened in the brightness. "Could you give me more information on this Sam character please?"

Jane looked to Lisa to give the information. "I can't do this Lisa; I feel sick talking about her in the past tense, I feel sick at the thought that she's dead."

Lisa took her hand; she was always the stronger of the two and she was always intent on looking after her little sister no matter what the situation. "His name is Sam Leonard and she was with him for a while. She seemed really happy when they first started seeing each other but after a while she started acting really strange."

"In what way?" Lang pushed.

"I don't know, she was a little distant and was always blaming their arguments on his friend."

"And what's this friend's name?"

"I don't know, like I said, she never gave too much away when it came to her relationship."

Jane kept her eyes on her Dad, knowing that he would make it all ok. She trusted her dad to keep her and Lisa safe. "Do you think she was killed on purpose, Dad?"

Preston smiled. "We don't know anything yet sweetheart, but we'll find out what happened to her, I promise."

Jane didn't doubt that they would find out what happened to Sarah. They were police officers and she knew her dad had never missed a case yet.

Lang turned from the window to face Lisa. "Hang on, Sam Leonard you say?"

"Yes."

"Sam Leonard, the actor guy?" Lang asked.

Lisa nodded. "So she said. At first I didn't believe her, but then she showed me a picture of the two of them and I had no choice but to believe her."

"You were never in their company when they were together?" Preston asked.

"No, again like I said, she was very private and didn't like to broadcast her relationship; maybe because he's so well known."

Preston and Lang stood up and smiled at the girls. "Thanks girls, you've been more than helpful." Lang said.

Lisa smiled but it didn't reach her eyes which glistened behind the tears she was fighting against. "Please find out what happened to her, I'd hate to think that someone would have wanted to hurt her."

Jane reached out and hugged her dad tight whilst still holding Lisa's hand. She couldn't believe what was happening.

"I'll see you tonight girls, I'll try to be home for dinner."

"I'll keep some food by for you if you aren't home on time, Paul." Janet's voice came from the kitchen door. Sorrow reflected in her eyes; she was hurting for her girls.

The girls made their way back upstairs and Preston kissed his wife goodbye before they left the house. They got into the car and Preston pinched the top of his nose. "I cannot believe this."

"They're nothing but innocent in all of this Paul, don't you worry about them, they're strong girls and they'll deal with this." Lang placed his hand on Preston's shoulder.

"I know Jim, I just hate that they're involved at all."

Lang started the engine. "So we're off to see the florist next. Maybe she'll know something to link with what the girls have said."

"Aye, maybe but I am not so sure anyone other than Sam Leonard will be able to help us," Preston replied.

Lang drove out of Preston's street and along to the main road. The rain had started falling again and along with it some hailstones.

"Jesus, this weather is mental. Do you think we'll ever get a break with the weather here?" Preston asked.

"Aye right, and I'm the Pope," Lang laughed.

Preston took the note from the dashboard that contained the florist's shop address and read it aloud, "Lynne's Flowers, Hyndland Road."

Lang nodded. "That's not far from here, just five minutes. In fact that isn't far from Henderson Manor."

"Well, it would make sense that she used a

florist nearby."

Before they knew it they had arrived at the little purple and yellow shop which was sandwiched in between a café and an independent book shop. They parked outside and went in to see the owner.

When they were inside, the gentle scent of various flowers filled their nostrils. A little bell above the door rang out pleasantly, to make the staff aware of the potential custom. The shop floor was colourful with flowers which Preston and Lang had no clue of their names, the only flower that Lang could name was a rose and daffodil and Preston was much the same. Preston realised that Lynne's Flowers would probably donate to Sarah's funeral.

"I'll be with you in just a second," a female voice came from a room at the back.

"It's D.C Lang and D.S Preston, Ms Prowse. We're here about Sarah Henderson," Lang called back.

Lynne Prowse popped her head out of what Lang had decided was the stock room. "Oh, of course. I'll shut the shop while we chat; tea?"

"No thanks Ms Prowse, we'll make this as quick as possible," Preston replied.

Lynne Prowse came out from the stock room and stood behind the serving desk, placing her hands on the counter. "I'll try to be as helpful as I can, I just cannot believe that she's dead. Sarah was such a loyal customer."

"How often did you deliver flowers to Sarah?" Preston asked taking notes as Lynne spoke.

"Sarah gave me instructions to deliver white lilies and purple pansies at the beginning of every month. She would always pay directly into my business account on the last day of the month- in advance you'll understand."

"And why is it that she had flowers delivered every month?" Lang asked.

Lynne shrugged her shoulders. "Why is that of importance?"

Preston's brow furrowed. "Because Ms Prowse, we're asking the questions here and we'd like to know the answer, to *anything* we see fit to ask."

Lynne shrugged her shoulders again. "She liked to put fresh flowers on the family burial plot to keep it looking nice you see." Lynne wasn't sure why she had challenged Lang on his question. She did feel slightly intimidated that there were two officers in her shop and all she wanted to do was sell flowers; she'd had no intention of annoying anyone.

"Burial plot?" Preston asked.

"Yes, there's a family burial plot outside the

back of the manor. They date back a century I think."

Lang was astounded by this but remained professional. "Ok, Ms Prowse did you notice anything about Sarah the last time you saw her?"

Lynne shook her head. "No. Like I said, I delivered Lilies and Pansies to her at the beginning of every month and the only words that were ever exchanged were pleasantries. I knew nothing about the girl."

Preston believed her. "Ok Ms Prowse. Thank you for your time and if you have any more information or think of anything else then please do contact us." He handed his card over.

"Good day to you Ms Prowse," Lang said as they left.

On leaving the shop, Lang thought about Lynne's statement and was unsure if there would be anything from it that would help their enquiry. "Onto Sam Leonard's house then?"

"Aye, back to the station first though, I want a bit of background information on him before we begin questioning. He's the only one whose number is on her records and had the most contact with over a certain amount of months so I want to make sure that we have all the relevant information on him that we need before we question him first."

They climbed back into the car and Preston drove them down Hyndland Road and crossed over Byres Road. The little cafés and delis were empty on account of the rain and the roads were jammed with cars and buses. No one wanted to be out in the crazy weather that Preston and Lang had experienced over the course of the day. They drove down University Avenue and the huge trees sheltered the street from the pelting rain which had once again begun to fall.

"So, any thoughts on this?" Lang asked as they proceeded to cross the lower end of Sauchiehall Street and then turned left onto Argyll Street.

"Aye, I think that Sam Leonard will be able to help us out with this. Even if the relationship had gone sour and the girl was so devastated that she had killed herself, it would still put an end to the enquiry."

Lang nodded, "Maybe you're right."

Preston pulled up outside the station and killed the engine. "Ok, let's see what we can find on this Sam Leonard."

The sun made another break in the clouds and shone down as they walked into the station.

CHAPTER TWELVE

Sam Leonard stood in front of the mirror as he brushed his teeth and watched the paste foam up and spill over his lips. He thought about what to do with his day off and wondered if he should contact his agent to see if any of the theatre productions coming up had shown an interest in him since his last performance. The bathroom smelled like men's shower gel and the condensation from the hot water in the shower ran down the gleaming white tiles. Sam felt good and was happy that he finally felt like his personal life was getting back to normal. Deep in his daydream, he heard Jenny call out for him from the end of the hall. He wrapped a towel around himself and popped his head out of the en suite shower room. "What's up?"

"There are some people here who want to talk to

you," Jenny replied; her voice uneasy.

Sam frowned. "Who is it?"

"It's the police."

Without warning, Sam's stomach flipped making him feel instantly nauseous. What would the police want? He quickly dried himself off and threw on a pair of stonewash denims and a black t-shirt. He reached for the handle on the bedroom door and made his way into the hallway, where he observed two men, each dressed in a suit. One was taller than the other and slimmer, the short one was plump; a size Sam did not care to think about for when he reached middle aged himself. Putting on his most confident gleaming smile he said, "What can I do you for gentlemen."

Lang (the plump one) replied, "We would like to talk to you about a Miss Sarah Henderson."

"Can we sit down?" Preston asked.

Sam felt another lurch in his stomach. "Yes, let's go through to the sitting room."

Jenny followed Sam and the two officers into the sitting room and sat down beside Sam, ready and waiting to offer support, lacking care for whatever the reason was as to why the officers were in their home in the first place.

"I'm D.S Preston and this is D.C Lang." Preston paused as Sam nodded, as if accepting their introduction. "Can you confirm that you know Sarah Henderson?"

"Yes, she's my ex-girlfriend."

Sam swallowed hard, he was quite sure that he knew what was coming next from the officer but he didn't want to hear it.

"We were called out to a property in Winton Drive earlier this morning, where Sarah Henderson was found dead."

Sam's stomach contents were like a demon trying to break free from hell. He made it to the bathroom just in time, spilling his guts like someone who had just eaten a dead animal. The violent wretches caused pain to his sides and temples but he managed to control his breathing and compose himself before returning to the sitting room.

"Are you ok?" asked Jenny, who was white with shock.

"Yeah, sorry about that." Sam felt ashamed with his reaction; he really had thought that Sarah couldn't affect him anymore. He guessed he was wrong.

"Mr Leonard, we would like to ask you some questions about your involvement with Sarah Henderson," Preston said.

Sam placed his hand over his abdomen again, as

if trying to control his stomach reflex. "Of course."

Lang retrieved his trusty notebook from the breast pocket of his jacket and flipped it open. He allowed Preston to do most of the questioning, giving him time to write everything down.

"So, Mr Leonard can you confirm the last time you saw Sarah Henderson."

Sam cast his mind back to the day that he ended their relationship; they hadn't parted on particularly good terms. "Around a month ago, maybe more; I'm not sure."

Lang scribbled away, trying to avoid missing anything that Sam was saying.

"Maybe more?" Preston asked.

"I don't keep a list of dates and times if that's what you mean," Sam replied, annoyed by Preston's tone.

"Ok, and could you tell us about the content of conversation that took place on that day?"

Sam hadn't allowed himself to think about Sarah at all since their break-up, let alone think about the day that he left the only woman who he ever had feelings for. "We broke up the last time I saw her." The sentence hung in the air, hovering over everyone in the room. Sam understood that Preston wasn't going to allow it to hang over them for any length of time, so he carried on, "She had become a little, shall we say obsessed. I couldn't cope with it so I ended it."

The room would have been silent, if it wasn't for the scraping of Lang's pen. He looked up from the notebook. "Obsessed with what?"

"Me, she was obsessed with me."

Lang glanced at Preston, unsure of what Sam meant when he used the word obsessed, so he went on. "Please elaborate Mr Leonard."

"She was stalking me!" Sam said with a raised tone.

Preston's brow furrowed. "Your own girlfriend was stalking you?"

"She was always a little jealous that my best friend happened to be female and so from the offset she and Jenny never really got on."

"Jenny?"

"That's me, Jenny Lawson," Jenny replied, offering support.

Preston glanced at Jenny, taking in the information that Sam had expressed. "So you never got along with Sarah; why was that?"

Jenny shook her head, "Sam just told you why, she didn't like the fact that Sam and I are best friends. She couldn't accept that he had another female in his life and that we lived together. She was always nice to my face and I never had any qualms that she would come between Sam and I, so I just tried to be nice and let her see that I wasn't a threat."

Sam was grateful that Jenny was aiding the interview, if in fact that's what it was; an interview. He couldn't get his head around the fact that Sarah was dead. She was *actually* dead and the police were questioning, he guessed, his involvement.

"It didn't bother you that your best friend's partner had a problem with you?" Lang asked.

"I didn't say that it didn't bother me, I said that I tried to be nice and prove that I wasn't a threat."

Lang regarded this; unsure as to whether or not Jenny *had* been a threat. "So what happened when you *were* nice to her?"

Jenny took a deep breath, allowing the intake of oxygen to calm her quivering nerves. She admitted to herself that she felt guilty that Sarah had passed away but she knew that it had nothing to do with her or Sam. Having the officers question them in their own home was what made her nervous. "*Nothing* happened, when I was nice or pleasant or kind or anything else that may be interpreted as friendly. She would either completely ignore me or just put on a sarcastic smile. She was always careful not to do it in front of Sam."

"And why was that?" Preston replied.

Sam interrupted. "If she was to do it in front of me then she would have known that I wouldn't stand for it. Jenny has been in my life since we were little and I'm not the sort to let a relationship with a woman tear apart my friendships."

All four fell silent for a few moments and the only sound to be heard was, once again, the scribble of Lang's pen. Lang noted everything that had been said by Jenny and Sam.

Sam hung his head low, his chin almost touching the top of his chest. "Are we done here?"

Preston nodded. "I'd say we're almost done here. I know that this must be very difficult for you but if you could just answer a few more questions we'll be able to eliminate you from our enquiries."

Sam lifted his head. "You're saying I'm a suspect in Sarah's death?"

Jenny got to her feet. "That's bloody ridiculous."

"I'm saying that this is procedure and we are trying to establish Sarah's last few hours before she died. We're not saying whether her death was intentional or not." Preston reassured them.

"Ok, but please make it quick." Sam said, accepting Preston's words.

Lang couldn't make up his mind about Sam and Jenny however, he *had* looked a murderer in the face on several occasions in his career and he was certain that these people were not killers; not intentional killers anyway. "So Sam, can you tell us what your relationship was like with Sarah before you split?"

Sam cast his mind back to the very beginning and remembered how much he had adored her, she was always smiling and laughing, then things changed quickly. She was always quiet around Jenny and never made an effort to speak to her or at least be civil. "Things were fine in the beginning, like a normal relationship is. We were always going out for dinner, drinks; that sort of thing. Then I introduced her to Jenny and she went weird."

"Weird, in what way?" Lang pressed.

"She would never want to speak *to* Jenny or *about* her. She was jealous and I confronted her about it. Of course she denied it but she never did anything to change the way she was around her."

"I tried to make things better between us," Jenny added. "But she just wasn't interested. I didn't want Sam to feel awkward when Sarah was in the flat and I was there. In the end I realised it wasn't me who had to change. She was an odd ball if you ask me."

"Jenny and I were getting anonymous text messages, phone calls and letters, among other things."

"What do you mean you were getting messages and letters; from whom?" Preston asked.

"Well, we couldn't prove it but we were pretty certain that it was Sarah. We were getting typed letters through the door saying things like, 'I hate you Jenny Lawson,' and 'you're a home wrecker.'" Sam said.

"Sounds like someone was jealous, does that necessarily mean it was Sarah?" Lang commented.

"That's what I thought at first but there was no one else I could think of." Sam replied.

"There were also photographs with the letters, of us together having coffee, or at the pub. It was starting to freak me out so Sam said he was going to end things with her. I said that doing so would make things worse but he went ahead and did it anyway."

Lang noted everything down, coming closer to his own opinions on the innocence of Sam and Jenny. "So, how did Sarah react when you ended the relationship?"

"As you can imagine, she didn't take it too well. She was incredibly upset and swore blind that she hadn't sent any of the hate mail to us. Then as I was leaving, she started to shout something about Jenny being the one who was sending the letters and making the phone calls; which is ridiculous. To be honest, by that point I didn't care if it was Sarah or not; our relationship was doomed from the *first* moment she shared her dislike and jealousy for Jenny. It had to end regardless of the hate mail or not. What made the whole situation worse was that I had fallen for her. Apart from all the crazy behaviour, she was actually a good laugh. We got on so well and I was genuinely sad when I decided that the best thing to do was to end it."

Both officers nodded as they listened. "I think that we have everything that we need here, thank you for you co-operation. We'll be in touch if we have any developments." Preston said as he stood up. Sam and Jenny joined him in stance.

Lang put his notepad back into his breast pocket and stood up. He shook Sam and Jenny's hands and followed his colleague to the front door of the flat.

Sam closed the door and Jenny hugged him tight. "Are you ok?"

"I think I'm in shock. She was fine when I left her, well not *fine* but you know what I mean."

"Sam, I don't think that Sarah would have killed herself because you ended things with her, she didn't seem like that sort of person, despite everything else." Jenny said.

"I am not sure of anything. I mean, we will

never *really* know if she was the one sending all of those photos and messages and making the silent phone calls but everything that had happened leading up to our split said that it probably was her. Maybe she killed herself to show me that she wasn't done with terrorizing us."

Jenny laughed gently. "I'd hardly say she was terrorizing us. She sent a few unsettling items but I'd say that's as far as she would've gone."

Sam made his way into the kitchen and took the whisky out of the alcohol cabinet on the wall. "Do you want one?"

"No, it's a tad early for me. You go ahead, it might help the shock."

He poured the whisky into a glass tumbler and threw it down his throat. It warmed him instantly.

How could Sarah be dead? She was the same age as Sam and had her whole life ahead of her. Surely she wouldn't want to kill herself over something like this?

"Do you think someone killed her?" Jenny suddenly asked.

"I have no idea Jenny and to be honest, I don't want to know. I split from Sarah for a reason and I still can't get away from her even though she's now dead. I thought that I could get over her quickly and now this happens."

They were quiet as Sam poured another whisky into his tumbler and with curiosity getting the better of him he wondered, if Sarah had been murdered, then who the hell killed her?

Jenny didn't mention Sarah's name again for the rest of that day.

CHAPTER THIRTEEN

"So, do you think he killed her?" Lang asked as they sat outside Sam and Jenny's flat.

Preston shook his head. "I don't think he did. Did you see his face? He looked like he'd been hit by a truck when we told him."

Lang agreed with Preston, he could see it in Sam's eyes that he was no killer. "I'm not so sure about that Jenny one, she seemed annoyed at our visit. You think maybe she had something to do with it?"

"No, I don't think Jenny had anything to do with Sarah's death either. I think that she disliked Sarah, for the reasons which she specified. Perhaps she feels differently about her relationship with Sam and Sarah picked up on it. Maybe Jenny knew this and that's where the problems started."

Lang shook his head as he reached down for a

water bottle at his feet. "Nah, I don't think so. They're *too* close, their friendship is solid. I think that's probably where the threat lay in Sarah's mind and that's why she took a dislike to Jenny. Probably didn't want Sam having such a close relationship with another woman, even if it was innocent."

Preston massaged his temples, the stress of the case was already getting to him. "You know I love this job but I can't wait for my retirement next year."

Lang laughed, "You and me both. We need to get back to Henderson Manor before we dream of long days in the sun and get a search started; see if we can find anything that points to how she came to her death at the bottom of those stairs."

Preston had already started the car, desperate for the day to be over. "Aye, unfortunately the sun loungers are just out of our reach."

The journey back to the manor was quiet, each officer dreaming of their retirement days. Preston had hoped that his last year would be easy; it wasn't looking that way. Glasgow had bred a society of junkies and murderers and in a lot of cases, each breed of scum had crossed paths. He was sick of dealing with them but was thankful that his days of being a beat officer and having to deal with them in the first instance were far behind him. Preston sometimes wondered how he had managed to climb the ranks over the years considering that on many occasions he had thought of giving it all up. He had seen people waste away on the streets Glasgow, junkies lying in shop doors, prostitutes selling themselves to anyone who would take them so that they could pay for their next fix, newly legal drinkers getting so drunk that they would pass out on the pavement. Yes; he was past all that now and was now working to finding the real criminals of Glasgow, but he couldn't help but wonder where the years had gone and how he had managed to get past all of the grit and grime of the job. Preston knew that he was good at his job but his body was telling him that it was time to start winding down and make some time for him and the family.

"You good over there, Paul?" Lang interrupted his day dream.

"Eh?"

"You're miles away."

Preston put his dreams of retirement to the back of his mind, he had a while to go before he would be there. They were driving up to the manor and the forensics team were still in and around the house. "Still busy I see?"

"Looks like it, maybe they've found something."

Pulling up outside the front door, they could see into the main hallway and the body of Sarah Henderson lay in its place of death.

"Isn't this job glamorous?" Lang said with sarcasm.

They entered the hall and took in the surroundings again. By now the team should have collected most of the evidence that they needed to decipher if the house was a crime scene or the scene of a tragic accident.

One of the head investigators approached Preston and Lang. "Hi, I'm Allan," he said. "I'm head of the forensics team today and you'll be glad to know we're almost done here, however one of our team found something that you may be of interest to you both."

"What is it?" Lang asked.

"Follow me," Allan said as he led them up the stairs.

Preston walked up with his back to the wall, trying to see the landing above. "Is it evidence of another person having been here?"

"Not really, we thought you might be able to make more sense of it."

They reached the top of the stairs and were led into a bedroom. It was a large room with almost floor to ceiling windows. The air in the room felt heavy and the room was in need of airing.

"So, what did you find?" Lang was becoming impatient.

Allan walked over to the bed and picked up what looked like a shoe box. "All the evidence that we need has been taken from this, photographs, fingerprints and what not. So you can have it for your part of the investigation. I have to say, some of the things in there are a little strange."

"I'll get an evidence bag from the car," Lang said. He left the room and Preston continued to observe the box.

"Can I have a pair of gloves?"

Allan handed him a pair of latex gloves from his forensic suit pocket. "Have a root around in there and tell me if you agree that the contents are slightly odd."

Preston opened the box as Allan held it in his hands and what he saw confirmed Allan's opinion. "What the hell?"

Allan nodded in agreement, "That's what I thought when I saw it."

Preston put the lid back on the box and Allan released it from his grip. "Cheers, we'll get this down to the station and get a proper look."

"I better get back downstairs. See you later."

Preston stayed where he was, waiting for Lang to come back with the evidence bag. Already he had come to his own conclusions about what had happened to Sarah.

"Got it, you ready?" Lang appeared by his side. He held the bag open and Preston carefully placed the bag inside.

"Aye, let's get this back to the station. You'll be interested to see what's in here."

They left the manor and made their way back to the station to examine the evidence.

***

"I think we should get Sam Leonard in to have another chat. This confirms a lot of what he and his friend said," Lang said.

They had laid the contents of the box on the table and had examined all of the items. Having heard everything that Sam Leonard had said about Sarah Henderson and seeing everything that was inside the box that they had collected from the house, Preston and Lang were ninety nine percent certain of the cause of death. But to be sure, they would invite Sam into the station to examine the items himself.

"I'll make the call," Preston replied.

"This case could come to a quick close," Lang said.

Preston nodded as he dialed Sam's number. "Looks like it."

The phone rang for a few moments before it was answered on the other end. "Sam? DS Paul Preston here, my colleague and I wondered if you could come into the station. We have something we want to discuss with you."

Preston hung up the phone, "He'll be here within the hour."

Lang gathered up the items and placed them back in the shoe box, not wishing Sam to see the evidence before anything had been explained to him.

"I'll grab the coffees then?"

"Any chance of chucking a shot of whisky in mine?" Preston asked.

If they could've gotten away with it, Lang would've used a whole bottle.

Chapter Fourteen

Sam walked towards the door at Pitt Street station and if it were possible, his stomach would win gold in the Olympic somersault trials. All sorts of scenarios were going through his head and he just couldn't agree with himself about what the police wanted to talk to him about that they hadn't already covered.

He opened the door and stepped inside. Sam had never had any encounters with the police before and he was worrying now about what would happen if the press got wind of the situation. He wasn't *that* famous but known well enough that if this got out then it would be all over the Scottish papers before he could blink.

Sam approached the front desk and suddenly his throat had become drier than the Sahara dessert. He found himself staring at the officer behind the desk, lost for words that would make any sense.

"Can I help you sir?" the female asked, after realising that Sam wasn't going to be the first to speak.

"Erm, yes; I would like to speak to D.S Paul Preston. I think he's expecting me."

The female officer smiled, relieved that there were no awkward silences. "Your name?"

"Sam Leonard."

"Have a seat please Mr Leonard; I'll have D.S Preston with you in just a moment."

Sam sat down on one of the cold, plastic chairs in the waiting area. He felt like a criminal and his stomach was now flipping around inside him so much that he felt like he was going to be sick; again.

"Mr Leonard," Preston's voice boomed. "Glad you could make it in on such short notice. Come this way please."

Sam stood up, wondering if his legs would be able to carry him. "D.S Preston, is there something wrong?"

Preston detected the worry in Sam's voice. "We have something that we would like to show you and it is important that you take the time to study it properly."

Sam felt a wave of confusion wash over him. He found himself in an interview room and Lang was sat on a chair at the table in the middle.

"Hi."

"Hello, Sam. Thanks for coming into see us. I presume D.S Preston has explained why you're here?" Lang replied.

Sam shook his head. "Not really. All I know is you have something that you want to show me. I'm confused, what is it that you have that would concern me?"

Lang glanced at Preston as Sam sat down on the seat opposite. "We do have something to show you. Don't worry, it's nothing sinister, we just think that you will understand it and will be able to explain it better than we can."

Sam's hands had become clammy, so he placed them on his knees hoping that the denim material would soak up the perspiration. "Can we just get on with it?"

"We went back to the manor house today and when we arrived we were handed this by one of the forensics team. What's inside is definitely something that you will want to see."

Sam observed the box with caution, almost like something would jump out and scare him half to death. "What's in it?"

Preston sat down beside Lang. "Open it and have a look. We've already taken a look and it definitely involves you. It was found under Sarah's bed."

Sam wiped his hands on his knees and put on a pair of latex gloves which Preston handed to him. He gripped the lid and when he lifted it off to look inside inside, he felt a mixture of shock and sadness. "What is all this?"

"We think that it all links with what you and Jenny were talking about earlier. The hate mail, the photographs and the phone calls, I think this proves it all."

Sam rose from his chair slowly as he peered into the box of items. He glanced at the two officers. "Can I take them out to get a proper look?"

"Be our guest." Preston replied.

Sam reached in and lifted out a photograph of him with Jenny in a café. "I remember this day; Sarah joined us for some food and then Jenny went home. Sarah and I went to the cinema."

Preston and Lang remained silent, allowing Sam to go through the rest of the box and take it all in.

He took out a number of different photographs and cuttings of Sam's appearances and productions in theatre. He shook his head and sighed as he looked over each item. "I don't understand why she did this?"

"Sam, there's more. There was a mobile phone in the box but we've taken it out and are having it analysed at the moment. However we did have a look at what was on it; can you tell us again, what the nature of the text messages and phone calls were?" Preston asked.

"When we got calls, there was never a voice at the other end. But the messages were nasty. Things like, *Jenny is a home wrecker, Sam is taken, Jenny needs to stay away from Sam.* But the worst one said; *If Jenny doesn't move out something terrible will happen to her.* I was more pissed off than Jenny was about this, she found it funny in the end. She said that it was sad that even though Sarah had me, she still felt the need to be nasty to other women in my life. I thought that I could change her behaviour but this obviously proves that she had a vendetta against Jenny."

Preston nodded. "The phone; it had messages on it that fit the description you've given. The prints on the phone match Sarah's and we just need to link the numbers and it proves that Sarah was your stalker."

Sam took a deep breath. "I suppose in a way I didn't really want to believe it. But this proves she was crazy. She didn't deserve to die though."

"Who does?" Lang added.

Sam put the items back in the box. "I can't look at this anymore. Do you need anything else from me?"

A gentle tap on the interview room door silenced all three men. Preston got up and opened the door. He turned and said, "I'll be back in a minute."

Preston took a piece of paper from the officer who knocked on the door. "Thanks for that." He looked at the paper and its contents before returning to the other side of the door.

Sam looked up expectantly, wondering if Preston had more news. Preston sat down opposite Sam and slid the piece of paper across the table. "Any of these look familiar to you?"

Sam studied it carefully. "They're all mine and Jenny's numbers. The messages are the ones that were sent to our phones."

"Sam, you can go now. We won't be needing your assistance any longer."

Sam looked across at Preston. "Is that it?"

"What else do you want me to say? You told us that you ended your relationship with Sarah Henderson because you thought she was stalking you and Jenny, now that we've proved that to be true, you want me to what, arrest her? Because

141

that's just not possible now, is it?"

Sam stood up, not sure how to reply. "Thanks for your time."

Sam left the room and was out of the station quicker than an athlete sprinter. What had just happened? He felt like he had been stabbed in the gut with a blunt knife.

He knew that it was ridiculous to feel sad for Sarah after everything that he had suspected of her had just been confirmed but he couldn't help it. Was she so alone in that house that when she found love she felt like she had to fight to keep it? It seemed that way. Their whole relationship had been a lie from day one and that little shoe box was proof of that.

His thoughts had distracted him from reality and he found himself outside his front door before he realised where he was. Sam put the key in and let himself in.

"Hey, what did they want?" Jenny said as she appeared in the hallway.

"They had a box from Sarah's house."

Jenny frowned. "A box?"

Sam made his way into the kitchen and lifted a beer from the fridge. "Yep; and you want to know what was in it?"

Jenny noted Sam's mixture of emotions. He

seemed angry, shocked, drained and sad. "What?"

"Us!"

"What do you mean us?"

Sam laughed a little, the disbelief of the whole situation seemed funny. "I mean photos, sick sadistic words on paper of how she hated you and hated me for *not* hating you. And a phone."

He gulped on the beer bottle and wished for something stronger.

"What was on it?"

"Only the fucking messages that we were getting just before I ended it. I mean, when I ended it and the messages and the tormenting stopped, I just assumed that she had decided to leave us alone. But oh no, she was dead; lying in a heap on the floor in her house on her own, dead."

Jenny didn't know what to do; she had never seen Sam this way. "What can I do?"

"There's nothing you can do. Looks like Sarah either killed herself or she just fell down those stairs by accident. I don't want to say what I think."

"Just say it, it might make you feel better."

Sam took another gulp of beer. "I ended it, then all of a sudden she dies. I don't know how soon after but Jenny, it makes sense but it's terrible for me to think that she killed herself. I think she threw herself down those stairs on purpose."

Jenny shook her head, "Would she be capable of that though?"

Sam finished the bottle in his hand, "Deep down, I really didn't think she was capable of doing what she did when we were together; seems like she was capable of anything."

Jenny hugged Sam as tight as she could. "It's over now though. As awful as it is, she's dead. She can't hurt us anymore."

Sam knew it was true, there was nothing that Sarah could do anymore. But it's what was in his head that could still torment him.

***

A week after the discovery of the box, Sam had decided that enough was enough and it was time to get on with life and forget what had happened. The phone call that he had received from DC Lang had helped him to take the first step.

"It seems from the coroner's report and the supporting evidence that Sarah Henderson's death was accidental."

"So that's it done then?" Sam asked.

"That's it done."

"Thanks DC Lang."

The conversation was short and fulfilled its purpose. Sam hadn't wished for it to go on any longer than necessary. He didn't want to know anything about a burial or a cremation, he didn't want to hear Sarah Henderson's name ever again.

Chapter Fifteen

Deborah updated her Facebook relationship status to 'seeing someone' and figured that it was enough to let people know that Sam was involved with someone. She wanted Sam to know how she really felt about him, completely uncaring of how complicated things would get. She had no idea that he would ever leap into telling her about his past, especially an ex- girlfriend and so, she wanted him to know things about her own life and past in return.

He walked into the pub where they had agreed to meet via text message and Deborah's heart fluttered. How can another human being make your heart do that? She waved him over, trying to avoid spilling the wine over the table as she did so. Her hands were shaking as if she was freezing, but it was the mere thought of his touch that caused it.

"Hello lovely," his voice floated across the air, reaching her ears with a pleasant buzz. All she could do was smile as he bent down to kiss her on the cheek, sending a ripple across her skin.

"How are you?" She managed.

"I'm fine; however I do want to talk to you about something."

"Ok," she said, unsure of what to expect.

Sam ordered a whisky and coke from the bar and knocked it back to ease the nerves, while ordering a bottle of white wine for them to share. What he was about to tell his new 'almost' girlfriend could potentially scare her off and he could be back at square one. Who in their right mind would want to go out with someone who once had a girlfriend who secretly stalked him and his best friend and then ends up dead? He figured that Deborah would find it all a little overwhelming and want to call it off.

"So, what did you want to tell me?" Deborah asked.

Sam took a deep breath, before spilling his guts about Sarah. He told her about how things were with her and Jenny and how Jenny had tried to be friends with her. He told her about the police turning up and announcing that Sarah was dead and that they were trying to find out if it was under suspicious circumstances. After the revelations tumbled across the table, the pair fell silent with Sam allowing Deborah some time to take it all in.

"I can't believe you just told me all that," Deborah said, feeling exhausted with all of the information she had just received.

"Are you glad I told you; because now you can take the time to decide if you really want to carry on with this, thing that we have?"

Deborah didn't like the sound of the phrase, 'this thing that we have.' Did that mean that he was trying to scare her off and he didn't really want her? Was this his way of telling her he wasn't interested, in the hope that she would think it was all too much and would want to leave?

"I'm glad you told me," she managed. There was no way that she was going to let him go after all the hard work she had put in to get him. She had made sure that she was in the right place at the right time and even though she had been as nervous as hell, she managed to catch his eye and gathered up his attention. She had allowed herself to go further than anyone else to make sure that she got what she wanted; yes it was a little far-fetched perhaps, but in this day and age you have to work to get what you want. She had ensured that she knew of every theatre date, production, colleague and anything else that she *should* know so that she would be in the same place at the same time. After everything that Sam had just said about Sarah, he could never know the lengths she had gone to, to make sure that she met him and lured him in with her seductive ways. It would surely freak him out and he'd would be likely to view her as psychotic, which was the last thing she wanted. She merely put herself into a situation that would work in her favour that was all; at least that was what she continued to tell herself. She had to convince herself that everything was normal, otherwise she was worried that she would crack.

"Do you really believe that Sarah was the one who sent all the messages and stuff?" she asked.

"Well, who else could it have been? It most definitely wasn't Jenny, even if Sarah said it was. Jenny and I have been friends since I can remember; if anything she would be the one to protect me from psychotic girlfriends."

Deborah nodded as she watched Sam open the bottle of white and pour it into her glass. She listened as it sloshed around inside the glass, realising that her brain was probably doing the same thing inside her skull. "I suppose it makes sense. You said she never really liked the fact that your best friend was female."

Sam eyed Deborah as he heard her words, unsure if he should ask his next question. "It doesn't bother you, does it?"

"What? That your best friend is a girl? Come on Sam, what are we, twelve years old?" Deborah gave her widest smile.

Sam felt the weight of the world leave his shoulders as the couple began to relax. He really felt that things were on the up, apart from the fact that the police had told him that his ex-girlfriend was dead. He still couldn't get his head around that part. He didn't like it but he could understand why he may have been a potential suspect had it turned out Sarah was murdered. But fortunately for Sam, she wasn't murdered. Unfortunately for Sarah, no matter what way she had died- she was dead and that was the end of it.

"So, did the police say that they would be in touch?" Deborah asked as though she had read his mind.

"Well, there's no need for them to contact me now. It was concluded as accidental death."

Deborah saw his expression deepen again and instantly regretted her question. It was plain to see he was still in shock.

"Why don't we forget about this for now and go back to your place. We could get some Chinese

150

take-out and a bottle of wine?"

Sam smiled and narrowing his eyes he replied, "That's what you call it these days?"

Deborah laughed, "All I want is Chinese food and wine, I don't have a clue what you're talking about."

The made their way out of the pub and down the street towards the Chinese takeaway place on the corner. Deborah was quiet, thinking about how their relationship might change if the police did conclude that Sarah was murdered. They would want to investigate Sam and anyone else who was involved in Sarah's life. When they found out that Sam had a new girlfriend, they would want to talk to her too. Deborah wasn't sure how she would deal with that if it did happen. She wasn't sure how anyone would deal with it.

***

Sam slid the key into the Yale lock and turned it to the right, allowing the door to click open. The hallway was dark and the flat was silent as he called out, "Jenny, are you in?"

No reply came, so he assumed that she was out. "Looks like we have the place to ourselves."

Deborah smiled as she shook her head. "Like I said, it's just Chinese food."

Sam flicked the light switch and was startled to see Jenny standing in the hallway at the entrance to the kitchen. Her hair had fallen over her face and her eyes were fixed on Sam and Deborah. "Jesus, Jenny you scared us half to death."

Jenny didn't reply, in fact she didn't move. She just cocked her head to one side, focusing her stare on Deborah through the strands of hair in front of her eyes. She smiled slightly, her teeth not showing as they hid behind her dried out lips.

"Jenny, are you alright?" Sam asked, placing the takeout bag on the floor by his feet.

Jenny did not reply to his question, instead she kept her gaze on Deborah, who had now taken a step behind Sam and was holding his hand. No word of a lie, Jenny was beginning to freak Deborah out. "Sam, what's wrong with her?" she whispered.

Sam broke his grip from Deborah's hand and took a few steps towards Jenny. He put his hand on her shoulder and she turned to face him. Sam noted that Jenny didn't look well, her face had turned almost grey and her lips were dry and cracked. "Jenny, what's wrong?"

She lifted her head, hair falling from her face to reveal eyes which showed no life within them. "Hello Sam." Jenny's voice was hoarse with a hint of playfulness behind it.

Sam looked over to Deborah, whom had now stepped backwards closer to the front door. "I think she's sleepwalking."

"Has she done this before?"

"Once or twice, when I was with Sarah; I think its stress related," he said as he placed his hands gently on Jenny's shoulders and guided her into her bedroom. "Take the food into the kitchen will you, I'll be with you in a minute."

Deborah nodded as she picked up the bag and walked cautiously into the kitchen. She froze when she heard Jenny say, "Goodnight Deborah."

The sound of her voice sent chills up her spine, allowing the hairs on her body to stand on end, each and every one of them to be precise. "Goodnight Jenny," she replied, trying not to allow the fear to come across in her voice.

She heard Sam close the bedroom door and soon he was behind her in the kitchen. He nuzzled her neck and wrapped his hands around her waist. "Do you want to skip the food?"

"Actually, no I don't. I'm quite hungry as it happens."

Sam laughed quietly, aware that it might disturb Jenny. "So, are you thinking food, then...?" The question hung in the air.

"I'm thinking that you don't ever give up, do you?" Deborah turned to face him and jumped as she saw Jenny in the hallway again.

"Hey you two, I could smell the food and I'm sorry to say that I'm a weakling when it comes to Chinese, any going spare?" Jenny asked with chirpiness in her voice.

Sam spun around, surprised to hear Jenny out of bed. "I've just put you to bed."

"Sorry?" Jenny said

"Yeah, you were sleep walking again."

Jenny shook her head. "I haven't done that for a while."

Sam nodded. "You want some rice and chicken balls? We ordered too much."

Deborah wasn't enamored at the fact that, yet again, she and Sam had been interrupted. Jenny wasn't as annoying as Deborah had first anticipated but she still didn't appreciate the fact that this was the second time Jenny had interrupted them.

"You don't mind do you, Deborah?" Jenny asked aware that she may just have gate crashed a date.

Deborah smiled as she shook her head. "Like Sam said, we ordered too much. In fact, why don't we go and work up an appetite so we can *really* enjoy this food?"

Jenny's eyes widened at the audacity in Deborah's tone. "I'll eat this in the living room." She left the kitchen and Sam and Deborah alone, not wanting to intrude when Deborah had just clearly stated what was on her mind, the boldness of some people.

"You said you were hungry," Sam smiled.

Deborah reached up and kissed Sam's lips gently. "I am hungry."

Sam reached down and took her hand in his and led her to his bedroom. She sat down on the bed, removing her shoes. "You said you thought it was stress related?"

"I think so, she'd never done it before Sarah and isn't aware if she did it as a child. It was when Sarah was sending those messages, the endless photographs of us together, the letters. I hated it, she just wore us both down. She swore it wasn't her and for a while I think I believed her. That was when Jenny started sleep walking."

Deborah held her hand out. "Come here."

He went to her, allowing himself to flop down beside her. "You're pretty amazing, do you know that?"

She smiled, feeling flattered by the compliment. "I am?"

155

"What kind of girl sticks around after finding out about all of my baggage?"

Deborah stood up and removed her dress, exposing her body. "I didn't find out, you told me about it. And while we are on the subject, I am not a girl but a woman who knows her own mind."

Sam placed a hand on either side of Deborah's waist, "I do like a woman who knows her own mind."

Deborah did know her own mind and as she allowed Sam to let go of his worries, she kept in mind the very strong possibility that this would have to end at some point. But for the time being, she drank in every ounce of Sam Leonard that she could.

CHAPTER SIXTEEN

Sam snored softly as he lay in Deborah's arms. She could smell the coconut shampoo in his hair and she let the scent fill her lungs. Had she fallen in love with him? She was quite certain that she had; not surprising really, considering the lengths she had gone to, to be with him. Deborah had followed everything that Sam had done over the last two years, at first due to a genuine interest in his work. But then something triggered inside her, something deep within that she couldn't explain and she knew from the moment she saw him in the flesh for the first time on the stage, she couldn't get enough of him. Deborah was aware that it would be a long shot that he would even consider going on a date with her, so when he offered to buy her a drink the night of the closing show, her heart had risen into her throat.

She watched his chest rise and fall as he breathed softly in his slumber, unaware of all the things in her head. Sam could never know the things inside Deborah's head; it would just ruin everything for everyone. He was so beautiful; conscious or otherwise, his skin was perfectly soft and to her, he was just precious. As Deborah continued to admire Sam, she heard footsteps outside in the hallway. She sighed, wondering if Jenny was sleepwalking again and hoped she wasn't. It had freaked her out the way Jenny stared at them both through the gaps in her hair which had fallen in front of her face. It was like she was reading Deborah's mind, which of course wasn't possible, but it scared her all the same. The footsteps had turned to a shuffle and were loud at times and quiet at others. If Deborah didn't know any better, she would say that Jenny was trying to scare her on purpose. She snuggled down under the duvet and cuddled into Sam. His skin on hers made her feel warm and tingly.

Suddenly, there was a loud thud outside the bedroom door and the sound of Jenny's screams pierced Deborah's ears. Sam sat up and was out of the bed before Deborah realised.

"What the hell was that?" He asked.

"I think it was Jenny."

Sam opened the door to find Jenny's lifeless body lying on the floor. He knelt down beside her and brushed her hair out of her face. "Jenny, can you hear me?"

"I'll phone for an ambulance," Deborah said, trying to mute the panic in her tone.

Jenny wasn't moving, she *was* breathing but she seemed lifeless. Sam began to move her into the recovery position and ran back into his bedroom to retrieve a blanket to cover her with. "Jenny, I'm here. We're getting you an ambulance."

Deborah was suddenly by his side. "It's on its way." She placed a hand on his shoulder. "I'll stay here till you get some clothes on and then I'll get dressed."

Sam was grateful for Deborah's presence; he wouldn't have been able to stay calm if she hadn't been there. "Ok, I'll be two minutes."

As Sam dressed himself in the bedroom, Deborah stroked Jenny's hair and stayed by her side. She knew she shouldn't, but for some reason she couldn't help but feel excited at what had happened. She tried to push the feelings to the back of her head. She didn't want those kinds of thoughts invading her mind again. "You do like to make a fuss, don't you Jenny. First the sleepwalking and now this, you'll have Sam worried sick." Her voice was soft, as if she were speaking to a new born baby.

Sam was, once again beside Jenny in his full attire. "Quickly get dressed so that we can go with the ambulance."

Deborah smiled inwardly but didn't dare show it. "They'll only let one of us in with her. You go, I'll go home and you can phone me later to let me know how she is doing."

Sam frowned, "You're not coming to the hospital?"

He wanted her to be there so much, he needed her support. Since Sarah, Sam hadn't considered being able to trust another female completely ever again; but Deborah did something to him which he couldn't explain. He didn't want to think about Sarah right now, he brushed her memory to the side and focused on getting Jenny to the hospital.

"Of course I'll come, I'll get a taxi."

The buzzer rang out louder than usual, perhaps because the night carries such stillness, everything sounds louder when the world is sleeping. Sam got up and pressed the release button and in seconds the paramedics were in the flat. Sam explained what had happened and before Deborah could blink, Jenny was on a stretcher and Sam was shoving set of keys in her hand. "Lock up for us please; we're going to the Western Infirmary. I'll meet you there."

He was gone and in an instant the flat was empty. Deborah went into Sam's room to retrieve her bag and made sure that all of the lights were out. She proceeded to close the door and as she did, she felt a presence behind her. She turned to face the inside of the flat, but of course nothing faced her.

She closed the door and put the key in the lock, turning it once and trying the handle to make sure that she had locked it properly. On trying the handle, she was shocked at how icy cold it had suddenly become.

As Deborah headed for the stairs, she pretended to herself that she couldn't hear the low growl coming from Sam and Jenny's flat.

***

On her arrival at the hospital, she was met with the usual A&E suspects; drunks, drug addicts and street brawlers. She sometimes really did hate Glasgow but now that she had met Sam, the place had become a little brighter, even tonight. Deborah took her phone out and sent a text message to Sam.

I'm here, where are you? Is Jenny ok?

On pressing send, she looked up at the main entrance to the A&E department. There was an old man outside smoking a cigarette and he was clutching on to a walking stick. She thought of her granddad and decided to check if he was ok. She approached him and he was clearly unaware that he had caught her interest.

"Are you ok?" She asked gently.

The man looked up on hearing Deborah's voice. "Aye hen, thanks." Smoke filtered from his mouth as he spoke. On seeing that she wasn't satisfied with his answer, he went on. "My granddaughter fell down the stairs tonight, broke her bloody ankle so she did. It's a bad one too, all puffed up an' that."

Deborah gave a sympathetic smile. "I'm sure she'll be ok, especially if she has you here."

The returned the smile. "Aye hen, she will that. She's tough as auld boots my Sarah, nothing phase's her."

Deborah felt the bile rise at the sound of his granddaughters name and it must have shown.

"Are you a'right love? You've went an awful funny colour so ye have." The man braced himself against his walking stick as he stood up straight, stepping on his cigarette.

Deborah swallowed hard. "I'm fine thank you.

It's just that, well my partner's friend collapsed tonight and I'm not so sure if she'll be ok."

Just at that, Sam came out from the swinging doors of the entrance. "There you are. She's awake."

Deborah looked at the man with sad eyes. He smiled at her. "Your friend must be as tough as my Sarah."

Sam was already pulling her inside. "Thanks," she mouthed as she entered the hospital. Was that guilt that ran through her veins at the mere mention of Sarah's name? Obviously it wasn't *the* Sarah but hearing the name and the fact that she had fallen down the stairs was enough to make her stomach lurch. She was pulled back from her thoughts when she realised that Sam was talking to her.

"The doctor wants to do some routine blood tests."

Deborah nodded. "And what will that tell us?"

Sam shook his head. "Hopefully nothing, maybe she was sleepwalking again, you know; after she'd gone back to bed."

Deborah hoped that was all it was, you don't just faint for no reason. "Can that happen?"

Deborah hadn't realised it but she was suddenly standing in Jenny's cubicle in the ward. "Oh, you're awake. How are you feeling?"

Jenny smiled weakly. "I'm not sure. I don't feel *great.*"

Sam was at her side, with Jenny's hand in his. Deborah's heart began to ache on seeing Sam so hurt by his friend's unfortunate illness.

"You didn't have to come here, you could've both stayed at home," Jenny's voice was weak. Her eyes scrunched at the pain in her stomach.

"What? You want me to call a doctor?" Sam panicked.

Jenny shook her head. "It could be food poisoning, I was sick earlier; after that bloody Chinese."

Deborah approached the other side of the bed. "Well, you did get out of bed to eat it. Maybe your stomach couldn't handle it sitting in there once you fallen asleep again."

Jenny's brow furrowed. "Erm, since when did you become a nutrition specialist?" She laughed quietly.

A nurse came into the cubicle. "I need to take some blood, could you wait outside please?"

Sam and Deborah waited outside, Deborah quite happily; she hated needles. "It probably is food poisoning, she had the chicken balls and we didn't."

Sam nodded. "That's true. It was just scary seeing her there, lifeless on the floor. I honestly got the fright of my life."

Deborah was hugging him now, wanting to take away the pain he felt for his friend but at the same time wanting nothing more than to be alone with him. "She'll probably get kept in overnight. They'll want to make sure everything is fine and with it being a Saturday they probably won't get the results straight away."

The nurse opened the cubicle curtain and stepped out. "You can go back in now."

Jenny had her eyes closed and seemed peaceful, her chest rising and falling slowly. "We shouldn't wake her." Sam said.

"I'm not asleep but almost. Go home and come back tomorrow," Jenny said softly.

"That's me told then," Sam laughed.

He kissed her on the forehead, Deborah didn't look. She couldn't look; it was too hard to see him be that way with her. Deborah knew she was being unreasonable and that he loved Jenny purely as a friend but she couldn't help but feel like he was becoming hers, only hers.

"We'll be back tomorrow first thing," Deborah said. She wanted Jenny to know that she would be looked after but she also wanted her to be aware that Sam wouldn't be alone.

They left, hand in hand and made their way out to the main road. The street was quiet, the pubs and clubs had closed two hours previously and the only life on the street was the ambulance workers going in and out of the hospital. Sam flagged down a passing taxi and they got in.

"Palazzo Apartments on Ingram Street please, mate," Sam said.

The taxi driver nodded and pulled out onto the road. They were silent on the way back to Sam and Jenny's flat and Deborah wondered if she would hear that low growl again once Sam fallen asleep.

She sincerely hoped that she wouldn't. Someone knew something about her which she did not want Sam to find out about. She would do anything to stop that from happening.

CHAPTER SEVENTEEN
(SIX MONTHS LATER)

He held a protective hand over her pregnant belly as they stood still, looking up at the house. It was marvelous, with high surrounding hedge growth which reached the height of the large windows at the front.

"I cannot *believe* this is our home," Jodie smiled.

"I know, a new start for all three of us," Patrick replied with a boyish grin.

Jodie turned to face him and she saw a twinkle in his eye. "Shall we go in then?"

Patrick nodded and handed over the keys to the front door. Jodie felt the baby flutter as she put the key inside the lock. She saw it as a good sign, this was going to be a wonderful place to start their new lives and bring up their first child. After everything that had happened in the last two years, they both deserved it.

She opened the door and stood still, looking into the entrance hallway and she drank in the view. The place certainly needed sprucing up a little but that didn't matter.

The house was huge, with old fashioned carpets and high ceilings. "I love it already."

Patrick was behind her, excited to show her the rest of the house. Jodie had viewed the brochure pictures from the auction, but she hadn't actually viewed the house properly.

"Come on, I'll show you the sitting room." He pulled her hand gently and led her into the room on the right hand side of the hallway.

The room was large, enough space for a dining table to fit eight around it, plus a three piece suite and still have plenty of room left over. The window was centered at the bottom of the room and stretched from two feet off the floor, almost all the way up to the ceiling. The natural light from outside gave the room a pretty glow which matched Jodie's mood and appearance.

"Come on, the kitchen is huge. You'll love it in there," Patrick was pulling her once more.

"Hey, you cheeky bugger, just because I'm the woman?" She joked.

Patrick led her down the hallway and through an arched doorway. He was right, she did love it. The kitchen ceiling was so high that there was no way that she would be able to reach it even standing on a chair. The large decorative light that hung down was beautiful, with butterfly shaped glass around each bulb. It did need a good dust and polish but Jodie had no clue how she would be able to do that with the height that it hung from. Patrick stole her attention away from the dusty glass butterflies and beckoned her to the large door at the end of the kitchen.

"Your outdoor space madam," he said. Patrick opened the door and natural light flooded the kitchen. The garden was partly paved with large neutral coloured concrete slabs, running from the door to the middle of the garden. Jodie could see a small pond in the far right corner, leading her to realise that the other half of the garden was covered in a healthy green grass, overgrown yes, but healthy looking.

"This will be perfect for our little one here," she said patting her stomach gently.

"It sure will."

Jodie felt her eyes begin to sting, but refused to allow any tears to fall. Patrick wasn't blind or deaf, he could hear her thoughts but would never invade her privacy by speaking out. "What's wrong?"

Jodie took a breath. "Nothing, I'm just feeling a little overwhelmed by it all. I mean, if you had told me two years ago that this was where we would be, a beautiful new home and a baby on the way, I wouldn't have believed it."

The last two years had been a mental struggle for Jodie. After the Ross situation, she had decided to lay off the psychic scene for a while and had taught herself to tune out from her ability, for two reasons. One; she knew that if she didn't, it would slowly begin to drive her insane, the last time had almost killed her and sent her mind into darker places that she could have imagined possible. Two; if she and Patrick were serious about starting a family, then that was all that she wanted to focus on and she didn't want anything getting into her mind set and screwing it up for her. Jodie would never speak ill of the dead, but in her eyes, there was now more to life than death. Of course she still liked the fact that she had this ability, after all it did prevent more deaths two years ago. But she knew that for the sake of her future and mental health, she could never go back there.

"I know. But we're here now aren't we?" Patrick stroked her hair.

Jodie smiled.

"Why don't you go upstairs and check out the rest of the rooms and you can decide which room will be the baby's. I'll go out to the car and grab our cases, and then we can start unloading the van."

"Ok," Jodie nodded as she watched Patrick head back to the front door. She closed the door to the view of the perfect garden and headed out to the main hallway. Patrick had left the front door open and she could see him at the van, unloading the cases. Jodie turned her back to the open door and faced the stairway which led to the upper level of the house.

She placed her hand on the rail on the left hand side and began the climb. Being eight and a half months pregnant did tend to take its toll when climbing a large, old fashioned staircase, she quickly realised this. The stairs reached a turn three quarters of the way up, and she was thankful when she saw that there were only another three after the bend.

"Right, now that I have conquered Mount Everest I can find your room," Jodie spoke down to her bump. She only had to take three steps forward before she came to the first room, which was on her left. She opened the door and found that it was dark and a little stale. "Oh god, I wonder how long these windows have been closed for."

She flipped the switch, but light did not fill the room. She sighed and made her way in to find the window. She opened the large, heavy curtains, lifted the safety latch and pushed the window up to let in some fresh air. She turned back to face the room, which was again, a little old fashioned looking but had some great potential. There was a mountain of space and she was almost certain that this was the room for the baby. Jodie looked up and could see that there were cobwebs in the corners of the ceiling and that some of the paper was coming away from the top of the walls. That wouldn't be a problem, they would be redecorating anyway. She smiled as she made her way down the hall to explore the next room.

"This can be the guest room."

The room was a little smaller than the last. It didn't have as much space but was still bigger than any room in the flat at Glasgow Harbour. More cobwebs lingered in the corners and there were a few cracks in the old paint job, goodness knows the last time it had been decorated.

She passed the bathroom, which was old and in desperate need of a white suite and new tiles. It would be too big a job for them to do with the baby coming and trying to settle in, they would just get someone in to do it. Jodie pictured what she

172

wanted in their new bathroom as she glanced quickly whilst making her way down toward the last room, which faced her head on.

She opened the door and was surprised to find that the removal people hadn't touched this room. It looked lived in but tidy. The bed was neat, as though someone had only just made it. The window was dressed symmetrically, just how Jodie would have dressed it. She walked in and opened one of the drawers in the large dresser to find clothes inside.

"Great, another job to add to the list," she sighed.

Jodie closed the drawer and walked over to the dressing table that still harbored perfume bottles and the odd scented candle.

"Patrick?" She called out. Jodie looked out of the large bay window in the centre of the back wall to see if he was still outside unloading the van. She could see that he was struggling with a large box which was labelled bedroom.

Jodie smiled and turned to go back downstairs when she heard a large thud coming from the hallway. Thinking Patrick had come into the house and dropped the box, she quickly moved to the top of the stairs, where she found nothing. She could hear Patrick's footsteps on the gravel outside, which would mean she was the only one inside the house. She shrugged it off, putting it down to the fact that the house was old and had been unoccupied for quite some time.

"Patrick, do you need a hand?"

"No, I'm fine. I just want to get the necessities in before it gets dark and then I can get the rest done tomorrow," he said as he dropped the box gently, just inside the front door.

"Ok, well I've picked the baby's room."

Patrick looked up to see Jodie coming down the stair case. "Great."

She glowed as she moved closer to him. He couldn't believe his luck at how far they had come. Ross Turner had almost destroyed them, but Jodie had bounced back and was stronger than ever. Patrick understood her reasoning for taking a step back from the church for a while, however, he did miss her at the church. So did the regulars, especially the elderly members. She had a special bond with them and was able to connect with them in a way that Patrick couldn't. She was sensitive to their needs from the church and they would always ask for her specifically.

"You ok?" Jodie interrupted his train of thought.

"Yes, just thinking about the baby's room. So, you want to show me and tell me your ideas?" He lied, not allowing himself to tell her what he was really thinking. He had agreed that he wouldn't bring up the church in a way that said he wanted her back until *she* initiated the idea; it was only then that they would discuss it. Now was not the time, he didn't want to put any pressure on her or the baby.

Patrick followed Jodie upstairs, listening out for the creaks and scrapes that he had heard on his first visit to view the house after bidding successfully at the auction. He had sensed then that there was something lingering there, but was not at all worried and still, he did not worry. Spiritually, nothing could be worse than what had happened to him two years ago. He had decided not to mention it to Jodie, knowing that she probably wouldn't pick up on anything anyway. Had she not learned to tune out, her pregnancy hormones would have thrown her off anyway. As they climbed the stairs, he heard the scraping sound coming from above him, just like from where he had heard it before. He wondered if it would amount to anything more.

"Do you hear that noise?" Jodie asked as they reached the top of the stairs. "I thought it was maybe a mouse or a bird when I heard it earlier."

"Yeah, I hear it. Can't think what else it could be."

Jodie's brow creased and then she smiled. "You seriously believe that's all it is?"

"Why not? Not every noise is a ghost, Jodie."

She paused for a moment more, uncertain as to whether he was genuine or trying to protect her from the ability she didn't want to face for the time being. She considered the latter for a brief moment and then let it fall out of her head. "So, are you ready to see this little one's room?" She asked as she opened the door.

"More than ready."

As they looked around, Patrick felt a sense of worth as he imagined his new life. His wonderful wife was carrying his baby and they were standing in their new home.

"You know, we'll never have to move again, we are set for life here," said Patrick as he pictured where the cot would go.

"I know, it's amazing. I'm so glad you found this place."

They were about to share their new lives together in a wonderful new home which could house a small army. However, Patrick wondered if it *would* only house them, or if the history of the house would become apparent.

CHAPTER EIGHTEEN

Jodie took out the dishes from the box that she had sat on the kitchen counter earlier in the day as Patrick unwrapped the fish suppers that had been delivered by the local chip shop. The scent of the fresh chips in newspaper made Jodie's mouth water. She couldn't wait to get tucked in.

"I have been looking forward to this all day," she said as she put the food onto the plates.

"Have you?"

"It's all this unpacking malarkey: it's given this baby a big appetite."

Patrick smiled as he took in his new surroundings. The kitchen was so big and he knew that it would be cold in the winter time. He watched as Jodie popped the first chip into her mouth. "Good?"

"Mmm, you have no idea," she smiled.

They made their way over to the large table that was situated at the back of the kitchen, near to the back door. "I think I would like to move this away from the door, it will be cold to sit near there in the winter," said Jodie.

"Yeah, I think so too."

They ate in silence, happily going over the events of the day. It had been very busy; with two removal men in and out with boxes and furniture. There was no way that they could have moved on their own with Jodie being pregnant. The opportunity to buy the house had come at a time which was almost perfect for them. The church had been doing well and Lomond Park had been accommodated every week for the last two years so money was in no way tight. Patrick's parents' had also kept by a legal document, which had only to be issued once Patrick was married. He had known about it and that it had been kept under wraps for years after his parents had passed away and his understanding was that he wouldn't be made aware of what the purpose of the document was until he was married. After the wedding, both Patrick and Jodie had forgotten about it, considering everything that had happened in the run up to the wedding. Patrick had just found his adoptive brother in the same instant that he watched him die and to top it off, had just solved Glasgow's first murder investigation involving a serial killer, he had also watched his fiancée go through hell as he tried to do so, so his mind couldn't have been further from a mystery legal document.

However, when they did remember about it a few months after their lives had settled down to normality again, Patrick was a little unsure whether or not he wanted to revisit his parent's deaths once again. He had taken a very long time to move on from their tragedy and if it hadn't been for Jodie then he was certain that he wouldn't be here today. Going back to the lawyer to go over legalities of it all was the last thing he wanted to do, it would just bring back the pain from the first time around. Having to go through all of their personal things and all of their finances, he hadn't wanted to face it all again. Jodie had convinced him to, as she was able to do with most things and after several signatures on various documents, a sum of fifty thousand pounds was paid into Patrick's joint account with Jodie. To say he had been shocked was an understatement.

It had been quite simple considering the amount of money that his parents had left for them. Patrick wasn't made aware of where the money had come from, had it been an estate or savings that his parents had been putting away in secret, he just didn't know. All the same, he couldn't have been more grateful.

They had celebrated quietly with a bottle of champagne and a three course meal in a restaurant in Byres Road; a nice little Italian with low lighting and a grand piano in the corner. Patrick and Jodie had discussed what to do with the money and had decided upon a new home, since they had been trying for a family.

They had searched for a few month, finding houses that were nice but nothing spectacular. Then Patrick had come across 'Henderson Manor.' Not quite a manor in this day and age but in its early days, certainly a manor house. The brochure hadn't done it much justice but enough to catch Patrick's eye.

He had kept it a secret from Jodie until he knew for sure that it was where he wanted to be. He knew deep down that she would love it. It was being auctioned for a lot less than it was worth due to the fact that the family who had resided there for over a century no longer existed. The last member of the bloodline had passed away suddenly and there was no named person in the legal documents to take the house. The last member of that family hadn't drawn up a will, so the house was taken to auction. Patrick didn't understand the whole legal process, but he didn't care, all he wanted was to see it for himself.

Having gone to see the house, he could see that it really had been a home for a lot of people from the same family. The house was very big and Patrick could feel the history once he stepped inside it for the first time. The staircase in the front hall way creaked in a way that said many, many people had used them. There was an outhouse that Patrick was told was used as a wash and laundry facility. On hearing this, he understood just how long the house had been standing for. The auctioneer had said that the property had belonged to one family since the early 1800s and only recently the last known family member had passed away suddenly. The front entrance to the grounds of the house displayed large sandstone walls and the two front pillars had 'Henderson Manor' engraved into them.

"It makes it sound a little creepy, like something you'd find in a horror film," Patrick had said to the auctioneer. Patrick made him aware that he wasn't at all spooked by the house and that he was just making a passing judgment.

On entrance to the grounds, the stones crunched

under his shoes and the fir trees that surrounded the grounds blew gently in the wind. Before he was even inside he just knew that this was the house that he wanted to spend his life in with Jodie and their new addition. The house was in a position where they could move in immediately and make the changes that they wanted, while living there. Patrick was determined, and it paid off as he was successful at the auction.

"Are you glad we found it?" Patrick broke the happy silence.

"I couldn't be happier if I tried, it's amazing."

"I don't know why I asked you that, I know you're happy."

They finished off their fish suppers and Jodie stood up to take the rubbish out to the bin at the back entrance of the house. She could feel herself starting to waddle as she moved across the floor.

What are you doing to me little one? She thought to herself as she opened the back door. She could hear Patrick start to wash the dishes as she went outside. The grounds were dark but there was a security light on and it lit up the whole area, allowing her to see into the fir trees and over to an area she hadn't had the chance to look at since moving in. She placed the rubbish into the bin and walked across the gravel and stones to the back end of the house.

As she drew closer she slowed her pace, unsure if her eyes were playing tricks on her. Her brow furrowed, almost like she was trying to see more clearly. Eventually, she realised that her eyes weren't playing tricks on her, what she thought she had saw was entirely correct.

Henderson Family
Here we lay together not able to go on
We trust in you to stay together
And keep the family strong
We worked hard everyday
To get to where we are
Our family ties will keep us together
For we are never really far

Here lies Ada Henderson
1871-1949
A loving wife to Walter and mother to George

Walter Henderson
1870-1950
A loving husband to Ada and father to George

George Henderson
1896-1970

A loving husband to Anna and father to Audrey

Anna Henderson
1898-1970
A loving wife and mother

Audrey Henderson
1957-1982
A loving wife to James and mother to Sarah

James Henderson
1923-2002
A loving husband to Audrey and father to Sarah

Helen Henderson
1921-2008
Wife, mother and grandmother.

"What?" Jodie whispered. She stared at the burial plots that were in her garden. "Is this a joke?" She said, louder this time.

She turned on her heal, half marching, half waddling back into the kitchen where Patrick was tidying up.

"You didn't get lost then?" He smiled.

"No, no I didn't get lost, but I did find something rather interesting," she returned the smile sarcastically.

Patrick looked up, he understood in her tone that something was wrong. "What is it?"

"Oh, you mean you didn't know that there are gravestones on our property?"

Patrick smiled, "Oh, that? I thought there was something wrong."

Jodie couldn't believe how calm he was. "What do you mean, *oh that*? Patrick, there are *gravestones*, burial plots on our new property!"

Patrick took her hand and led her to the kitchen table. "Did you read them?"

"Yes, there are bloody seven of them under there," her head was in her hands.

"What's wrong? It's only a few memorials of the people who used to live here. The first man to have gone in there was born over one hundred years ago, in this house by all accounts. I think it's a nice history to come with the place. Come on, there had to be something to come from a house this old. It gives the house character."

Jodie nodded, knowing he was right. But she still couldn't believe that there were dead people in her garden. "Yes, but I didn't actually think we'd get the remains *and* the history."

Patrick laughed. "Hardly. Come on Jodie, you of all people should know that this isn't going to turn into a zombie fest. It's just that, the family who owned this 'manor' as they named it wanted the family history to stay here as long as possible. Each one of them lived here, reared their children here and died here. They ran a whisky firm by all accounts; Henderson Whisky funnily enough."

Jodie rolled her eyes. She knew fine well that there was nothing scary about death, yet she was still surprised that there were graves in her garden. "I know. Well, so long as we don't end up in there that's all I care about."

Patrick smiled. "Very funny, come on, let's get up and unpack our bedding. I'm done for the day."

"And if you hear from any one of them, keep it to yourself. I'd rather not be aware of an old spirit wandering around our house while I'm in the bath." Jodie was laughing, however she wasn't joking. She really didn't want to know about anything spiritual until the baby was born. She didn't need the stress, remembering how ill it made her when Patrick was working alongside the police and Ross was going around strangling people made her shiver. She didn't want to become ill with stress when she was pregnant with her first child.

"I won't say a word."

As they climbed the stairs to their new bedroom, both were unaware of the presence already appearing before them.

Ada Henderson knew fine well that Patrick was the only person who would be able to help her and the rest of the Henderson family bring home what was rightfully their own.

CHAPTER NINETEEN

The gravel was surprisingly smooth yet cold on his bare feet as he made his way across the grounds, towards the Henderson memorial plot. He had decided to call it a memorial plot rather than graves or burial plot. Even though having them on the grounds of his house didn't bother him at all, he still would rather that Jodie felt comfortable in her own home. So if that meant changing the way that they referred to it, then that was what they would do.

He found that he was walking slowly and realised that his legs felt as if they were full of lead. His eyes were focused on the memorial plot and he was aware that he felt worried but he couldn't figure out what he was worried about.

Help us!

Patrick stopped when he heard it, a female voice

that sounded frail and distant. He continued to walk, again feeling as though he was fighting against a force pushing him back. But he wouldn't give in, something was telling him that he had to get to the side of the memorial plot.

She's missing, came another voice now, a man this time, still frail but not as distant.

Patrick tried to focus on his goal, getting to the memorial plot. He put all of his energy into taking one step further and by the time he reached the plot he felt physically drained. What he didn't expect to see was what shocked him more than the struggle to get there. The plot was empty. He could see that the plot was actually split into three sections and all of them were empty. Patrick wasn't scared of spirits but he had never experienced a situation where bodies had gone missing before. And not just any body, bodies that were meant to be buried at his house. He was nervous to look round and find all seven spirits standing there, waiting for him.

"Who are you referring too?" he said aloud, hoping to get a name. However he wasn't so sure a name would help, the family had been here for over a century.

We should be together, came the first voice again.

Patrick wasn't sure if he had the strength for

another spiritual mystery. The last one had almost sent Jodie over the edge with panic attacks and sleep deprivation. He couldn't afford any of that to happen now.

"I had to pick a haunted house didn't I?" he said as he turned to face the house, fully expecting an audience. When he didn't find one, he decided to go back inside. The security light began to flicker and just before it went out completely, he felt a coldness creep over him. The hairs on his body stood on end and he began to shiver, realising that for some reason he was only wearing a pair of boxers and a t-shirt.

He felt a cold hand place itself upon his right shoulder just as the light went off and he turned around startled to find the face of an old woman so close to him that, had she been alive, he would have felt her breath on his face.

Help us find her!

Patrick found himself alone in the back grounds of the house, cold and with sore feet. He looked around for the woman who had appeared to him. She was nowhere around. When he thought about it, he couldn't remember why he was outside in the first place. All he could think of was that he was trying to get to the memorial plot and that it had taken all his strength. His legs no longer felt heavy, so he walked over to the plot, remembering that it had been open and empty. He approached with caution only to find everything as it should be. The plots were not open and certainly not empty.

Patrick looked up at the clear sky and breathed a sigh of relief. "I was sleepwalking." He couldn't understand it even though he was relieved that it was all just a dream. He hadn't done it since he was little. He went back inside as soon as he realised and was now more than aware that he was outside in the middle of the night, semi naked.

As he entered the kitchen, Jodie came in through the hall's entrance. "What are you doing?" She said as she rubbed her eyes.

"I was bloody sleepwalking. I woke up outside," he replied as he shook his head in confusion.

"You haven't done that since you were little."

"You're telling me. Don't know what that's all about."

Jodie filled the kettle. "So I can't sleep and you're walking around in the land of nod. Fancy a cuppa?"

Patrick nodded. "I'll just go up and get some clothes on; it's a bit chilly out there."

Jodie laughed. "Well you will be cold if you're wandering around outside in your boxer shorts."

As he made his way up to their bedroom,

Patrick couldn't help but think that there was a meaning behind the dream. It had felt very real to him and he couldn't help but think that whatever the meaning of it was, it had led him out the memorial plot. And those voices, they were so real and they had passion in their tone. They had been looking for someone. Someone they claim is missing, but missing from where?

Patrick entered the bedroom and pulled on a pair of tracksuit bottoms and put on a pair of thick socks to warm his toes. He walked over to the window and looked out over the front entrance of the manor. He scanned the long, gravel covered drive and noticed that the front gates were open. Patrick was quite sure that he had closed them after the delivery men had left.

Help us find her, was whispered into his ear. He jumped not only at the voice but also at the reflection in the window. Patrick spun round but there was no one behind him. He realised that he had been right, the dream did mean something and it *had* led him out to the plot. Patrick decided that he would communicate and find out who exactly was contacting him and why. But not now, it was too soon.

"We've only just moved in for God's sake."

He switched off from the connection and went

down to join his wife for a cup of tea, leaving the spirits of goodness knows who to wait until he was ready for them. Patrick really hadn't expected something to come up in this house, or at least not so soon. He didn't want Jodie to know, so he kept it to himself, allowing her to enjoy the pregnancy in peace.

As he entered the kitchen, he found that Jodie had already made his tea and had laid his mug on the kitchen table, across from where she was now sitting. "So; barefoot?

Patrick shook his head. "I know. I haven't a clue why, maybe because we're in a new house on the first night. Maybe my mind was trying to work its way around the place while I slept."

Jodie knew fine well there was something that he wasn't telling her and she was, in all honesty a little pissed off that he was keeping it from her. "You said that this was a fresh start for us."

Patrick looked up, uncomfortable with the indirect approach she had taken for what she really wanted to say. "It is a fresh start." His throat was beginning to dry up; she really did know how to get his pulse racing.

"Then why the lies?" she was smiling but it didn't reach her eyes.

"Lies?"

"Why were you really out there? I believe you were sleepwalking but I don't believe you when you say you don't know the reason behind it." Jodie tapped the mug with her index finger, the nail creating a 'ding' sound against the porcelain. She watched as he sighed heavily, knowing that she had quickly worn him down and that he was about to tell her what was really going on.

"It's nothing for you to worry about, really. I can handle what-ever it is that's going on here by myself."

"So, there is something going on?"

He looked down at her bump, knowing that any potential stress could be harmful to their baby. Patrick certainly didn't want to be the one who put his baby or wife in harm's way. "Like I said, nothing for you to worry about."

"You said that the last time. It was something you and the police would work on and I didn't have to worry. Then look what happened, I almost died. I don't know about you but I do not want anything like that to happen ever again, especially now that we are going to be parents."

Jodie had grown since Ross Turner had almost killed her. It had taken her a while to get over being kidnapped and held hostage while he planned to kill her in a gas explosion. For two months she couldn't close her eyes without seeing the inside of the boot that he had used to transport her to his flat. She still couldn't remember much of that, all she could remember clearly was being in that room, the door boarded up and a montage of those voices, telling her to stay calm, be strong, play him at his own game. Ross Turner had been a vile man but a very clever one, using Jodie at his advantage would have been a murderer's dream had his plan not been foiled by the help from the spirits of his victims. Jodie had vowed never to allow herself to become a channel for anything like that ever again and after she had mentally recovered, she decided to switch of her psychic ability and concentrate on her own life. When she found out she was pregnant, nothing on earth would stop her from protecting her family. Jodie understood that the spirits that came to her and Patrick weren't always looking for a killer but she never wanted to take that chance again. Jodie understood that Patrick needed to carry on, he was running the church and his success in catching Ross alongside was what drove him to continue his work in the church. If he could help more people, then he would.

"I am serious. If you don't want to worry then I don't have to tell you."

"Patrick, that's ridiculous. You're my husband

and this is our new home, if there is something happening here, I want to know about it."

Patrick knew that this was leading to an argument and either way Jodie would be the one who suffered from it. If he didn't tell her then she would be angry at him for keeping it from her and if he did tell her what happened out at the plots, then she would worry about the effect it would have on him and their relationship, not to mention the baby.

"You've got me over a barrel here."

"So, tell me. You know it's a strain if you don't."

"You're sure you want to know, earlier today you said you'd rather not know?" Patrick pressed, willing her to change her mind. She nodded, showing him that no amount of stalling would change her mind or make her rethink.

"Ok, I'll tell you." Patrick moved around to the same side of the table as Jodie, he wasn't so sure why he did this but he felt it necessary. "I was led out there, to be shown something."

"Shown what?"

"The plot outside; when I got out there, in my head the plot was open."

"In your *head* it was open?"

"Yes but not only that, the plot was empty. There were no bodies inside."

Jodie shook her head. "You're sure about this?"

"I was told that there is someone missing from it. That I had to help find her, that they should all be together."

Jodie took his hand, "Who's missing?"

Patrick shook his head. "I have absolutely no idea."

CHAPTER TWENTY

"I can't believe he's mine!" Jodie said as she stared down into baby Lewis's eyes. He had the most beautiful eyes that she had ever seen. They were deep blue in colour and so alert.

"Ours," Patrick smiled.

Jodie nodded, "Yes, of course ours. But what I mean is that he is *mine*. Nothing else has ever felt like mine before, nothing like this. He belongs to us, we created him. I don't think I have ever or will ever love anything as much as him ever again."

Patrick felt like his heart would burst, pride and love had completely consumed him. Jodie had been amazing during Lewis's birth and he was so incredibly proud of her for bringing him into the world safely. He owed his life to her now for giving him the best gift that you could ever possibly give.

"Unless we have more that is?"

Jodie laughed gently, "Let's give this little one time to settle first before we start creating a football team."

Patrick stood up and moved across to the window in the hospital ward. It was stifling hot outside and the hospital staff didn't allow fans to be brought in, in case of spread of infection.

There were three other beds on Jodie's ward, all of which were unoccupied, which they found strange. However Jodie wasn't complaining, she had some time to herself. Lewis had fallen asleep in her arms after feeding and she gently placed him in the little hospital cot beside her bed. She covered him with a small blanket and watched as his little chest moved gently as he breathed softly.

They were getting home the next morning and Jodie couldn't wait to get Lewis settled into his new home. "I can't wait to be home and be a family with you both."

Patrick turned from the window and smiled widely. He drank in the fact that he was now a dad, wholly responsible for the tiny person in the cot beside Jodie's bed. He couldn't be happier and he loved how much he loved Lewis and Jodie right at that moment. He took in the perfect picture of his wife and his son sitting by the bed and understood that he would have to make sacrifices for both of them for the rest of his life.

"Do you fancy a tea?" he asked Jodie.

"That would be nice."

Patrick kissed Lewis on the head as he slept and made his way down to the café in the Southern General hospital. He took his time, walking slower than he normally would, considering his new responsibility and what it would mean for the career side of his life. Being a psychic medium had its rewards but it also meant meddling in another being that had proved dangerous for him and Jodie in the past. Of course that would never happen again but he just wasn't sure that he ever wanted to take that risk. The risk was even higher now that Lewis had arrived and Patrick never wanted to put him in any kind of danger because he could speak to the dead. Lewis wouldn't even be here if Ross Turner had succeeded in his plan. Fortunately, Patrick had been one step ahead.

Patrick found himself in front of the tea and coffee machine and pressed for two teas after sliding the coins into the slot.

Walking back to the ward, he heard Lewis crying. His heart swelled at the sound of his son's heartbreak. He entered the ward and found Jodie rocking him gently as she stood by the window. She looked up as she saw Patrick, "Wind."

"Is he ok?"

"He will be. Just need to rub his back and he'll be fine."

Patrick placed the tea on the bedside stand and was at Jodie's side in the blink of an eye. He held his arms out, "Can I?"

Jodie handed Lewis over, who was grumbling in the process. He was tiny in Patrick's arms and Jodie felt tears sting her eyes. Lewis grumbled a little more and then settled in his dad's arms. He looked up at Patrick's face, trying to make sense of the colours and shapes that were in his line of sight.

"Seems ok now," Patrick said, gently swaying Lewis back and forth.

"You're a pro," Jodie wiped the tear that threatened to fall.

Jodie felt a sudden bout of tiredness creep over her and she climbed into the bed. Resting her head on the pillow, she watched as Patrick placed Lewis back into his cot.

"Go to sleep Jodie, you'll be home this time tomorrow and everything will be perfect." He looked up, expecting protest but she was already asleep.

"Well little man, you've only been in the world eight hours and already you're tiring your poor mum out."

Patrick sat in the chair next to the bed and watched his wife and son as they slept peacefully. He knew then that he had to consider the possibility of giving up his place in the world of mediums. It wouldn't be easy but if it meant a better life for his family then that's what would have to happen. There would be a lot to do, he would have to find someone to take over the church and find a full time job to pay for the house. But he didn't care what it took, so long as Jodie and Lewis were always happy and safe.

"You sure you really want to do that?" He heard Jodie ask.

Patrick smiled, "You're not supposed to listen to my private thoughts."

"They're only private if they don't involve me and our son." Her eyes were still closed.

"It's the best thing for all of us."

Jodie nodded gently, "I know. It's just been such a big part of our lives for so long, you're sure you really want to throw it away?"

"I'm not throwing it away. I am going to find someone to take over. Obviously I will still run it until the right person comes along. I need to give it up for us, for Lewis. I can't just live for the dead anymore Jodie. I need to do this for Lewis."

Jodie didn't argue, she knew that there was no

way to persuade him to keep going with the church. In a way she was glad, the whole Ross situation had put her off the spirit world. It had only brought bad luck to their door and she certainly didn't want any of that now that Lewis had arrived.

She slept soundly at the thought that Lewis was at the forefront of every decision Patrick would ever make.

CHAPTER TWENTY ONE

"What do you fancy for lunch?" Sam asked as he looked at the menu. He and Deborah were going strong, their relationship had moved quickly and Sam had been happy at the prospect. In fact, he couldn't have been any happier if he tried. Months of dates, talking and spending time together, Sam had come to fall in love with Deborah and he had forgotten all about his troubled past.

"I think I'll have the omelette with a side order of vegetables," Deborah replied.

The sun shone brightly through the window and it warmed their skin. Deborah had been blissfully happy in her relationship with Sam since Jenny's weird episodes had calmed down. Sam had been attentive, loving and everything else you could imagine to make their relationship as perfect as she had always wanted.

Their love hadn't blinded them in all fairness as there were still strange happenings within the flat. The happenings were small things that you mightn't notice or if you are one to think logically you would have explanation for. Keys jingling quietly as they hung on the key hook, the kettle switching on by itself and walking out of a room one minute and the next walking back in to find all of the windows open as wide as they could go. Sam was honest only with himself and found it hard to come up with reasonable explanations for the events which were taking place in his home. He was always reassuring towards Deborah and Jenny though, and would laugh off the events. Deborah wasn't stupid, she knew what was going on scared them all but she preferred to go along with Sam's uncaring attitude. She knew it wouldn't last.

The waitress made her way over to their table to take their order. Without looking up from her little pad of paper she said, "What can I get for you?"

Sam looked up to greet the waitress, only to discover he recognised her. "Claire?"

Claire glanced up from her pad and beamed a smile at him, "Well, you've not been in for a while. How've you been?"

Deborah's stomach lurched as she watched her man engage in conversation with another female.

This female was pretty, with short dark hair and rosy cheeks; this is not good. Deborah cleared her throat to distract Sam.

"Oh, Deborah, this is Claire. She has been a waitress here for a long time. You've actually met before, on one of our first dates." Sam said happily.

Claire smiled at Deborah, happy that his crazy friend Jenny was nowhere around. "Hi."

Deborah returned the smile however it barely lifted the corners of her mouth. "I'm sorry, I'm having trouble placing you."

"Likewise, it must have been a quick introduction." Claire replied.

Sam turned from Deborah to face Claire again. "She'll have the omelette and a side order of vegetables and I'll have my usual."

Usual? Deborah suddenly thought. *How often is he in here without me?*

Claire scribbled the order down. "I can't stay and chat, this place is mobbed today. I'll have it with you shortly."

Deborah watched as Claire walked back to the kitchen and disappeared behind the door. She turned to Sam, not wanting to spoil the afternoon.

"She seems nice."

Sam nodded; completely unaware that Deborah was gritting her teeth and wringing her hands together. "Yeah, she's worked here for ages. Just know her from coming in all the time."

"With Jenny?"

"Not always. Sometimes come in for a takeaway before work, especially if I'm rehearsing. She always throws in an extra sausage or toast."

Deborah smiled through her anger and knew that the best thing to do would be to change the subject and steer Sam from wanting to come back to this café again; from wanting to see Claire.

"What do you want to do tonight?" She asked.

"Sorry babe, got rehearsals at the theatre tonight. Will probably be out to well after midnight, the show is less than a month away so it'll be all go for the next month."

Deborah grinned. "If you have to work then you have to work. I'll just wait up for you. Maybe there'll be a surprise on your arrival."

Sam returned the grin, knowing exactly what she meant. "I'll make sure I get my lines perfect in that case."

Claire returned with their food and Deborah found it best not to look at her. After their meal, Deborah excused herself from the table and she made her way to the bathroom. She sat down on the seat and tried to rid herself of the jealousy that had taken over her mind. She knew that Sam was head over heels with her and she knew that he would never cheat on her but there was something in Claire that she didn't like. Perhaps the fact that she was pretty and Sam engaged in pleasant conversation was a factor, also knowing that Sam had a usual meal choice and that she wasn't always with him when he was in the café.

Deborah's thoughts were interrupted by two females entering the bathroom. They were giggling and she recognised Claire's voice straight away.

"He just gets better looking every time I see him," she heard Claire say.

"I know, he is just flawless; that jaw line, his hair. He looks even better in real life than he does on telly," girl number two replied.

"If he was single I would definitely ask him out."

Deborah smiled as she opened the cubicle door. She met Claire's eyes in the mirror and Claire's rosy cheeks drained away.

"Uh…" was all Claire could say.

"You're right, he is better looking in real life. And you know what else?" Deborah spoke as she casually washed her hands.

Girl number two didn't know where to look. "We're just messing about."

Deborah ignored her. "He's fantastic in bed too.

208

And he's all mine, so if you were planning on waiting until he's single; you'll be waiting a very long time."

She stuck her hands under the hand dryer and even though her heart wanted to burst out of her chest, she kept her composure.

"Look, there's no harm here. It's just a bit of girly banter," Claire tried to fill the silence.

Deborah turned to face her and as the hand dryer switched itself off, the silence which filled the room was chilling. She didn't reply to Claire's words, she simply walked through the girls and left the bathroom.

Girl number two turned to Claire. "Jesus, she's a bloody head case!"

"That's nothing; you should meet his friend Jenny. I don't know what it is he does to women but after that I don't think that he will be back in here, not without *her* anyhow."

Girl number two shook her head and went into one of the cubicles. "You think they're a threesome?"

Claire laughed. "No. I don't know but whatever the relationship between those three, it's weird. The funny thing is, he seems to be oblivious to it."

Deborah walked away from the opposite side of the door when she heard the flush of a toilet.

Sam looked up as she appeared at the table. "You ready?"

Deborah nodded as she picked up her coat and followed Sam out to the street. "Ready as I'll ever be."

CHAPTER TWENTY TWO

Jodie was happy that she had all the time in the world now that she had settled Lewis into their home at Henderson Manor. She had mentioned to Patrick about perhaps changing the name on the plaque at the front of the house from Henderson Manor simply to McLaughlin or something else a little less creepy. The name Henderson Manor did not suit the modern day reality that the house was now a part of. It almost sounded more like a horror was being filmed on the grounds rather than a new family building a life there. Patrick hadn't understood the urgency in her suggestion and thought that there were more important things that they should be thinking about rather than the name of their house.

"I just don't like it, when Lewis is at school the kids will make fun of him," she had stressed.

"You think the kids at his school won't like him because his house has a name? Come on Jodie, don't be ridiculous!"

She knew it sounded unreasonable but something inside her didn't feel right, Henderson Manor sounded like the setting of some old legendary horror tale. "I'm not being ridiculous; I'm just saying I want to change it. And anyway, we're not called Henderson, we're McLaughlin, so if anything it should be called McLaughlin Manor or McLaughlin House."

Patrick nodded, "And we can start calling it that if it means that much to you. We'll change the plaque too but not now, we have to decorate this place and if you haven't already noticed, it's going to be a big job for me."

The conversation was left at that and Jodie didn't mention it again. She wanted to focus on how to be a good mum to Lewis and for their new family to work, she thought it best to forget about renaming the house. It was a little ridiculous how strongly she felt about it and she couldn't quite put her finger on why she felt the way she did about the name. Jodie put it down to the fact that she wanted the house to be in their name and not some other family who had no living relatives left.

"I'm not speaking or thinking ill of the dead,

you'll understand," Jodie had said aloud as she watered the flowers next to the memorials at the back of the house. "I just want this to be *our* home. Time moves on and things change; we won't completely erase you from the house. We couldn't even if we wanted to, there's too much history here; a coat of paint and a roll of wallpaper couldn't erase that."

Since Patrick had told Jodie about the connection which he had made to one of the deceased Henderson family members before Lewis was born, nothing else had happened, which Jodie was glad of. Whatever meaning was behind the message had obviously not meant enough for them to carry on contacting Patrick.

Jodie looked up when she heard Lewis babbling from his pram. She had moved the seat upwards and pulled the hood up to shield his little head from the sun. Even though it wasn't hot, she didn't want to risk him burning. His little eyes darted back and forth, taking in the bright colours and sounds around him. He spotted his mum as she approached the pram and his little legs began bouncing up and down. His pink, toothless smile melted Jodie each time she looked at him.

"Hi baby, are you laughing at mummy talking to herself?" She asked softly as she lifted Lewis from the pram.

At eight months old, he was as bright as a button and smiled constantly which reminded Jodie each day, why she had decided to give up her place at the church. Spending every day with her son had made her realise that life was much more than death. With the greatest of respect for the dead, Jodie knew that her heart no longer lay with them and all she wanted was to be a mum and a wife.

"Come on baby boy, let's get you to the park and see if we can feed those ducks."

Walking with Lewis had become a daily occurrence and she had managed to get back to her pre-pregnancy weight. Jodie enjoyed walking around the park with Lewis, listening to him babble to himself and coo as the gentle breeze touched his face. She would never have thought a baby's voice could be so tranquil.

As she reached the park bench that she sat on each day, she put on the back brake of the pram, made sure that Lewis was covered with his blanket as he slept and took out her book. The weather was pleasantly warm for late February and the breeze had faded and so Jodie felt comfortable to sit there for as long as she could.

Feeling content that Lewis would have his full

two hour afternoon nap, Jodie opened her book and began to lose herself within the pages of a story far from the world she knew to be reality.

"Hello," came an unfamiliar voice which startled her.

Jodie looked up and saw a young woman sitting beside her on the bench. Lewis was still fast asleep, cosy under his blanket.

"Hi," was all Jodie could manage. Well, it was all she wanted to manage; whoever this person was had interrupted the peacefulness of reading and escaping from the world for just a few hours. She lowered her head back into the book and scanned the page, looking for the words her eyes last read.

"Is this your son?" The woman asked again.

No, I stole him from the hospital! Jodie thought sarcastically but thought better to answer more politely. "Yes, he is."

She didn't feel comfortable with how close the woman was and discreetly shuffled along the bench by leaning into the prams basket underneath to check her mobile phone, even though she knew it was switched off.

The woman stayed in the same place on the bench and continued to look at Lewis as he slept.

"Can I help you with something?" Jodie said, hiding the irritation in her voice.

The woman smiled, "Sorry, I just like to sit here sometimes. I hope you don't mind."

Jodie shook her head, "I don't mind. I sit here every day at this time, I have never come across you."

The woman smiled again and looked across the duck pond ahead of them. "My mum used to bring me here when I was a baby. She told me when I slept in the pram; she would sit here and read, just like you are now."

Just like I was, until you interrupted me, Jodie thought. And then she instantly felt guilty. She could tell that this woman was reminiscing about her mum, who was obviously no longer with her. She had spoken to enough people in the church over the years to understand when someone spoke fondly of a past loved one.

"Are you ok?" Jodie found herself asking.

"It just reminded me of my mum telling me that when I saw you. It was nice to see that this bench is still being used for that purpose."

Jodie felt this woman's heart aching but she sensed that it wasn't just for her dead mother.

"I'm Jodie," she said with a smile.

"Nice to meet you Jodie; and who is this little chap?" the woman asked as she peered into the pram?

"This is Lewis, he's my first."

The woman looked at Jodie and said nothing. She just stared into her eyes, as if searching for something.

"What?" Jodie asked. She frowned at the woman, not knowing how to take her.

The woman's eyes were suddenly dark and shadows began to fall over her face. "You are living in a house that you no longer feel comfortable with. You don't know why you suddenly feel this way but you will soon find out; and when you do, you'll want to get out of there and stay away. Bad things will happen in that house, you don't want your little Lewis to experience any of it."

Jodie was stunned by the woman's sudden outburst of words. She said them with kindness though; her intention wasn't to frighten Jodie but to warn her.

"Hang on a minute, how do you know about my house?"

"Let's just say I knew the family who lived there once."

The woman stood up, smiled down at Lewis and then cast her eyes upon Jodie once more. "Think about what I have said. Something will come into your life that you have been trying to keep out since you found out that you were going

to have your baby and you won't be able to stop
it."

***

Lewis cried loudly, and Jodie opened her eyes.
She had fallen asleep on the bench and her book
was on her lap at the page she had opened it at. She
picked Lewis out of his pram and noticed on her
watch that he had had his two hour nap; which
meant that she had had a two hour nap.

"Jesus," she whispered to herself. "How could I
have fallen asleep in the bloody park?"

She put Lewis back in the pram and covered
him again with the blanket. As she made her way
toward the gate which led to the street, she silently
cursed herself.

*How the hell could I be so bloody stupid, anyone
could have taken him?*

As she passed the last bench of the park before
the gate, she saw a woman sitting there. The dream
flashed into her mind and she remembered that the
woman in her dream was the woman now sitting
on the bench.

As Jodie passed through the gate, the woman
smiled at her, and waved to little Lewis as he
chewed on his fingers. Jodie walked quicker.

Lewis began to giggle as the woman waved to
him until he and Jodie were no longer in her line of

sight.

CHAPTER TWENTY THREE

"See you in the morning," Claire called out as she left the café. Every Friday the café had a late license where customers could bring a bottle of wine and have a meal. The only thing was it was open until midnight and somehow Claire always ended up on the early shift the next morning. The air had grown chilly and she wrapped her coat around her tightly as she walked along the street to the flat she shared with her mum. She turned up the side street at Kelvin Hall and knowing that her mum would kill her if she knew she had taken that route, Claire increased her speed to get home.

The breeze caused the bare trees to sway, creating a low hush in the air which harmonized with the rush of the canal below. The lights along the street which housed the old Transport Museum were dimly lit and the stars twinkled above her.

Half way along the street, she became lost in her thoughts about what life would be like had she completed her university course. She would've been able to get her mum away from Glasgow and the memories that tempted her lips back to the bottle. Claire knew that her mum was getting better as the years went on and that the flower shop was doing well. It kept her busy and her mind off the booze but she couldn't help but worry that it would always be part of her. Claire knew that there was nothing that she could ever do to change the way her mum was but she would do everything that she could to keep her mum busy. That was why she decided to help her mum develop her hobby of gardening and develop it into a business.

After her dad died from cancer ten years previously, she watched as her mum spiralled into depression which drove her to drink. It started out as a few glasses of wine at night, then it quickly progressed to a bottle, then two and before Claire knew it her mum was drinking a litre of vodka every two days. The drink almost killed her and the only thing that stopped it from happening was the thought that Claire would be left on her own without any parents. Claire was strong for both of them and as her mum got better she went out to work and kept the household running.

This had brought them closer together and Claire not only had a mum but a best friend and a sister. That was why she was always worrying but would never let it be known.

The flower shop was what kept her mum going during the day and at night Claire would cook and they would have a meal together, except of course for a Friday when Claire worked late.

Claire had become so lost in her thoughts that she hadn't noticed she was being followed. The figure behind her kept a safe distance and stayed within the shadows of the old Transport Museum building. Claire crossed the empty car park and heard the leaves crunching beneath her shoes. The sound merged with the sounds of the wind and the rushing of the canal that she didn't even hear the fast approaching footsteps behind her.

At first she thought that she was being mugged and so held onto her bag as tight as she could, however it wasn't until she saw the glint of the blade sparkle under the moonlight that she knew this was more than a mugging.

She let go of her bag and tried to run but the person in black grabbed at her hair and pulled her back. Claire tried to scream but the sound wouldn't come as the shock took over. The pain in her neck came in waves and seemed to spread over her whole body. She put her hand up to protect herself and felt that her neck was wet. On observing her hand, even in the darkness she knew that it was blood and lots of it.

The person who had stabbed her was gone, she hadn't noticed them leave and she hadn't cared; she just wanted to get home. Her legs would no longer carry her and so she collapsed to the cold ground with the gravel crunching under her weight.

Claire looked up at the building where she shared the flat with her mum and could see that the kitchen light was on; she was *that* close to home.

Suddenly she found she couldn't breathe, everything was happening in slow motion. She reached for the bag that she had ditched in the hope that she could phone an ambulance but she couldn't move her body.

A car passed by on Old Dumbarton Road, heading towards the children's hospital but with the car park in almost complete darkness, no one saw that Claire was sprawled on the ground, taking her last breath. There was nothing that Claire could do but hope that it would be over quickly. She had always been afraid of an early death from her experience with her dad; however she found peace in the fact that if there was a heaven then she might get to see him again.

Her eyes filled with tears at the realisation that she was about to die on her own, on the ground of a car park outside her home and there was no one around to help her. She closed her eyes to allow the tears to fall.

She never opened them again.

CHAPTER TWENTY FOUR

Walking along the road in the rain at six o'clock in the morning with an excitable dog on the end of the lead was not his idea of fun but fifteen year old Gregory had no choice. His mother had told him that if he wanted to go on the family holiday he had to find a way of earning some spending money or it just wasn't going to happen. So he had offered to be the one to walk the family dog; every day. He hadn't believed that his mum and dad would actually make him keep his word but he was wrong.

With the cold wintery weather truly making its presence known, Gregory couldn't help but imagine walking along the beach in Lanzarote and feeling the hot sand beneath his feet. The cool water lapping around his toes and the sound of the gentle Canary Island breeze whirling around him was enough to accept walking Dennis, the hyperactive Labrador puppy. At six months old the thing was close to fully grown and he was almost pulling Gregory off his feet.

"Wait!" Gregory said in a firm voice.

The dog ignored his command and continued panting his way up the street. Gregory's images of Lanzarote were blown from his mind as the wind picked up, causing a strong gust to uplift the crisp packets which littered the street and create a cyclone of colourful foil.

"This is just great for a Saturday morning," he said to himself.

Gregory was doubtful that the sun would shine today, what with the rain and wind during the night. The weather had been reasonable when he had gone to bed but it had woken him in the middle of the night with the rain lashing off the window. His immediate thought was that his alarm clock would be going off in a few hours and the knowledge of taking Dennis for a walk was not what he had in mind for his Saturday morning. But it would only be for twenty minutes and then he could take Dennis home and climb back into bed. That was, if Dennis didn't drag him home instead; the damn dog was so strong and full of energy all of the time.

"Slow down you stupid mutt," Gregory said as Dennis almost strangled himself trying to pull them along the street.

They turned down Bunhouse Street, away from the main road into the city centre and the old museum building sheltered them slightly from the wind. Dennis stopped suddenly and barked once. Gregory took no notice as he continued to walk however, Dennis continued to bark furiously and his tail whipped from side to side. Gregory looked down at the dog as he continued to bark and wag his tail. Dennis never barked unless the door went or they were just about to go out.

"What is it boy?"

Gregory allowed Dennis to lead him towards the car park and by the looks of it, Dennis knew where he wanted to go. Bunhouse Street car park was empty and there was nobody else around. The trees cast large shadows across the car park and the street lights twinkled behind the branches blowing in the wind. Before Gregory knew it, he was standing by himself and he had let go of Dennis's lead. He watched as Dennis sniffed around the bulk on the ground and his tail had stopped wagging.

"What have you found boy?" Gregory called.

Dennis barked again, allowing Gregory's

suspicions to grow. He knew that it was likely to be what he expected but he didn't want it to be. He approached the dog slowly and on his approach the dog would normally become excited; but not now. He reached the bulky heap and looked down; what his eyes saw were not what a fifteen year old boy should have to see. There was a lot of blood along the jaw line and the upper part of the body. The gash in the neck was neat, where he presumed a knife would have made its entrance.

Gregory was frozen to the spot for a few moments; not sure what he should do. He jumped as his mobile phone rang in his pocket. His hands scrambled in his pocket to find the device.

"Hello?"

"Gregory, if there is a shop open, grab some milk," his mum's voice was on the other end of the phone.

"Mum?" his voice shook.

There was a silent pause.

"You've lost the dog again, haven't you?" She whined.

Gregory shook his head slowly, "I've found something."

"What is it?"

Gregory swung his body away from the bloodied corpse as he retched. His mum could hear this on the other end of the call and began to panic. Putting the phone to his ear he spoke. "I'm at the old museum, you'd better come quickly. I've found a body."

Chapter Twenty Five

Lang held up his badge to the uniformed officer guarding the forensics tent and he lifted the material to allow him and Preston inside.

"Yet another Glasgow murder," Preston sighed as they looked down at the woman on the ground.

The flash of the camera reflected the bright white material of the tent and Lang could feel another headache threatening. He massaged his temples as he took in the scene. "What do you think; unprovoked?"

Preston nodded, "Possibly; a jealous boyfriend perhaps?"

"Could be a number of things at this stage; we'll need to ask the next of kin as much as we can to determine the company she keeps..."

"Kept," Preston corrected.

"Aye, we'll need to find out where she worked,

who she worked with, if she had any, what is it the kids say these days; beef with anyone?"

Preston smiled. "Why are you doing that? Act your age man."

Lang beckoned the forensic officer in charge. "Do we have an identity on the girl yet?"

The forensic officer nodded. "Yes. According to her student card her name is Claire Prowse. She was twenty three years old and her address is Forty Four Ferry Road, which if I'm not mistaken is just down there." He pointed in the direction of the flats at the bottom of the main road.

"Jesus, she was on her way home." Preston shook his head.

Lang narrowed his eyes as they exited the tent. "We'll wait until they've moved the body before we inform the next of kin. We don't want them seeing this and knowing that it's their daughter or whatever."

Preston and Lang went back to the car, all the while Lang still massaging his temples.

"You ok there Jim?"

"Eh?" he looked up. "Aye, just got a headache."

"Another one?" Preston asked. "That's the fourth this week. You'd better get to the doctor and get that seen to."

Lang nodded. "I will. But we've been too busy

for me to get away."

Preston climbed into the car, shaking his head as he did so. "Always excuses with you."

"What are you; my mother?" Lang snapped.

"I'm just saying that if you've got a constant headache maybe you need glasses."

"Then I'll go to the bloody optician."

There was silence. Lang had been snappy for weeks and Preston was getting a little bit sick of it.

"Do you know what? Next time I won't bloody bother."

Lang put his seat belt on and was glad that Preston had shut up. There was enough going on with Preston's imminent retirement and now a new murder enquiry. He didn't have the want or the time to be going to the doctor.

"Let's just go and wait for the call that the body has been moved so we can inform next of kin and start trying to piece together her last movements."

***

Linda Prowse dialed her daughter's number for the millionth time that morning but she still couldn't get past the voicemail. It just wasn't like Claire to stay out all night and not tell her mum where she was. Something definitely wasn't right. Linda punched the local police station's number into the keypad.

"I'd like to report my daughter missing."

Linda explained the situation to the officer at the end of the phone and before she knew it the buzzer in the flat was sounding. On opening the door, she instantly recognised the officers.

"You're the two officers who I spoke to when Sarah Henderson died."

Preston smiled, completely unaware of how to answer that considering what they were about to tell her. "Can we come in Mrs Prowse?"

Linda opened the door wider and welcomed them in. "You see, my daughter Claire. She hasn't come home from work last night and if she had planned on staying out she would have told me and she hasn't. I can't get her on her mobile and well, I just started panicking. All I could think to do was to report her missing."

"Mrs Prowse, we actually have some news about your daughter." Lang hated this part of the job. He was glad he didn't have to do this part too often. Usually it would be uniform that would take this responsibility but seeing as they already had knowledge of Claire Prowse's demise, they saw it as the best thing to do to be the ones to deliver the news.

"Oh god, what is it?" Linda Prowse clasped her hands together under her chin, eyes glistening with threatening tears.

Preston took a deep breath before he began. "A body was found in Bunhouse Street car park at six o'clock this morning. We believe the identity to be Claire; I'm sorry Mrs Prowse."

Linda Prowse fell back onto the couch, her hands still clasped together under her chin. "I want to see her."

Lang nodded, "Of course. We can arrange for that today."

Preston sat down beside her. "Is there anyone you can call?"

Linda Prowse shook her head. "It was just the two of us."

Lang turned to face the door, disgusted that yet again they had had to tell some poor woman that her daughter had been murdered. Professionalism took over and he turned to face Linda once more. "I'll make the call and arrange for an official identification, Mrs Prowse."

Linda didn't take any notice. She turned to Preston, who was trying to stop himself from imagining what it would be like if it were one of his two beautiful girls. "What happened to her?"

"Mrs Prowse, Claire has a stab wound to the neck. She was murdered."

Linda Prowse stared through Preston, like he

wasn't there.

Silence filled the room and Preston stood up as Lang entered the room. "We can take you now Mrs Prowse. Are you sure you want to do this so soon?"

Linda Prowse was already on her feet. "Yes, I want to see her. I need to see her to really believe that it is her."

Denial was evidently sailing through Linda's mind as she followed Lang and Preston out to their car. Her face failed her attempts at bravery and Preston was sure she would cave at any moment. She didn't say anything as they made the journey to Glasgow City Morgue. On arrival, Preston and Lang led Linda Prowse down a long, white corridor which smelled of death and decay. Of course the place was clean but Linda could smell nothing other than death masked with bleach. It turned her stomach to think that her daughter may be lying on a cold concrete slab somewhere in that building.

"What do I have to do?" Linda asked suddenly, her voice cracking.

"We'll sit outside and wait to be called in. You will go into the room, one of us can accompany you if you'd like. All you have to do is tell us if it is Claire and you can leave as soon as you wish afterwards." Lang found he was speaking with the softest voice he had ever used. It seemed to help his headache. The bright white walls did not.

"I'll go in by myself."

"Ok, that's fine. Take as long as you need." Lang replied.

Linda Prowse sat down on the cold plastic seat outside what, to her, looked like the doorway of an office with a mirrored window beside it. Forever and an eternity passed by inside what turned out to be just a few minutes and a pathologist invited Linda inside. Her stomach flipped and turned and she could hear her footsteps sounded like thunder. Her heartbeat echoed in her head and she could hear the blood rushing in her ears. Everything slowed down and became blurry as she watched the pathologist lift the crisp white sheet from the head of the corpse on the concrete slab. She looked down and saw her daughter. Her face no longer smiling and full of light, instead shadows cast across her pale skin and dreadful fear filled Linda. Had her daughter suffered terrible pain and dread in her last moments? And who had put Claire Prowse on that slab?

"Yes. That's Claire."

Linda turned before the pathologist covered Claire's face and she was out of the door and back on the plastic seat next to Preston and Lang.

"It's her; my baby girl. It's her." Linda said, with a mixture of shock and anger in her voice.

"Thank you Mrs Prowse. I can't imagine how hard that must have been for you to do." Preston said.

Linda stood up and the officers rose with her. "Find the bastard that murdered my daughter before I do."

CHAPTER TWENTY SIX

Sam had managed to cover up his real feelings about the things that had been happening in his flat over the past year or so. Deborah and Jenny had been scared at first but seeing Sam calm about the situation made the girls calm and so things seemed relatively normal for them. But deep down, Sam knew that these things were happening for a reason, even if he didn't want to admit it out loud. He had never really considered life after death until he started to experience the things which were happening right under his nose. The slamming of doors, the windows opening, the kitchen appliances turning themselves on and off... how can that explained rationally? He had managed to hide most of it from the girls although they would occasionally witness small things, like tapping sounds and the temperature dramatically dropping.

Standing outside the main entrance to the church, he found himself clutching at the small cutting from the advert in the paper about the West End Spiritualist church and all its offerings. Sam had never given the 'afterlife' a second thought until recent events made him question what was really going on in his and Jenny's flat. All he knew now was that he was standing outside the church, ready to go inside and try to figure out what was going on.

"You ok there, son?"

Sam turned to find a little old lady looking up at him and smiling kindly. She was half Sam's size and was clutching at her handbag.

"Yes, I'm fine thank you. Is this the West End Spiritualist Church?" Sam already knew that it was; he didn't know why he was asking.

"Aye it is, son. This here is the best place to come if you're looking for comfort after the death of a loved one, or if you're looking to find peace. Is that why you're here?" Her voice was soft but with a broad Glaswegian twang behind it.

"You could say that." Sam returned the smile.

He followed the old lady inside and found that there was already a building audience. Sam didn't know entirely what he was going to say; if he were going to say anything at all. He felt slightly ridiculous that he had come to someone who claimed to speak to the dead about some bumps in the night in his flat. However, he had no other ideas and had hoped that this medium could shed some light on the subject.

"It's your first time, is it?" The old lady asked as she sat down beside him.

Sam nodded.

"You'll like it here; Patrick is spot on almost every time he gives a reading."

"Patrick?"

"Aye, Patrick is the medium for tonight. There are others but he and his wife Jodie are the best of the bunch, although since Jodie had the baby, she doesn't really do readings anymore. Shame really, she was always great at making you feel better about a loved one's passing."

Sam tried to concentrate on the stage at the front of the room. For some reason he felt terrified and he didn't understand why.

"Don't look so scared, son. You'll be fine."

The bustle of the room distracted Sam for a little

while before the demonstration began. He watched the people that poured into the room and wondered why they were here; who they were here for and if it would make them feel better. Sam watched a man approach the stage and realised that he had picked a seat in the front row.

Nice one, Sam, he thought to himself.

The bustle of the room lessened until there was silence and everyone turned their eyes to the man who was now standing two feet above them on the small stage.

"Good evening everyone and thank you all for attending tonight's demonstration. As many of you are already aware, my name is Patrick McLaughlin and I am the head medium at this church. Are there any newcomers in the audience this evening?"

Sam reluctantly raised his hand, wishing he had sat at the back to get a look at who else was new.

"A few tonight, well I will welcome you all and give you my quick spiel before I move onto the readings. My aim is to provide you with as accurate a reading as possible from whoever may come to me tonight. If I come to you and offer you information, all I need for you to do is say yes if you understand or no if you don't."

Sam felt his palms begin to sweat. *Why am I so bloody nervous?*

"I do not aim to scare, upset or give anyone negative information during the readings and so if you feel any of these things I need you to tell me that you do not wish to continue and I will move onto someone else."

The little old lady nudged Sam and when he turned to her, she winked at him. "That never happens, he is always fantastic," she whispered.

"Let's begin."

Patrick fell silent along with the audience and his eyes scanned the room. A few moments passed and he nodded a few times, as if agreeing with something. Sam almost got up and left, but froze in his seat when Patrick's eyes fell on his.

"Sam?"

Sam's eyes widened and his throat almost seized up. He nodded.

"You've come here for help this evening."

Patrick moved along the stage slowly, back and forth; saying nothing for a few moments.

"It seems you have had a visitor and you wish for them to leave?" Patrick enhanced the last word to make it sound like a question, even though he and Sam both knew that it was not a question but a confirmation.

"Yes, that is correct; I think."

Patrick nodded, "I do not wish to continue this

reading in the public gallery. We will meet at the end of my demonstrations tonight, if that is ok with you."

Sam was shocked and before he knew it, Patrick had moved onto someone else entirely.

What the hell does he know?

***

Patrick closed the door of the church when the last person left and turned to face Sam. He was surprised that Sam had stayed at all; he had fully expected to see him leave as soon as he had said they would speak after the demonstration.

"So, you have something to say that can't be said in front of an audience?" Sam asked. It sounded like an interrogation; it wasn't meant that way.

"I didn't say it *couldn't* be said in front of the audience. I just thought that out of courtesy for you that it would be better if we spoke in private."

"And I suppose that you'll charge me a fee for that?" Sam asked.

Patrick shook his head. "No, I offered for you to stay."

Sam nodded in defeat. He had expected to have to pay an up-front fee before any words were exchanged. Patrick led Sam to a small room in another part of the building and offered for him to sit down.

"So, you seem to have a lot on your mind." Patrick said.

"You know?" Sam asked.

"I have been made aware of your visitor."

"Visitor?"

"The bumps in the night, the photo frames falling off the walls, the items going missing and turning up somewhere else?"

Sam couldn't help but smile, "You think I have a ghost?"

Patrick returned the smile which slowly turned to a grin. "Why else would you be here?"

Sam couldn't believe what he was hearing; come to think of it, he couldn't believe that he was considering it to be a possibility.

"No way, ghosts don't exist. This is ridiculous."

Patrick nodded. "So why are you here then?"

Sam couldn't reply, in all honesty he didn't know why he had come to the church.

"Desperation I suppose."

Patrick sighed. "I'm not one to force my ability on anyone, so if you're not sure that you believe in what I do then you're free to leave. I'm not going to waste your time and I certainly don't want to waste my own."

Patrick left the small room and made his way

into the main hall. He began stacking chairs and was shocked to see that Sam was helping.

"I didn't say I don't believe in what you do, I'm just saying that I am not sure what to believe."

Sam had thought of multiple ways to explain what had been going on in his and Jenny's flat. But nothing seemed reasonable, not when he had seen things with his own eyes on more than one occasion. Yes, photo frames fall down all of the time, loose hooks or bad hanging to blame for that. But how do you explain the frames not just falling down but flying across the room?

"If you want my help, I'll gladly oblige. However if you don't then I wouldn't be offended. Many people have come here before out of sheer curiosity and found that it is just not their cup of tea. But you've come here for a specific reason, am I right?"

Sam cleared his throat as he stacked the last chair. "Yes there is a specific reason but in my head it's not logical."

Patrick was not surprised to hear that. "It never is logical in my line of work. If you really do want me to help you, then you have to let me help you. If not, then that's fine. Good luck with sorting it out."

"How much do I pay?" Sam asked.

Patrick laughed. "I'm not going to charge you

anything. It's only a few moments of my time to find out what's going on."

Sam shook his head. "I don't know if it will be just a few moments."

"What do you mean?"

"I mean, that what-ever is in my flat has steadily got worse as time has gone on."

Patrick frowned. "Well then, for me to really understand it, I'm going to have to come to your house."

CHAPTER TWENTY SEVEN

As the bulb flickered for the umpteenth time that evening, Jenny decided to go out. Jenny was not at all one for believing in ghost stories however being in the flat alone when the bulbs in most of the rooms were flickering and doors were seemingly closing on their own made her skin prickle. She made her way through to her bedroom to collect her handbag when a sound from the kitchen stopped her in her tracks. Being frozen with fear prevented Jenny from going to the kitchen to investigate and so instead of turning around she kept moving toward her bedroom door.

Jenny.

Not only did she hear it but she felt it to. An ice cold breeze on the back of her neck and she swung on her heel to where she had heard it. Nothing or no-one stood behind her but she knew that something was not right. Jenny wanted to call out but what good would it do? If she got a reply she would probably die from a heart attack and if she didn't get a reply then she would probably die from fear of waiting for one. Instead she decided to grab her handbag and leave as quickly as she could. Jenny rushed into her bedroom and hooked her arm through the straps. She then reached for her coat and didn't dare look in the mirror. Reaching for the handle of her bedroom door, she stopped.

"I didn't close the door," she whispered to herself.

A gentle rush of air brushed the side of her face and her body convulsed with fear. Jenny grabbed the handle and pulled the door open. Stood on the other side of the door was Sam and she screamed with fright.

"What?" Sam jumped back.

Jenny dropped her bag and coat and slumped down onto the bed, covering her face with her hands.

"Are you trying to send me to an early grave?"

"What is it?" Sam asked as he entered the room.

Jenny looked up. Her hands were shaking so much that she had to place them on the bed at either side of her to keep them steady.

"It happened again."

Jenny stopped talking when she saw another man come into her view.

"Who's this?"

Sam looked behind him and saw Patrick standing in the doorway.

"Oh, this is Patrick McLaughlin."

Jenny smiled gently, looking for more information.

"He's a medium."

"A medium?"

Patrick entered the room and held out his hand.

"Nice to meet you; you must be Jenny?"

Jenny shook Patrick's hand and tried to control the involuntary jittery movements.

"Are you ok Jenny?" Patrick asked.

Jenny shook her head.

"I gather that from you being here, Sam has told you what has been going on?"

"He mentioned a few things."

Sam interrupted.

"I told Patrick that I wasn't sure how to explain things, so he offered to come and have a look around."

Jenny stood up from the bed.

"For what price? Surely your kind doesn't come cheap?"

Patrick smiled.

"Actually, this is not usually in my job description. So I am not charging anything."

"What were you so frightened of when we first came in?" Sam asked.

Jenny told him about hearing her name and the bang from the kitchen. Patrick listened as he took in his new surroundings. Something definitely didn't feel right. There was a heavy presence in the flat and it wasn't a happy one.

"Can I have a look around?" Patrick asked.

"Of course; it's not a big flat so you can't get lost." Sam replied.

Patrick disappeared from their sight and Jenny fell into Sam's arms.

"You looked terrified when you opened the door."

"I was; I am. What the hell is going on in here?"

Sam shook his head.

"I have absolutely no idea."

Jenny pulled away and ran her hands through her hair, not knowing what to do or where Patrick's visit would lead them.

"Should we go with him?" Jenny said.

The pair left Jenny's room and went into the kitchen where they found Patrick, who was stood by the breakfast bar and staring out of the window.

"Anything?" Sam asked.

"Has this been happening the whole time you've lived in this flat?" Patrick replied.

Jenny shook her head.

"No, only in the last year or so. It has become progressively worse though and to be honest it is scaring the shit out of me."

Patrick nodded as he gazed around the kitchen.

"Ok. And how long have you lived here?"

"About two and a half years." Sam replied. "These flats have been up for about three. And I own the property."

"Why do you ask?" Jenny prompted.

"Just trying to establish all the facts."

Patrick left the kitchen area and made his way into the living area. He stopped suddenly and Sam almost walked into the back of him.

"What is it?" Sam asked warily.

"Who's Sarah?"

Jenny gasped at the sound of her name.

"She's my ex. And yes, before you ask; she's dead. And no; I didn't kill her."

Sam's attempts at comedy failed him miserably when neither Patrick nor Jenny even cracked a smile.

"Why do you mention Sarah?" Jenny asked.

Patrick turned to face them both.

"Your relationship with her didn't end well, did it?"

Sam's head began to ache. This can't be happening. He knew what Patrick was about to say next and suddenly wished that he hadn't gone to the church at all. He would rather not know.

"No, it didn't end well. But there were many reasons for that and the police have proven that my reasons were factual."

"Police?" Patrick asked.

Sam nodded and Jenny sat down on the sofa.

"Sarah kind of lost the plot when we were together; hated the fact that I was living with Jenny. She became jealous, so jealous that she started to send hate mail to Jenny. And I would receive photographs of Sarah and me together and Jenny and me together. On the back of them she's written, *he's mine* and *she's dead.* She did a lot of really sick stuff and tried to make it look like someone was stalking me when it turned out to be her all along."

Patrick frowned. "How did you know it was her that was sending you those things?"

"When she died the police turned up asking me questions about her and the how things were between us the last time I had saw her. Anyway, they found a bunch of photos, letters and other stuff in a box in Sarah's house. They confirmed to me that it was most likely her who was stalking us." Sam stopped talking for a few moments. "I didn't want to have to go through all of this again."

"I'm sorry. But if you want me to help you I have to know everything."

Jenny sniggered. "If you're so psychic, then how come you don't know it all already?"

Patrick didn't retaliate. He smiled gently and considered his answer before he spoke.

"Because, Jenny I'm not a mind reader. I'm a spiritualist medium and I don't always have the full background."

Jenny opened her mouth to reply when music began playing. It was coming from the other end of the flat and it was getting louder by the second.

Sam raced through towards the music to find it was coming from his bedroom. It wasn't the fact that music had begun randomly playing that was giving him chills but in fact it was the song. Elvis Presley, The Wonder of You.

"No way," was all that Sam could say.

Patrick turned the music off and turned to Sam.

"She used to sing it all the time, didn't she?"

Sam's face was drained of colour. What was normally a fresh rosy face was now the look of death.

"*All* the time."

253

Sam didn't want to believe it however he knew what Patrick was about to say next.

"Sam?" Jenny placed her hand on his shoulder.

Patrick looked at the terrified faces of the people standing in front of him and knew that they understood.

"When Sarah died, I don't think that she went very far. I think that she is here, in this flat."

Jenny shuddered.

"Oh my god, this is ridiculous." Her faked confidence failed her; she couldn't hide the fear in her voice.

"It explains a lot though, doesn't it?" Sam looked down at her. "Question is; why is this happening?"

Patrick hadn't anticipated this at all.

"I think she has some unfinished business. But not with you."

They all jumped at the sound of Sam's mobile ringing loudly in his pocket. He took the phone in his hand and looked down at the screen.

"Excuse me please," he said as he left the bedroom and went into the hall to answer.

Jenny was left standing in Sam's room with Patrick and she looked him straight in the eye.

"Do you honestly not know who she could be here for?"

Patrick shook his head.

"Do you think it could be me?"

"I don't mean to scare you but if what Sam said about the stalking is true then it is a possibility."

Jenny's eyes glistened against the moonlight filtering through the window.

"She hated the fact that we were; are best friends. She wanted him to stop being friends with me. She hated me. I could see it in her eyes. Of course she denied everything and I just kept my mouth shut whenever Sam spoke to her about me. You think that she wants revenge?"

Patrick narrowed his eyes.

"Revenge for what?"

"For not getting her own way and for not getting her claws into Sam. For dying before she could really do some serious damage?"

"You really think that Sarah was so jealous of your friendship with Sam that she would have gone on to do something far worse?"

Jenny shrugged her shoulders. "Who knows, she was pretty crazy when Sam broke up with her."

Patrick rubbed the back of his neck. "How did she die?"

"The police said that it was accidental. She fell down the stairs in her house apparently. She lived by herself in a huge house that was left to her in some family will. I seriously thought that Sam was set for life when he first started seeing her; clearly he wasn't."

Patrick sat down on the bed, wondering what to do next.

"Are you alright?" Jenny asked.

Sam entered the room just then, still holding the phone.

"That was Deborah on the phone. She's coming over."

Patrick's mind was working overtime as he tried to piece together all of the information he had received so far. But something didn't feel right.

"Sam, what did you say Sarah's surname was again?"

"I didn't say, but it was Henderson. Sarah Henderson. Why?"

Patrick stood up and ran his hand across his head.

"Jenny said that Sarah lived in a huge house that was left to her in a family will, is that correct?"

Sam nodded.

"Ok, well in that case, I think I've bought Sarah Henderson's house; Henderson Manor."

CHAPTER TWENTY EIGHT

Sam felt completely deflated after Patrick had left,
almost like someone had pricked him with a thin
needle and the air was slowly releasing from a
puncture wound somewhere on his body. How
much of a freakish coincidence could it be that
Patrick had come to buy Henderson Manor? Surely
he had made some sort of mistake or jumped to
conclusions. There had to be many women out
there with the name, Sarah Henderson. Jenny
didn't seem to think it was a coincidence, she was
almost certain that Patrick had gotten it right and
that on some level, Sam was meant to meet Patrick
because he would know what to do. Deborah on
the other hand, didn't believe a word that had
come out of his mouth, even if she hadn't had the
chance to meet him herself.

"There is no way that he's telling the truth; he

wants to suck money out of both of you." Deborah said as she handed Sam a hot coffee.

"But he said that he wouldn't take any money from us," Jenny said as she sipped on a glass of wine.

"Of course he said that. He's not going to take anything off you straight away, is he? He'll *'delve'* a little deeper into it and when his mind hits a *dead end*, so to speak, and then he'll say that he needs to start charging you a fee."

Deborah was furious that this had happened. How dare this Patrick person put Sarah into Sam's head. It had taken him long enough to forget her and what she had done to him.

"Deborah, I really think that this is all too close to be a coincidence," Jenny said, "I really think that he's right and that he can help us."

"Are you seriously suggesting that this flat is haunted?"

A wave of confusion crossed Jenny's face. How else would you explain it?

Deborah turned away from Jenny and looked into Sam's eyes.

"Listen, baby this is all nonsense and the sooner you start to realise that, then the better off we'll all be."

Sam shook his head. He couldn't just leave

things hanging like this.

"No, something isn't right. And maybe this place isn't haunted or maybe Patrick has made a mistake. But until I know for sure, I can't let this lie."

Sam stood up and went to his jacket that was handing over the back of the single recliner across from the sofa.

"What are you doing?" Deborah asked.

"I'm phoning Patrick. I need to speak to him."

"But he has just left. See; look what he has done to you. You hear her name after all this time and suddenly you can't think of anything else."

Jenny nodded. "She's right Sam. Just leave it until tomorrow, when your head is a little clearer. You're just a bit shaken because he told you that it's Sarah."

Sam swung on his heel. "See, you said it yourself. *It's Sarah,* so you admit that there is something going on in this flat and that there is a strong possibility that it could have something to do with her."

Deborah tried to keep the venom from her voice as she spoke but it was a hard task to carry out. "I'm sick of hearing *her* name. She is dead! How can she be doing any of this when all she is, is dust in the ground now?"

Sam ignored her and began to dial. Deborah flapped her arms in the air in defeat and stormed into the kitchen.

"What's her problem?" Jenny asked quietly.

Jenny understood and agreed with Deborah's point but at the same time she wasn't the one to experience what had been happening in the flat and she was also not around when Sarah was creating merry hell. Her thoughts were interrupted by Sam's voice.

"Patrick? It's Sam here. We need to talk, can we meet?"

***

Patrick had sat Jodie down earlier that evening and explained everything to her. He was worried that she would have gone crazy when she found out. What she had done was far worse.

"You seem really quiet. Are you ok?" Patrick asked her.

"I'm fine."

"Every man knows that when his wife uses those words it usually means the exact opposite."

Jodie didn't respond as she put Lewis's lunch for the next day into the fridge. Mashed up sweet potato with broccoli; he was a vegetable lover at a young age.

"Jodie, I can't just ignore this, you do realise that?"

She didn't respond, instead she left the kitchen, went upstairs to their bedroom and closed the door, leaving Patrick alone with his words.

Lying on the bed, she listened to Lewis's soft breathing and wondered what on earth Patrick had been thinking. How could he offer to bring his work home for a complete stranger and bring all this into Lewis's life?

He had explained to Jodie about Sam and how it had turned out that they were living in the house of his ex, whom was now 'haunting' him and his flat mate. Jodie's response was flat and lifeless.

"You'll remember the night I was sleepwalking, when we first moved in? And I told you that some spirit told me someone was missing and they wanted my help to find them? Well Sarah Henderson isn't in that plot. I think it's her who I've needed to find."

Jodie's response was relatively flat and lifeless. "Are you serious?"

"Jodie, I didn't ask for this, it's just come around. You chose to leave this part of your life behind but I am still very much a part of it."

"Did you not learn your lesson after what happened the last time?" Jodie had said as she stacked the dishwasher.

"That was different."

"Not so much, we just lived in a different house then. It affected our personal life, I almost died at the hands of an absolute lunatic. Why can't you see that you are tempting fate by getting involved in something like this again?"

Patrick had shaken his head at this point. "I'm not getting involved with a killer, I am helping someone who is having trouble with something and it turns out that it comes back to this house."

"Yes, THIS HOUSE!"

Jodie rarely lost her temper with Patrick but when he was being stubborn to the point where it affected their son then she wasn't going to stand back and be little miss quiet.

"Jodie, it will be over before you know it."

"You know what Patrick?" Jodie tried to calm herself. In anger, her emotions became jumbled and tears would flow; something that she hated about herself. "I love you more than anything on this earth, except for Lewis. And I am *not* going to allow you to bring someone else's problems into this house and disrupt his little life just because their ex-lover used to live here. That is my final word on the matter."

They hadn't spoken much after the conversation

and Jodie had hoped that her words had been strong enough for Patrick to understand that she was dead against the idea.

As she lay on the bed, she propped herself up, resting the side of her face on her hand and watched Lewis as he slept in his cot. She knew that he should be in his own room soon but she just couldn't bear the thought of him sleeping alone. The door opened slightly and Patrick's head appeared in the gap.

"Can I come in?"

Without waiting for an answer, he entered the room. He caught a glimpse of his son asleep and knew that what Jodie was asking was completely appropriate. However, something inside him just didn't feel right when he considered ignoring it. Had his house not been at the centre of what was going on in Sam's flat then it would be easy to pass it onto another medium. But it was and so he felt like he had to do something.

"We agreed after Ross that we wouldn't let work life affect home life," Jodie said quietly.

"Yes, we did agree."

"So, what's changed?"

Patrick sat down on the bed, next to Jodie and without taking his eyes off his sleeping son.

"This house and it's direct involvement with

Sam. And it's for that reason why I can't ignore it, Jodie."

Jodie sighed and fell back onto the pillow. What could she do? When Patrick had something in his head that he had to do, there was no stopping him. And that is what bothered her. Not even his son could stop him, so what did that mean for them?

"Patrick, if you bring this to our home, I will take Lewis and I will not be back until you can prove to me that we're your number one priority."

Patrick felt like he had just been punched in the stomach.

"Are you serious?"

Jodie could only nod.

Patrick stood up and slowly walked over to Lewis's cot. Watching his beautiful baby boy was the most tranquil feeling he had ever experienced and his heart felt like it would burst with love and pride.

"Jodie, I think that you and Lewis should leave and when this is finished you'll come back and things will be ok."

Jodie stood up and feeling winded, couldn't think what to say.

"You're right, you and Lewis are my number one priority and that is why you and he shouldn't be in this house until I can sort things out. There are burial plots in our garden for Christ sake and Sam is being harassed by his dead girlfriend who, funnily enough, used to live in this house. So for both your safety and wellbeing I think it is best that you move out for a few days until I can get this sorted."

Jodie was still, with no words. How could this be happening?

"Are you serious?" She asked.

"I don't want you to go, Jodie. But you're right; you and Lewis cannot be around this anymore. You have chosen to give up being a medium to be a mum to our beautiful boy and I don't want to be the one who forces this on you."

Jodie opened the wardrobe next to Lewis's cot and pulled out two hold-all's. She began to pack some items for herself but mostly Lewis's things.

"I'll help." Patrick said.

"No!"

Patrick stood back, feeling helpless at the situation. This house was supposed to be their new start, together as a family after what had happened with Ross.

Jodie must have been thinking the same thing.

"The only way we will ever work, Patrick, is if you give up the church too. We will only work if both our heads are at the centre of this family. It was ok before Lewis came along. But now that he is here, it's not ok for you to be working to help the dead and we're side-lined."

Patrick watched as Jodie packed the rest of the bags.

"I'll be at my parents until you've decided what you want more."

Chapter Twenty Nine

Sitting wallowing in his own pity, was not something that Patrick did often, however tonight he felt was an exception. He wondered what it was that he was doing, Jodie was gone from their home with their son and all that he could think about was the fact that some stranger was being haunted by some spirit who had once lived in his house. He knew it was ridiculous and that any other normal person would forget about it and get on with their own life; but Patrick felt a niggling in his stomach each time he tried to push it to the back of his mind. Would it have been better if they just sold the house and moved somewhere else? A new build without any history perhaps, or just somewhere that they could live in peace.

Patrick became distracted from his thoughts when he heard a sound from upstairs. He got up from the armchair in the sitting room and began to climb the stairs. He was getting sick of this life and not for the first time he began to seriously consider giving up his place in the church. It just wasn't worth all the hassle. He peered up to the landing and realised that the loft hatch was open. Patrick knew that he hadn't left it open. He jumped when the doorbell sounded and was opening the door before he knew it.

"Sam, come in."

Sam entered the house and stood still, memories flooding back to the last day that he saw Sarah.

"This place hasn't changed much."

"That's what having a baby does to your plans," Patrick replied.

"So, to be honest I don't really know what I'm doing here. But I had to come, gut instinct told me to."

Patrick nodded. "I know how that feels."

Patrick led Sam to the sitting room, having forgotten about the loft hatch. They both sat down and were silent for a short time.

"It feels strange being back here." Sam broke the silence.

"I can imagine."

"The last time I saw her was in this room, you know."

Patrick eyed him as he spoke, wondering where this was leading. "That day didn't end well?"

Sam shook his head. His face was shadowed by a sadness that shouldn't have been there. He was with Deborah now, he was happy. Things should have been getting better. But something told him something wasn't right.

"You ever get that feeling when you know something isn't right."

"Yes," Patrick replied. "In fact, I have that feeling right now."

"You do?"

Patrick stood up and Sam followed.

"I know that you probably don't understand what is going on in your flat right now, but I think I have a fair idea and considering that your ex used to own this house and you have come here tonight, that tells me that you're willing to find out."

Sam nodded.

"What are you thinking?"

Patrick began to walk towards the stairs.

"If you want to find out for yourself and you want my help, we have to do something that you probably won't feel that comfortable with."

Sam felt sick but he had to stop the feeling of uncertainty in his stomach.

"I'll do anything to stop what's going on in my

home."

***

As Patrick took his place across from Sam on the floor, Sam felt like his heart was trying to burst out from his chest. He could hear the blood in his ears rushing around as the adrenalin took over and a feeling of fear and readiness flooded his veins.

"I cannot believe I am going to do this."

Patrick smiled, remembering his first experience of a séance. "Normally there are more people involved but seeing as it is just the two of us then we may as well get started."

"Will it work if it is just the two of us?"

"So long as there is something that you need to know beyond what I can tell you, then yes it should work."

Sam took a deep breath and closed his eyes. Sarah Henderson's face flooded his mind. At first she was smiling, the way she always used to before she changed.

I didn't change, Sam. Things changed.

Sam opened his eyes, expecting to see her standing right there in front of him. The only person who was in front of him was Patrick.

"I assume from your expression you heard that too?" Patrick asked him.

Sam didn't answer, instead he thought it best to keep quiet and listen. He felt a change in the environment around him, it became colder and his toes became icy.

You have to help her. She is lost!

A different voice this time that only Patrick could hear.

Sam continued to sit quietly and seemed to be in a trance, listening intently to which he would only hear silence as the other voice filled Patrick's head.

Our girl needs your help. She has been accused of things which were not her fault.

Patrick opened his eyes to find Sam staring at him.

"I don't hear anything. Do you?"

Patrick closed his eyes, not willing to break the connection by speaking to him.

Sarah did not fall down those stairs. She was pushed!

Anna Henderson's voice was soft and clear, as if she were sitting right behind Patrick. She spoke with soft determination and Patrick could feel her energy becoming stronger the longer he listened.

Our lovely grand daughter's life was taken needlessly from her. She was the only one left to carry on the family name. That chance was snatched away from her. Someone who she loved and trusted took her life from her.

Patrick did not reply as he listened to a voice to which the belonging corpse lay in his back garden in a family burial plot. No wonder Jodie left.

You have to stop her before it's too late and she hurts someone else.

Patrick wasn't too sure where this was heading.

Sarah's time was forced upon her and she's in limbo, she can't get to you to ask for help, her energy is far too weak because she wasn't ready to go. That's why I am here.

Patrick opened his eyes. Anna Henderson was in his line of sight. Her hair was white with very fine, auburn strands running through it. Her glasses were thick and big frames surrounded her eyes. Her voice certainly didn't match her appearance.

"Patrick?" Sam's voice snapped him back to reality.

"Sorry, I was miles away. What is it?"

"It's not Sarah who's been causing havoc in my flat, is it?"

Patrick frowned. "Why would you say that?"

Sam didn't know whether to smile or run.

"Because I heard everything that you just did."

Patrick, Sarah was murdered. And by someone that she knows.

Sam stood up and then climbed back down the

loft hatch.

"Sam, wait!" Patrick called after him.

Patrick clambered down the loft hatch and was met by Sam's gaze. "You heard all of that?"

"Yes, I feel sick. How is it possible that, not only did I just hear the voice of a dead old woman, but I also just heard that Sarah was murdered?"

Patrick shook his head. "Maybe you're psychic?"

"Not funny."

Patrick closed the loft hatch and thought about the revelation they had both heard.

"Who would want to murder Sarah?"

"Someone she knew apparently. But I can't think of anyone. I never got to meet her friends and her family were all dead."

They found themselves in the kitchen. Patrick opened two beers and they sat at the table.

"I always found this house spooky," Sam said.

Patrick smiled but it barely lifted the corners of his mouth. "Now you know why."

Sam looked around the kitchen and took in its vast size. The ceilings were so tall you would need a large ladder to reach it. The place had such an old, vintage feel to it. With its size and lack of human occupancy, it should have felt empty. It didn't feel empty at all. It felt full.

"Do you think a house like this can remember things?"

"Ha, you even sound like a psychic."

Sam stood up and walked to the door which led outside to the grounds of the house. As he looked out, he could see the headstones. He remembered Sarah showing him once and it had scared him a little at first. But then, it made him think that the house had a bit of character; something that a lot of Glasgow's houses didn't have anymore. New builds were modern copy cats of one another with no feel to them. Sam had kind of grown to like the house before things had begun to go sour between him and Sarah.

"I mean, there is so much history inside this house. Do you think that because the Henderson family are the only family ever to have lived here, apart from you, that they will always be here?"

Patrick considered this. "I think that once Sarah has justice, the Henderson family will be just that; history. They will go off to where ever it is you go to when you die. They won't rest until Sarah's killer is behind bars."

CHAPTER THIRTY

Paul Preston had done nothing else but think about his retirement from the moment he had decided on a date. All he kept thinking of was he and his wife Janet lying on the beach six weeks of the year while the sun would beat down, washing away any stresses that they had. It was the only thing that would keep him going in the job. He only had six more months left as an officer and he would be done. The only thing that he would miss would be working with Jim every day. They had been partners for as long as he could remember and Paul couldn't imagine he would have lasted as long as he had without Jim by his side. He savoured his days off, but he savoured his days on more, those were the days which etched him closer to retirement.

Paul lay back on the reclining chair in his living

room, relaxing after dinner. Janet had cleaned up the kitchen and gone out to the bingo with Barbara, who was Paul's new step mum. Janet teased him about it but in all seriousness, Paul was glad that his dad had found someone after his mum, Liz had passed away from cancer five years previously.

Thomas Preston, who was also known to many as 'Auld Tam' was in his seventies and full of life; more so than some people in their early twenties in this day and age. He had been through a troublesome time since Sadie had died. At one point Paul had worried that his mum's death would kill his dad. He had sunken into himself and refused to go out or spend time with anyone other than Paul. It was a wonder he had come to meet Barbara at all; they couldn't have been more opposite. Barbara was a full of life, easy going lady with a lot to give. When she had met Tam at a charity gig for cancer, she had seen something in him which was hiding and bursting to come out. He had gone along to the gig only to support Paul, who had done a ten kilometer run with other officers, to raise money for Cancer Research. Paul and some of his colleagues were going to stand up and present the charity with a cheque for five thousand pounds, which they had raised during their run. It had turned out that Barbara was a volunteer fundraiser for the charity and got talking to Paul and Tam that evening. Tam would never had admitted to liking Barbara had it not been for Paul teasing him about it. It was from then on that Tam and Barbara had become companions. Paul and Janet had felt a wave of relief wash over them when they began to watch Tam return to his old self. He began socializing again and before they knew it, he had moved in with Barbara at her house. She had even dragged him into the twenty first century and he was now dressing with more style and using technology. He owned a smartphone, which Paul didn't even understand and he was using social networking. He would keep in touch with old school friends through Facebook and seemed like the happy Tam everybody knew and loved.

Paul heard the front door open and a voice called through.

"Paul, are you in?"

It was Tam and he sounded jovial.

"In the living room dad."

Tam waltzed in and sat down on the couch, removing his bonnet and jacket.

"What you so cheery about?" Paul asked, failing to hide the smile from his face.

"Uck, Barbara's only gone and won two grand

at the bingo!" He slapped his thigh as he chuckled away.

Paul's eyes widened. "Are you kidding?"

"I widnae joke aboot something like that son, it's nae good tae dae that tae the heart."

Paul stood up and walked over to his dad. He held out his hand and helped Tam up from the couch.

"This deserves a wee dram, don't you think?"

Tam rubbed his hands together. "Aye, noo yer talking son, noo yer talking."

They both walked into the kitchen and Paul pulled out a chair from the dining table, where Tam took his place. Paul opened the drinks cupboard and pulled out a bottle of whisky and two glasses. As he approached the table, Tam was tapping away on his phone.

"Who are you texting now?" Paul asked.

"Barbara, I'm suggesting a night away at that fancy hotel doon next to the bridge, what dae ye call it again?"

Paul shook his head as he laughed. "Too expensive, that's what I call it. Why do you want to go there anyway?"

"My beautiful lady has just won two grand, what else would we be spending it on?"

Paul poured the whisky into the glasses and

passed one across the table to his dad. It was great to see him so happy.

"So, other than winning at the bingo, what else have you and Barbara been doing?"

Tam sipped at the whisky and savoured the flavour. The warmth of the liquid trickled down his throat and he let out a gasp of pleasure as it did so.

"Uck, no much son. Ye know, at oor age we're just glad we're still breathin, eh."

"Nice and morbid dad, thanks for that."

Tam chuckled away to himself as Paul poured more whisky into their glasses.

"Aye, well ye just never know. I mean, look at Wee Rab, he died just the other day there. Just dropped doon deed while he wiz eating a fish supper. Poor auld bugger."

Paul almost spat his whisky back into the glass.

"Wee Rab died?"

"Aye son, did a no tell ye? Uck sorry aboot that, time gets away fae ye at this age. I must've just forgot."

Paul was in disbelief. Wee Rab had been his dad's neighbour since Paul had been a little boy and he was one of the nicest men you could ever meet.

"I can't believe it. How did you find out?"

"Norma phoned to tell me. She's cut up, the

poor soul. She went tae get him a napkin fae the kitchen and when she got back he'd collapsed on the floor. Died fae a heart attack."

Paul practically threw the whisky down his throat and poured another one. "When's the funeral?"

"Monday, ye going?"

Paul nodded. "Should pay my respects. I've known the man since I was a wee boy. Poor Rab, poor Norma."

Tam nodded and finished his whisky. They heard a key in the door.

"Dad?" A voice called.

"Uck, wee Janey's here."

"Grampa?" Jane replied.

Jane Preston appeared in the kitchen doorway with a big grin on her face. "Hi Grampa, nice to see you. How are you?"

"Barbara won at bingo."

Jane hugged her dad as she spoke to Tam. "Oh really, that's great, how much?"

"Two grand apparently." Paul answered.

Tam got up from his seat. "Excuse me, nature calls."

As Tam left the room, Paul put the whisky back in the cupboard. It was too early in the day to drink the rest. Jane sensed the tension.

"Dad, what's wrong?"

"Your Grampa just told me that Wee Rab died."

Jane frowned. "Who's that?"

Paul shook his head and led them into the living room. "Never mind, I'll tell you about it later."

***

Tam switched the bathroom light off and as he walked past the room to his left, he saw the computer sitting on the desk which Jane often used for her university course work. He walked into the room and switched it on. Tam had been terrified of technology before meeting Barbara and had no idea how anyone could work anything remotely more challenging than a typewriter. As he waited for the computer to load up, he looked around the room and saw pictures of his family dotted around the walls. There were photos of his wedding day to his late wife Liz, photos of his granddaughters Jane and Lisa and various holiday snaps. They made him smile. It was good to see Liz in a photo smiling; it helped him to forget the pain in her expression when she had been suffering from cancer.

The screen lighting up distracted him from the photos and he clicked on the internet icon. Google Chrome filled the screen and Tam typed into the search bar to find Facebook. As he clicked on it, he searched his mind for his log in details, however he found that Facebook was already logged into someone else's page.

"Jane, ye forgot tae log oot ya silly girl. Fraudsters are all over the internet don't ye know," Tam said under his breath as he looked at Jane's profile picture.

As he moved the mouse up to the log out icon, he noticed something that wasn't right. His eyes scanned the screen further and he found that the name didn't match his granddaughter's photo.

He clicked on the photo album and found photos of Jane with a man around the same age as her. He didn't recognise the male in the picture and the 'about' section was absolutely nothing to do with Jane.

"Grampa, what are you doing in here?" Jane asked.

"Oh, jeezo Jane, you scared me half tae death there!"

Jane walked over to the computer screen and stared in disbelief.

"Jane, I think there's something wrong with Facebook. It's your picture but the name isn't yours."

Jane nodded. "It's for university, I have created

a character page for one of my projects. Don't worry Grampa I haven't been hacked or anything."

Tam stood up from the computer chair and smiled. "Awe, that's a'right then. For a minute there I was thinking, who the hell is Deborah Bell?" Tam laughed as he walked out the room. "Just a'ways mind an' log oot. Ye never know who's trawlin' the internet, hen."

Jane returned his smile. "Will do Grampa."

Jane quickly deleted the Facebook account for Deborah Bell and switched the computer off.

"Shit!"

Chapter Thirty One

It's only a matter of time now. I mean, what am I going to do when it all comes out? Maybe I can just take off somewhere and not come back. But how can I leave him? How can I leave them? This is all just one big mess.

"You fancy a cup of tea Jane?" My mum asked as I stared at the television.

"No, thanks. I'm going to head out now."

My mum just smiled. She was the loveliest mum on the planet. This was going to kill her when she found out. It would be a lot easier if I wasn't in love with him or if I was one of those people who was devoid of emotion. To be perfectly honest I don't even know how I got to this place. It was meant to be a one night thing, where I could just fulfil my lust for someone and move on. But from the minute he kissed me I was completely hooked on him, his scent, his touch, his voice; everything that he stood for.

"That's me away dad."

"Ok love, you be safe. There are a lot of bad people out there."

I smirked inside.

There it goes again, that part of me that I hate. It can hide from me for months at a time, then it rears its ugly head when I least expect it. I hate that part of me. And if I hate it, others certainly will when it presents itself, which it will, eventually.

"I know how to protect myself dad. It pays to have a high up in the force officer as a dad," I said.

He kissed me on the forehead and I heard Lisa call down from the bedroom.

"See you soon Jane."

"Bye!"

My Grampa Tam tried to stand up but I stopped him.

"Don't get up."

I bent down and hugged him tight. It killed me that he had found that Facebook profile. It kills me that he thinks of me as someone kind, loving and upstanding. If only he knew, if only all of them knew.

"Have a good night hen, look after yersel."

I put my coat on and pulled my phone out of my

bag. I had three missed calls from Sam. I wondered what was wrong. It must be something; last time I saw him he said he was going to see that bloody psychic, Patrick something.

"Bye!" I called just before I closed the front door.

I was out in the night, on my own and to be honest, to have so many good people in my life I had never felt so alone. I was scared of the person I had become. I mean, what happened to Sarah was... crazy. I hadn't planned it and I had never in a million years wanted to physically hurt her, or anyone else for that matter.

But when it came to Sam, no one could understand how much it hurt. To watch him, hear him with someone else. I know, it started off as just a silly crush, after watching him as an actor in small time telly shows and stage shows. I was on placement in the theatre and I just couldn't take my eyes off him. He never noticed me, not once. Then all of a sudden, mine and my sister's best friend drops the bombshell that she's going out with him. I mean, how the hell did that happen?

I was absolutely distraught; my heart wasn't only broken, but shattered. It was one thing to know he may have a girlfriend but to know it was my best friend and hear all the sordid details of their sex life and how much he treated her like a princess, that was something else entirely. It was then, if I remember correctly that something inside me snapped. All I wanted was Sam and at that precise moment, I didn't care who got hurt in the process; so long as it wasn't me. I began doing things that would put a strain on their relationship. I listened intently to how Sarah had been a little jealous of Jenny and how she found it strange that Sam could be so close to another female and not have feelings or find her attractive. I listened as she explained to Lisa and how she had briefly spoken to Sam about her feelings and he had assured her that it was nothing to worry about.

Then I had an idea. What if I implemented something that would split them up, something that would keep them apart forever? So, I started to do things that would make Sarah look like a crazy jealous girlfriend. I started taking photographs of Sam with Jenny, looking happy and 'couple' like. I also took photos of Sam and Sarah together, Sam on his own, doing his own thing. I sent letters, messages and all sorts of stuff that made it look like Sarah had been stalking her own boyfriend. It drove them both crazy. So much so that he ended it with her.

I had been in her house when it happened. I heard the whole thing. I got excited when I heard him tell her it was over and she screamed and cried like a stupid, needy little bitch. Not only did I get excited but I was also scared to death at the person I had become. But I couldn't stop myself. It was like an obsession. It was then that the whole situation begun to get out of control and my plan strayed from a break up mission to something far worse.

**

My hands stayed in the position that they had taken to push Sarah down the stairs. Well, I say push, she sort of fell. When she asked me to leave, all I wanted to do was shut her up, tell her that she would never have Sam the way she wanted and that he didn't want her anymore. But I didn't say it, I just looked her in the eye and she could tell that I was smug about something.

She had come into the bedroom once Sam had left and saw me standing at the window, watching him walk away; she looked confused to see me there.

"What are you doing here?" She asked.

"I've come to see if you're ok?" I replied. "You've not been around much."

Sarah looked at me with sadness in her eyes, "I suppose you heard all of that."

I smiled gently. "Yes, are you ok?"

"No, I'm not. He won't listen, he thinks that I've been stalking him and his friend Jenny," she said.

I frowned. "How can you stalk your own boyfriend?"

Sarah was beginning to pace the floor, she was becoming anxious. Her eyes were a picture of crazed devastation. "You tell me how I can stalk my own boyfriend. Jesus, I wouldn't know where to bloody start."

I watched her as she paced back and forth, her brow glistened with sweat and I swear I could hear her heart banging around inside her chest. She stopped suddenly and looked in my direction. "How did you get in here?"

I hadn't thought of this one. Shit!

"I asked you a question."

I remained calm, "The door was open, I did knock but there was no answer so I tried the door and it opened. I just assumed you were in. I didn't think that you'd leave a house this size open for all and sundry to waltz in."

"Like you did you mean?"

I couldn't risk her finding out what I had been doing so I had to try to sway the subject back to Sam being unreasonable in thinking Sarah had been stalking him.

"You think maybe that it was Jenny? Maybe she was jealous of you and Sam?"

She didn't reply to my suggestion, she was

quiet. Too quiet; she was thinking.

"What is it, Sarah?" I asked but still she remained silent.

I watched her as she sat on the edge of her bed and I could see that her brain was working overtime. I was frozen; rooted to the spot. It was like time had been paused and the only people exempt from it were her and I.

After what felt like a lifetime, she looked at me with caution. She rose from the foot of her bed; I was still standing at the window. Her voice was almost a whisper.

"Oh my god, I can't believe that I haven't worked it out before now."

"What are you talking about?" I asked, curiously.

"It's you. You're the one who's been stalking him."

"Don't be so bloody ridiculous!" I spat.

She walked towards me slowly, eyeing me from head to toe. "It's not ridiculous, it makes perfect sense."

I laughed, "And how the hell do you work that one out?"

"When I told you who I was going out with, you couldn't have been more critical. You said things like, *He's only after one thing, He'll drop you for some theatre star, He's not that perfect and he'll break your heart.* And when I told you that I thought I had fallen for him, you couldn't even look at me."

My heart began to pound and my head began to throb. My palms had become clammy and all I wanted was to slap her in the face and get out of there but my instinct told me to remain cool and deal with what was coming.

Sarah began to smile and her eyes sparkled with the tears that were beginning to fill them yet again. "You're the one who has been sending the notes and photographs. You're clever, I'll give you that. I don't know how you've done it but you have."

She began clapping sarcastically. I was beginning to feel angry and I couldn't tell if it was with her or the fact that she had rumbled me. She had figured out what I had been doing and in all honesty, I hated the fact that she was being so smug and proud about it. I felt a burning desire in my stomach, it rose to my chest and then to my throat, like I would explode. But I pushed deep down, back to its pit. I wanted to launch myself at her, kill her right there and then. But I just couldn't bring myself to move. So all I said was, "So what if it was me?"

She shook her head. She couldn't take her eyes off mine, as if she was searching for answers, for the friend she once knew. Then she asked, "Why didn't you just tell me how you felt?"

I was stunned. Sarah sounded sad, not at all smug as I had initially thought. What could I say? Why *had* I done this? Even I wasn't sure how to explain it.

"Because I could," the words were out of my mouth before I had even thought of them.

Sarah walked to the door. My emotions were through the roof, I couldn't decide if I felt guilty, sad or pissed off.

"I still don't get why you're here?"

"I wanted to hear him tell you to get out of his life!" I snarled. I was surprising myself at how nasty I had become.

Sarah suddenly lost it; she began screaming through gritted teeth. She ran at me quickly as I stood at the window and grabbed me by the arm. "Get the fuck out my house before I phone the police and have you done for harassment!"

I pulled my arm from her grip and slapped her across the face, the stupid bitch had no idea what was about to happen and neither did I.

"Listen Sarah, you do anything of the sort and I *will* kill you, understood?" I hissed.

Sarah took no notice and grabbed my arm again, this time with more force and began to drag me out to the top landing of the hallway, all the while laying blows down on my head and shoulders. "I said out!" she screamed again. "You were supposed to be my friend and this is how you treat me. You're a psycho!"

I managed to shake her off and pushed her away. I hadn't meant to push her down the stairs, I just couldn't see where we were positioned on the landing because I was trying to protect myself from the raining blows to my head. I hadn't even seen her begin to fall, I only heard it. She thumped down, gravity pulling at her all the way to the bottom. No sounds or pleas came from her throat. I only looked up when my conscience told me something was wrong. When I did, I was horrified at what I saw. A twisted neck, a badly broken leg (I only knew it was broken from the angle in which it positioned itself once the body was still) and open eyes.

For a few moments I was thinking, *Shit! I have just killed her.*

And then as I looked on at the badly positioned corpse I thought, *Hang on, this is what I wanted, her out of the way.*

My advantage was that nobody had seen me enter the house, so straight away I am not able to be placed here visually. Second advantage is that I had stashed everything in a box under her bed. The hate mail, the notes, photographs of Jenny and photographs of Sam. A list of dates, times and places where Jenny had been with Sam, all of which were beautifully crafted by me, someone who had never met these people in person and the mobile phone used to send the messages. I had taken their numbers from Sarah's phone one evening when she had first started seeing Sam. I knew that they would suspect her and that Sarah would suspect Jenny. I was careful of my ways. I obviously couldn't have handwritten the notes, as that may have caused me problems. I made sure that all of those were typed on a computer that couldn't be traced back to me. Third advantage, I had made damn sure that I would not leave any prints behind, so I wore the black leather gloves that Sam had given Sarah as a gift; which she had raved about. Oh well, looks like they came in use for something other than winter. I'd stolen them from her on the night that I had taken Sam and Jenny's numbers from Sarah's phone. I needed something he had touched, something that would smell of him and would allow me to feel a little closer to him.

I decided that this was a blessing in disguise and that what had been done couldn't be changed. So, I slowly made my way down the stairway. I stepped over her body and took a last look before I made my way to the back door. She looked uncomfortable once she was dead. Her frame all twisted and out of shape; she must've bounced off every stair and piece of banister on her descent to have been looking like she was once she reached the bottom.

I know that it was not possible, but she looked through with those dead eyes. I hadn't thought about it before, what it would feel like to be stood over the body of the person I had killed. Well, like I said before, I didn't *mean* to push her down the stairs, I just meant to push her away from me and then she accidentally fell down the stairs. Either way, I had to leave, I couldn't risk being here a minute longer.

I bent down to have a closer look at her face, I guess you could say that curiosity got the better of me. I had never been that close to a corpse before. Her eyes were glazed over however there was a look of terror on her face. She must have known that she was going to die as she tumbled down.

I thought I would do the decent thing and provide her with the smallest amount of dignity and close her eyes, of course ensuring that I kept the gloves on.

I had the most horrid thought that she would jump up and finish me off and it almost stopped me from doing it. Of course she didn't, although I did have an unnerving feeling. Yes, I know I had just killed someone but I couldn't help but feel the hairs on my neck prick up when I touched her face. It was almost as if she was telling me that she was still there. My irrational thoughts quickly dispersed as I realised I would never have to deal with that woman again as long as I lived. And neither would Sam.

As I stood up, I looked around for any evidence that would have indicated my presence but couldn't point anything out, so I took a deep breath and made my way to the back door.

I slipped out unseen and made my way home. Sam's nightmare, as far as he was concerned was over, he had ended things with Sarah and then I killed her. But no-one would know about that; no one could ever know about that.

My brain was in over drive as I walked home. Everything that I had done in the last few months was because of my desire to split Sam and Sarah up. She asked me why I didn't just tell her how I felt. I had to be honest with myself and admit that I just couldn't answer that question, I really didn't know why I hadn't told her, it could've been the fear of rejection on her part or the fear of embarrassment. Whatever the hidden reason, it just didn't matter now because Sarah was lying at the bottom of the stairs in that huge house as dead as I am alive and for some strange reason I felt nothing. Nothing for Sarah but absolutely every feeling that is possible for a human to feel, towards Sam.

It's true, I am in love with Sam and I always have been, ever since Sarah met him. It was a crush at first from all of his TV and theatre work. I could always handle my feelings when it was just a crush, when he was just some actor on the stage. But when I found out that he was going out with my lovely friend Sarah, something inside me changed. I instantly changed the way I felt about my friendship with Sarah and I just couldn't stop the overwhelming feeling of wanting to see her suffer.

I know that my love is stronger than any other kind out there, as I have never heard anyone talk about their feelings the way I know my own. At first, I really did try to suppress these feelings because I knew in my heart and in my head that they were not healthy. But as time went on and my feelings for Sam grew, they began to burst out of me. I couldn't tell anyone, I didn't think that anyone would understand it.

If my feelings had been visible to the human eye, I'd imagined that they would look like a huge rainbow rising from my chest. As time went on, some of those beautiful rainbow colours which I imagined pouring out of me turned to a dark, not so pleasant shade. A shade which made me understand that my feelings were beyond love. I had become unhealthy in my feelings for Sam. You may go as far to say that I had become obsessed.

I am not proud of what I did to Sarah, but I am certainly not ashamed either. I was only doing what was best for the good of my heart. It was aching to see him with a potential future partner that wasn't me, even if it was my best friend. And she was my best friend for a while but I had to do something to scare her away.

You see, I hadn't ever *planned* to kill anyone. All I wanted was for Sam to notice me and perhaps fall for me the way I had fallen for him. I wanted him to be happy, but I just couldn't bear the thought of him being with anyone else.

I could never let that happen.

So now you'll understand what happened to Claire Prowse.

CHAPTER THIRTY TWO

I put the key in the door of Sam and Jenny's flat and paused before I turned it. What if that stupid psychic had started putting ideas in Sam's head? What if he had begun to suspect me?

"Don't be so ridiculous," I whispered to myself as I turned the key and opened the door.

I entered an empty flat; how comforting to know he was still with the psychic. I switched on the light and almost jumped out of my skin when I saw my own reflection in the mirror on the bottom wall facing the door. All this psychic talk was freaking me out. I dumped my handbag in Sam's room and went into the kitchen to switch the kettle on. I saw a bottle of wine sitting in the wine rack and decided that it looked more appealing than a mug of hot water with a tea bag floating around inside it. I reached up to retrieve a wine glass when I heard the front door open.

"Hello?" Sam's voice was smooth as silk as it floated through to the kitchen.

"Hi, do you fancy a glass of wine?" I called back.

I looked up to see his anguished face in the doorway. He nodded in reply.

"What's wrong?" I asked.

Sam pulled me into his arms and held me close, so close in fact that I felt like I was going to pop. "I went to Patrick's house."

I pulled away and looked up at the beautiful face which was tormented by his dead ex girlfriend. How could she still be in my way when she was dead?

"And?" was all I could manage but with a positive tone behind it.

"Did I mention that he has bought Sarah's old house?"

His eyes searched mine, though I am not so sure what for.

"Small world, eh?" Shit! Of all the houses in Glasgow, the psychic had to buy fucking Henderson Manor.

"He's pretty sure that he can figure out what's going on in this flat and he is certain that it is something to do with Sarah."

He released me from his embrace and opened

the bottle of wine. "You having one?"

I just nodded. I listened to the glugging sound from the bottle and when he finished pouring mine, I gulped a large mouthful down.

"Deborah, it's not going out of fashion," he laughed as he watched me.

I smiled. Why couldn't I speak? He was going to start getting suspicious. I had to change the subject. "Let's put the telly on and get more comfortable with that wine."

He smiled and followed me into the lounge. I felt his strong presence behind me and wished that everything and everyone could just disappear. I switched on the television and the news was just starting. We settled down on the couch and Sam draped his arm over me. I began to settle a little more now.

A recap of the recent headlines; it is thought that the recent discovery of a woman's body in the West End is murder. She was found to have one knife wound to the neck and was discovered by a young teenage dog walker at around six o'clock yesterday morning. She has now been named as twenty five year old Claire Prowse. Police are appealing for witnesses.

"Isn't that the girl who works in that café around the corner?" I heard Sam's voice distantly.

"I don't know, they've not shown a picture," I

said, trying to hide the dryness in my voice.

Just as the words were out of my mouth, there it was filling the screen; Claire Prowse's face.

"I thought it was her. Jesus Christ, that's a shocker."

I watched as the reporter went on to give more detail about the circumstances surrounding her death but I didn't hear anything. It was as if I had suddenly gone deaf.

"How could someone do something so callous?" I said, with as much emotion as I could push into the words.

"I know, it's awful; to think that she served us food not so long ago. She was really friendly." Sam said.

I know, I thought to myself. I remember just how friendly she was and how cocky she had been when we were in the bathroom of that restaurant; hence the reason she's bloody dead.

We heard the front door open and the sound of Jenny's high heels tottering down the hall.

"Hey; ooh, wine," her eyes widened and so did her smile as soon as she saw our glasses.

"The bottle is in the kitchen," I said, welcoming the distraction.

"Hey, Jenny; you remember that Claire girl from the café around the corner?" Sam called after her.

My stomach was lurching and I felt my head begin to throb. This just wasn't happening. I couldn't keep up the pretence much longer. I was pretending to be someone else to keep hold of my man. What the hell was I doing?

"Yeah; why?" Jenny was suddenly in the lounge clutching at a large glass of wine.

"She was murdered yesterday."

Jenny looked at the television and then back to Sam. "What the hell happened?"

"A knife wound to the neck apparently," I added. I didn't want to seem too quiet or they would get suspicious. *I* would be suspicious of me. What was I thinking about? Of course this would be on the news. But it's ok, because I wore protection. I wore the same gloves I was wearing when I killed Sarah. So my prints wouldn't be accounted for. It was strange for me to think about how I had killed Sarah and I had been wearing a pair of gloves which Sam had given to her as a gift.

"What the hell is the world coming too, when a girl can't walk down the street for fear of being stabbed in the neck, I know I wasn't the nicest person in the world to her, but no one deserves that?" Jenny said, shaking her head in disgust before sipping at her wine.

We watched the rest of the news in silence and I

tried to stop my shoulders from tensing up. I couldn't believe that we were sitting together, watching the news of a girl who had been murdered by *me* and my boyfriend and my friend were none the wiser.

Yes, Jenny and I *had* become friends as I had spent so much of my time at their flat. The more time I'd spent there, the more I had come to realise that Jenny was no threat. Of course, I knew she wasn't a threat; I was the one who had created that illusion, but with Sam having become so precious to me, I couldn't help but worry that someone, anyone could have snatched him away at any point. I would go as far as to say that she was one of my closest friends. But I knew that all of this was a lie; all of it. The only truth was my absolute unconditional love for Sam. I don't think there is anything on this earth that he could do that would make me second guess my love for him. If he told me that he had murdered someone in cold blood, I genuinely think I would be ok to move past it. But I know that there is no way he would feel the same. If he knew what I had done, what I have done to be with him, then he would cut all ties with me.

I had to remind myself that this little fantasy story that I was living would be coming to an end relatively soon. Sam knew me as Deborah Bell, mysterious and fun. I hadn't ever given him the opportunity to meet my family because there was absolutely no way around it. I mean, how the hell would I explain firstly that my name is not my name? And secondly, Lisa would instantly figure everything out. My sister was like my dad in that sense, she had traits of being a good detective and not a lot of things got past her. That is why I had kept all of this a complete secret. I didn't mention anything about a relationship with anyone. The only thing I ever mentioned was my friend from university. I didn't divulge any information about how I met her, who she was or where she was from. That would have been too dangerous. She would have worked it out in a second, even though she had never met Sam when he was with Sarah. Sarah had told her so much that she would have put two and two together.

My head was spinning from it all and even though I watched the screen, I was not listening to the words spoken by the reporter.

"I think I am going to head to bed. The wine has muddled with me." I said smiling.

"Ok, I'll be in soon. I want to watch the rest of this and see if there is anything else on that girl Claire." Sam said.

I felt sick.

"Ok, goodnight." I bent down to kiss him and then went to Sam's bedroom.

I undressed as I sat on my side of his bed and looked at the little photo in the frame of us together. Jenny had taken it; we had been sitting in the kitchen having dinner when she took it. It was my favourite thing to look at if I was feeling sad or scared, except for the real thing of course.

I crawled under the quilt and lay my head on the pillow. Memories of the night I killed Claire swirled around in my mind. She hadn't even seen me coming; she was just walking along the car park on her way home from work. It had all happened so quickly. I had taken a knife from Sam's kitchen and gone to the café to wait for her in the shadows. Sounds sinister I know, but I had to do something. She was too friendly and I know that guys like Sam may read the signs wrong- especially Sam. He is so lovely and he would read her signs of lust and passion as signs of friendship and end up in a compromising situation. What had really put the icing on the cake was the conversation in the bathroom in that café. The stupid bitch hadn't realised what I was capable of.

Claire didn't protest, she didn't shout out or plead. It was quick and easy, which scared me. It scared me how easy it was and how much of a thrill it gave me. Her life was in my hands and it was up to me whether she lived or died. I chose the latter. There was no choice really; I had to do it for the good of my heart. To be honest, I knew that what I was doing was wrong and I would be caught eventually but until that day was upon me I would do anything to keep Sam in my life. I knew it would hurt him when he found out what I was, who I really am.

As I drifted off, I felt the bed dip on Sam's side. I smiled gently at the thought of him cuddling in to me and falling asleep.

"Night baby," I said sleepily.

I felt his arm slide around me over the top of the quilt and I felt his breath on my ear.

"Not long now Jane."

The words that were whispered harshly into my ear made me jump out of the bed in fright. When I turned to face the bed, Sam's side was empty. It was then that I realised that the voice was female.

Sarah Henderson wasn't going to let me forget what I had done to her. And I was sure that she wasn't going to let me forget about Claire either.

CHAPTER THIRTY THREE

Sam woke up to find that he was no longer sharing his bed with Deborah and that she had left a note on his bedside table. It read; *Gone shopping, will be back soon. Love you. D x*

Sam stretched out and got out of bed. The room was cold and so he put on a pair of tracksuit bottoms and a t-shirt. He yawned and on exhaling he saw a white mist appear in front of his face. Was it *so* cold that he could see his breath? He was startled by the crash behind him and when he turned back to face the bed he saw a photo frame on the floor, face down with broken glass surrounding it.

"What the hell was that?" He found himself asking.

He picked up the frame and inspected the area around it. There was nothing that could have knocked it over, there was no breeze and he was no where near it.

Something made him look up at the mirror on his dresser and he drew back in fear of the face staring back at him. Sarah Henderson.

You are one big fool Sam.

Sam watched as the eyes became narrow on Sarah's face as she looked out at him. Her mouth did not move but he heard the words. What did she mean?

Sam closed his eyes and hoped that when he opened them, she would be gone from his sight. He felt himself begin to shiver and as he opened his eyes, he was relieved to see that she was gone. Sam got dressed quickly and grabbed his phone and the photo frame. He searched for the name in the phone's address book and pressed the call button.

"Patrick, its Sam, I'm coming over, I have something to show you."

"You sound shaken up, are you ok?" Patrick replied.

Sam exited his building and was half way down his street already. He didn't want to be in his flat any longer than he had too.

"Not really, I'll be with you in about fifteen minutes. I'm just getting in a taxi now."

Sam ended the call and told the driver where to

go. All the while, he clutched at the photo frame and replayed Sarah's words over and over in his head.

***

Sam walked up the gravel driveway towards the main entrance to Henderson Manor. He eyes scanned the entire building and thought about Sarah's death. What a lonely way to die. He found himself outside the door and before he could ring the bell, Patrick opened the door wide and invited him inside. Without saying a word, Sam handed the photo frame to Patrick.

"What's this?"

"It's a picture of me and my girlfriend Deborah."

Patrick frowned. "Why would I want to see this in such a hurry? No offence."

Sam turned away from the stairs to face Patrick. "Because when I woke up this morning, alone may I add, it was knocked off my bedside table with such force that it smashed."

Sam searched Patrick's face for answers. "There's no way you could've knocked it over by yourself?"

Sam laughed loudly. "So *you're* a sceptic as well as a psychic?"

Patrick shook his head and looked down at the

photo. "Who did you say the girl in the picture is?"

"Deborah, she's my girlfriend."

Patrick walked to the kitchen and Sam followed him, not daring to look at the bottom of the stairs. He had a horrible feeling that he would see Sarah lying there and he was already beginning to feel guilty about her death.

"Sarah's death wasn't your fault Sam, you didn't kill her."

"Someone else did though. I think she's trying to tell me something about her death. Why else would my flat have all these weird things happening in it?"

Sam looked up from the floor as Patrick sat down at the kitchen table. Patrick wasn't looking at Sam, he was studying the photo.

"This must have come down with some force for it to have broken into shards like it has."

Sam was quiet for a moment. He tried to put into order the words that he wanted to say. "Sarah was in my bedroom this morning, straight after that frame was knocked down. She spoke to me but her lips didn't move. It was like I heard her voice in my head."

Patrick nodded. "That's the way it normally goes. What did you hear?"

"She said I was a fool."

Patrick was quiet.

"What's wrong?"

"I think you're right, I think that Sarah is trying to tell you something about her death."

Sam sat, down across from Patrick. He feared the outcome of the events leading him to Patrick.

"So what do we do about it? I mean, this concerns both of us. After all, this used to be her house."

Patrick put the photo frame to one side and thought for a moment. He couldn't sort this alone, if Sarah was murdered, he had to involve the police. He knew the outcome of her death was concluded as accidental because Sam had explained it all to him. Patrick knew now that it wasn't accidental but he had to find a way of proving it to his sources.

"I have connections in the police. I'll get in contact with them today and see if they'll entertain me."

Sam sat back and seemed to relax at Patrick's words. "You think they'll listen?"

"They have in the past. I can't say for sure that they will again. You don't ask you don't get."

CHAPTER THIRTY FOUR

DS Paul Preston and DC Jim Lang were sat in the office, doing the least enjoyable part of the job; paperwork. If they had picked a job that was purely office based, they would have died of boredom long before now.

"My dad came over last night after dinner," Preston attempted to fill the silence.

"Oh aye?" Lang replied.

"Seems Barbara won big at the bingo."

Jim Lang laughed; in knowing Tam well enough he could tell what was coming next.

"I assume he wanted her to spend big on him?"

The shrill ringing of the phone pierced their ears and as Preston reached for the receiver he said, "Aye, he wanted to book them into some posh hotel down next to the Erskine Bridge."

Lang smiled and shook his head as Preston

turned his voice to that of a professional.

"D.S Preston speaking."

Lang continued shuffling papers and busying himself when one word made him look up.

"Patrick."

Lang narrowed his eyes and mouthed, "What does he want?"

"The Sarah Henderson case was closed last year Patrick."

Lang frowned.

"By all means, although I'm not sure how I can..." Preston pulled the receiver away from his face and stared at it.

"That was weird."

"What did he want?" Lang asked.

"He wants to talk to us about Sarah Henderson."

"Why?

Preston shook his head. "He said he has some information that may contribute to her case."

Lang stood up and walked over to the white board in the office. They seriously didn't have time to be mucking around with this ghostly nonsense again. There had been a brutal and callous murder and the last thing Lang wanted was Patrick hanging around saying the poor girl had come to him in his sleep or some other crap like that.

"Well, unless he's brought her back to life then I doubt there is anything we can do for him. What's he got to do with her anyway?"

"God knows but he sounded pretty certain on the phone."

Preston and Lang had been working on the Claire Prowse case over the last few days and they had hit a brick wall with the lack of evidence. There had been no murder weapon, no prints at the scene; nothing. Her face stared out at them from the white board in the office and Lang wondered, like he always did, how people could be so cruel, for such a young girl to die in such a brutal way baffled him.

"It would be more helpful if he had a lead on the bloody Prowse case, that's what we need right now." Lang said through gritted teeth.

"Her phone records should be back by the end of the day and the CCTV from the café where she worked should provide us with information on the people she had come into contact with over the last few weeks. If we spot the same person more than once, we need to speak to them."

"And the CCTV from the street cameras?" Lang asked.

"That should be back at the same time as the footage from the café."

Lang turned his back on the white board and exhaled loudly, demonstrating his frustration.

"I'll grab us some coffee, we're going to need it if Mr McLaughlin will be joining us."

Some things never change, Preston thought to himself.

***

Patrick walked into the station and felt a wave of déjà vu wash over him. He was transported back to the first time he walked through the doors of Pitt Street police station and remembered feeling scrutinized by Lang and not quietly by any means. He remembered the worrying look on Jodie's face when he had told her he was going to the station to tell the police about his knowledge on the murders of the girls in the city centre. He still thought about them from time to time. Patrick remembered how he felt when he imagined what it would have been like not to help them but to ignore them. It would have niggled away at him and their families would never have found justice.

That was how he felt walking into the station now, that niggling feeling in the back of his mind. Jodie had been so supportive the last time that it had almost killed her. Ross had almost killed her. Patrick tried not to think about that part of his life and what it may have been like had he not been adopted. It made him sick to his stomach. Now his mind was asking him if what he was doing now was the right thing for him, for his family. Jodie had walked away with Lewis, the two people in his life who he would take a bullet for, yet they were gone and here he found himself standing in a police station, once again fighting for the dead instead of the living. He just could not stop himself. Patrick could feel it in his gut that what he was doing was the right thing for the long term although he could not explain how. He knew Jodie and Lewis would be waiting for him when all this was over with. He just didn't know how long it would take.

"I'm here to see D.S Preston and D.C Lang," he said to the officer behind the desk.

Patrick waited for a few moments before he was greeted by Lang.

"Patrick, long time no see," Lang offered his hand.

Patrick shook his hand and then followed Lang back to his and Preston's office. Walking down the corridor took him back to that day again. Where he bared his soul to the two officers for the first time and remembered how Lang was having none of it. Preston had been kinder to Patrick and was willing to listen. He had the sneaky suspicion that history would repeat itself.

Lang opened the office door and allowed Patrick to go inside first.

"Patrick, nice to see you, to what do we owe this pleasure?" Preston stood up from his seat.

He heard the door close behind him and could be sure that he felt Lang's eyes burn into the back of his head. They all sat down and Patrick tried to figure out how to place his words.

Lang eyed Patrick with scrutiny, just like he did the first time they had met.

"You investigated the murder of Sarah Henderson last year."

Preston nodded.

"And her death was concluded as accidental." Lang added with certainty.

"Well, I bought her house earlier this year."

Again, Preston was silent. However, he heard a very loud sigh come from Lang. "Oh course you did."

"And what do you mean by that?" Patrick replied, failing to hide his annoyance towards Lang's ever so sceptic attitude.

"Gentlemen, it's like old times," Preston shook his head. "Patrick, unless you have something concrete that would make us consider looking into the death of Miss Henderson again then I'm afraid you're wasting your time."

"And ours," Lang said.

Patrick wanted to punch Lang square in the jaw but refrained from it. The thought of prison wasn't so appealing to Patrick.

"Like I said, I bought her house at auction earlier this year. Everything was fine until I got a visit from a Sam Leonard only a few days ago, telling me that he thinks he is being haunted by her."

Preston frowned.

"He's her ex-partner; we questioned him about her death. He knew nothing about it."

"He didn't know anything. Sam came to me for help and by pure coincidence it turned out that I had bought his ex-girlfriend's house. I made connections with other members of the Henderson family." Patrick was interrupted.

"Dead, I assume?" Lang asked with sarcasm.

"Yes, actually, there's a book of family archives in my loft. The house has a lot of history to it and the family were very wealthy. Sarah was the last surviving Henderson. Anyway, as I was saying I made a connection with one. Her name was Anna. She made me aware that Sarah was murdered."

Lang got up from his seat and walked to the

white board. "You see this here, Patrick?" He pointed to a picture of a young girls face. "This here is a murder enquiry and involves one dead girl and a loose killer. This is what's real, not your silly little ghost stories. So, if you don't mind."

Preston stood up. "He's right Patrick, we can't do this anymore. You had the chance to work with us and you turned it down. We did our job; this set up," his hands flapped back and forth between himself and Patrick, "it's dead and buried. Sorry mate, there's nothing we can do."

Patrick got up, feeling defeated. He made a last attempt. "There's one more thing. Sam gave me a photograph and there's something about it that I can't quite put my finger on. I was wondering if you could have a look."

Preston shook his head. "Right, what is it?"

"A photo of Sam and his new girlfriend Deborah, the frame was damaged by an unknown force this morning. Sam said he witnessed it himself."

Patrick produced the photo and just as he was about to hand it to Preston, he felt it pulled from his grasp.

"Did you not hear me the first time?" Lang said as he looked down at the picture. He fell silent as his eyes set on the people in the picture.

320

"What is it Jim?" Preston asked as he saw Lang's expression change.

For once, Patrick was still unsure what was going on. He knew there was something about that picture but he could not place what it was.

"What did you say her name was?" Lang asked quietly.

"Deborah, her name is Deborah Bell."

Lang looked up and met Preston's eyes. "That girl's name is not Deborah Bell." He said as he handed the photo to Preston.

"What?" Patrick asked in confusion.

Preston took the picture from Lang's hands and looked down at the faces. His stomach lurched and his face became pale.

"What's wrong?" Patrick asked.

Preston couldn't find his voice, his lips had gone dry. After what seemed like an eternity of silence, he finally uttered the words which changed everything.

"Jim's right. Her name isn't Deborah Bell, her name is Jane. Jane Preston. That's my daughter."

Patrick frowned, was he hearing this right, "Are you sure?"

"Of course he's bloody sure. You think he wouldn't know his own daughter?"

Preston sat down on his chair. "Why is she

going by a different name? And how does she know the ex-boyfriend of Sarah Henderson?"

The three men fell silent in the office. What now?

CHAPTER THIRTY FIVE

Patrick had called Sam and asked him to attend the station to meet with Preston and Lang. Preston was still very confused about the photograph which pictured his daughter Jane with Sam Leonard, even though Patrick had informed him that Sam had referred to her as Deborah Bell. There had to be some sort of mistake, surely. Preston had sent Lang away to see his doctor since he had been complaining about the persistent headaches and so he was alone in the office when Sam had appeared. Patrick sat down beside Sam, across from Preston and at that moment he had never wanted his colleague by his side more. He and Lang had a strong relationship and even though they could be snappy with each other, they had become the best of friends over the years. Their families had come together through the years for dinner parties and social gatherings and Preston couldn't imagine what his life in the force would have been like had Lang not been a part of it. Lang had felt the very same way and looked at Preston like a brother. It never did affect their work though, when something needed done it would be done properly and with precision.

"Paul, Sam is here to explain everything." Patrick said quietly.

Patrick had gone outside to meet Sam and had not explained in full why he had been called in. Sam understood that he was to explain why he thought that Sarah's death was not accidental, however Patrick was now beginning to slowly piece together how this assumption had come to be.

Preston stood up and shook Sam's hand.

"We meet again," was all he could manage.

"Has Patrick explained everything about my flat and his house?" Sam asked.

Preston nodded as they all sat down.

"So, you think we could be right? You think that Sarah may have been killed intentionally?"

Preston ignored the question.

"The photograph that Patrick brought in," he slid open his drawer and lifted the frame out. "Can you tell me who this is in the picture with you?"

Sam looked at Patrick and frowned. "Her name is Deborah. She's my girlfriend."

"Deborah you say?"

Sam nodded, unsure as to where the conversation was headed but with a gut feeling that it was not going in the right direction.

"Deborah...?"

"Bell," Sam drew out the surname slowly.

Preston turned the frame to face him and looked down at his daughter's face.

Patrick had gone into a minor daze and could see how this was going to pan out. He knew that what was about to happen would end Preston, and his career.

"You see, Sam. The woman in this picture is not called Deborah Bell. Her name is Jane, Jane Preston; my daughter."

Sam dipped his head forward slightly and laughed.

"You can't be serious? I'm trying to figure out if I'm being haunted by my ex who may have been murdered and you're pulling tricks like that?"

Preston remained sullen faced. This was not the kind of joke that would make him laugh, or even crack a smile.

"No joke, Sam. This *is* my daughter. Jane."

Sam looked at Patrick for support. Patrick shook

his head.

Sam got up quickly from his chair. How could this be happening?

"Forgive me for being a tad slow on the subject, but you say her name is Jane?"

Preston nodded again, beginning to understand the potential horror that could be about to tear his family apart.

"But Deborah and I have been together for close to a year, give or take a few weeks. I would've known if she was lying."

Preston shook his head. "And did you know that Jane and Sarah Henderson were best friends before she died? She and my other daughter were devastated when they found out what had happened to her."

Patrick had been quiet to allow Sam and Preston the time to unravel the mystery of what had been going on. He heard the handle on the office door turn and he spun around slowly on his chair to find Lang peep his head in. Patrick got up and went outside.

"You're back quick, everything ok?"

"Never mind that, what's going on?" Lang pushed Patrick aside and went into the office.

When he sat down and listened to the conversation, he was astounded by the revelations.

"Am I hearing this right?" Lang asked.

Preston was angrier than he had ever been. But he wasn't sure who he was angry with. He just could not believe what his daughter had been doing and he was angrier that he hadn't seen it.

Sam was slumped on the chair in front of Preston and felt like he had been knocked over by a truck. He had been living a lie for the past year. He had been dating someone who wasn't real, someone who had lied and betrayed his trust.

"Why would she pretend to be someone else?" Sam asked.

Patrick had been quiet for long enough. "Paul, I'm sorry to say this but I think you need to get Jane in for questioning about the death of Sarah Henderson."

Preston didn't want to admit it but Patrick was right. Everything that had been said over the past half hour led them to believe that Jane knew more about Sarah's death than she had first let on, one way or another.

"Paul, you know you can't be the one to deal with this. It'll have to be me or passed on to another team." Lang's voice echoed in Preston's ears.

Preston nodded in disbelief. His life had just changed dramatically in the blink of an eye.

"You just continue to work on the Prowse case and until I can get someone to deal with this, I will take it on. You ok with that?"

"Aye."

Lang led Sam into another room. He walked down the corridor, massaging his temples in rhythm with his walk. He was not prepared to let his health issues get in the way of work now, not after what had just happened. Preston needed him now more than ever and he could not let him down with his own problems. He would tell him when the time was right.

Sam stood beside the table in an interview room and his mind was going crazy. He felt like he was in one of his plays, like this wasn't really happening.

"Sam, we need you to talk to Jane."

Sam nodded. "It feels so strange when you say Jane," his eyes began to fill. "I've known her as Deborah the whole time. How could she do this?"

Lang shook his head. "How do you think it feels for D.S Preston back there? He's in bits and we need you to help us fix this."

Sam felt sick. "How can any of this be fixed?"

Lang sat down at the table and gestured for Sam to sit down too. The room matched Sam's mood; cold and gloomy.

"I am going to need you to phone Jane, arrange to meet her. Try to get the truth out of her."

Sam wondered how it could be possible. "I'm not so sure I can do this."

Lang bit his bottom lip and shook his head. "You don't have much of a choice son."

CHAPTER THIRTY SIX

I sauntered around the shops on Buchanan Street and for the first time in a long time I actually felt normal. No one knew who I was or what I had done and certainly no one cared. I looked at the people around me, going about their business with loved ones or on their own and I felt, safe. I thought about going back home to Sam after my shopping trip (even though I had not actually purchased anything) and it made me smile. I could not stop smiling to be honest. I looked in the shop windows and I looked up at the cloudy, bleak sky over Glasgow. It did not alter my mood that was for sure. I felt my mobile vibrating in my jacket pocket and I took it out to see Sam's name lighting up the screen. I smiled once again.

"Hey babe, what's up?"

"Can you come back to the flat?"

Something was wrong. His voice sounded, flat. It made my stomach flutter and not in a good way.

"What's wrong?"

"Nothing, I just want to ask you something."

He sounded odd. The kind of odd when you know something bad has or is going to happen and you know it is totally out with your control.

"So, ask away. I'm on a shopping trip babe; you can't ask a girl to interrupt a shopping trip, can you?" My attempt at humour failed.

"Just come back to the flat as soon as you can please."

The line went dead.

I began to panic, my skin began to tingle and my heart began to pound. My stomach felt like it was twisting inside to the point where it was going into cramps and I could feel tears begin to sting my eyes.

That's it, I thought. *He's had enough and wants to end it.*

I suppose I knew that this day would come eventually; I mean how could I spend the rest of my life with him when I was living my life as a lie? I turned and made my way back down Buchanan Street and turned left onto Argyll Street. As I walked past people in the street, I felt like I was being watched. Every set of eyes I made contact with bore into me like some sort of demon. Then I realised that every set of eyes I looked into were Sarah's eyes. She was everywhere and in broad daylight. It was like she was there, right in front of me, as alive as I was.

Of course I knew it was ridiculous but the more I tried to block it out the more I saw her. Then, the low hum of conversations all around me turned to one voice, with one word being said over and over.

Murderer!

I tried to be strong, I tried to show that I was not scared of her tormenting. It was then that I saw the other one. Claire Prowse. I did not just see her the way I saw Sarah, I saw Claire the way she was the very last time I saw her; lying on the ground with a stab wound to the neck. She was on every corner, every shop doorway. The street was littered with the vision of her death.

I put my head down and began to walk faster than my legs could carry me. Without looking up, I found my way back to Sam's flat and climbed the stairs slowly, slower than usual, to try to compose myself. My time with Sam was about to end and I was not so sure how I would react. I worried about my reaction. I honestly did not know if I would simply allow him to end things and I could go back to being myself, Jane, or if I would react differently.

I tried not to think about the latter, it concerned me that my reaction could physically harm Sam. I was sure that I would not be able to carry on living without him. The thought of life without Sam suffocated me.

I put the key in the door quietly and went inside. The place was silent, eerily silent.

"Hi!" I called out as cheerfully as I could.

"I'm in the kitchen." His voice was what I could only describe as dead, like his feeling for me had become I could only presume.

I walked into the kitchen and stood in the doorway, my bag swinging by my side and my stomach cramping so much I thought I would vomit right there on the kitchen floor.

"What's all the hurry to get me back?" I said, failing to hide the shakiness in my voice.

Sam's eyes were red, not from tears but from anger. I had never seen him look so mad. It scared me a little.

"Why haven't I met your family yet?"

What? I thought to myself. *What an odd way to initiate a break up.* "Excuse me?"

"I mean, we've been together for a long time now, you've met what little family I have. Why haven't I been introduced to yours?" His eyes blazed.

"I told you, my family aren't that nice. We have a history and not a good one. I don't want to spend any time with them and I certainly don't want you to have to either."

Sam shook his head. "So your sister Lisa, you don't get along with her?"

The vomit rose so quickly it startled me but I managed to keep it down. *How the hell does he know about Lisa?*

"I don't have a sister called Lisa, where did you get that from?" I asked. My hands had begun sweating and my stomach was so sore that it was travelling down to my thighs.

"Don't lie to me, I know." He stood up and walked over to me, with a look on his face which made me realise that this was not just a break up. He knew; he knew everything.

"You know what?"

He grabbed my chin and jolted my head up so I could look him dead in the eye. "You know *exactly* what I'm talking about Deborah."

I pulled away from him, shocked at his aggression. I was speechless; I never knew he had it in him to be so brutal.

"Or do you prefer Jane?"

It was then that whatever strength I had left had disappeared and been replaced by blind fear. I ran out of the flat and didn't look behind me.

CHAPTER THIRTY SEVEN

I found myself staring up at the house where it all began; my other life. The life which I thought I was able to control, the life in which I believed I could create and be happy. It turned out to be something which at first was incredible, I had never felt love like it in my life and to be honest before Sam, I never really believed that such love existed. He made me feel more alive than I had ever felt before, he made my heart beat to the point where I thought I would explode. Truth be told, I would have taken a bullet for that man; I would die for him. When we first came face to face, I could never have imagined getting to this point; in actual fact it was never meant to get this far. Had I just been honest from the very beginning, things may very well have been different.

Knowing that he had discovered my secret

changed things, he looked at me with disgust when he called me Jane. How had he found out? How could he know without me being the one who told him?

Of course, I figured out that it had to be the psychic. Ironic really, considering I believe them to be the biggest liars ever to have walked the planet. He was the only person I could think of and with everything that had happened in Sam's flat, it had to be the only explanation. My real name kept ringing in my ear with Sam's voice behind it. I never thought I would hear him call me Jane.

As I looked up at Henderson Manor, I wondered if this Patrick would be inside. I found myself knocking on the door and for a split second, bile had risen to my throat as I imagined Sarah answering the door. Of course, she did not.

My knuckles made contact with the thick wooden door and I heard the sound echo behind it. The early signs of winter were beginning as I looked up at the sky and saw the stars begin to twinkle. It was so cold and I could hear the gravel crunch beneath my feet. I believed it to be possible that if I ever saw Sam again, it would be my last time. I could feel it in the air and in my blood.

I heard footsteps approaching the front door but I was surprised when it opened to see a female standing inside. She looked at me with uncertainty.

"Can I help?" She smiled gently.

I couldn't speak.

"Are you looking for someone?"

I nodded.

"Are you ok?" She asked.

I finally managed to find my voice. "I used to be friends with the girl who last lived here."

We both stood in silence for a few moments. I had no idea what I expected her to say. I had no idea who she even was.

"Why don't you come in?"

I stepped over the threshold and averted my eyes from the staircase. Something made me question my own sanity. But then; I was already able to answer my own question. I knew I had lost it, but nothing could stop my irrational behaviour when it came to Sam.

"It's always hard to lose someone. Were you both close?"

Why was she being so nice to a complete stranger? She had no idea who I was and she had just opened her door to me. She seemed so kind.

"I'm Jane," I said. My voice cracked.

"I'm Jodie." She held out her hand.

Something caught the corner of my eye and I turned quickly to look.

"This is Lewis, he's a little rascal."

Shit! What the hell am I doing here, in this house? This isn't Sarah's house anymore, this is a family home; the psychic's family, the psychic who had just wrecked my life.

"I bet he is," I said with a smile.

The baby was strapped into a pram and it was then I realised that she was wearing a coat.

"Oh, I'm sorry, were you on your way out?"

"No, actually we've just arrived. Long story but we've been away for a while."

Probably would have been better for her if she had just stayed away. If this Patrick character wanted to go messing up my life, then he would pay for it. I had killed in this house before, I could certainly do it again if I had too.

"I should go; you've obviously got a lot on your plate. I just miss her, that's all."

Jodie shook her head. "Don't be silly, you came here for a reason. Stay for a cup of tea at least."

CHAPTER THIRTY EIGHT

Patrick sat behind his desk in the church and wondered how his life had taken such a turn for the worst. Jodie had taken Lewis and left to stay with her parents until he was able to decide what was more important to him; his family or his work in the church. To say the last few years had proven difficult for them would be an understatement.

When Patrick had become involved with the triple murder case in Glasgow two years ago, he could never have foreseen that he would have had such a personal involvement. It almost tore them apart and Jodie had almost died; hence the reason that she had given up her place in the church and decided to close the door on that particular part of her life. Patrick on the other hand had still felt like he had so much to give and decided to continue his work with helping people in the church. It was not until Lewis came along that he began to question his work and how it would affect his son; he continued with it all the same. When Sam turned up, Patrick knew he could not ignore him, when all said and done; Patrick's house was directly involved in the situation.

Patrick filed away the last of the papers on his desk and ran his hand over the top of his head.

"What the hell am I doing?" He said out loud.

Patrick picked up his phone and dialed Lang's number.

"Jim, it's Patrick. Listen, I can't be a part of this anymore. It's ruining my marriage, I know you're probably quite thrilled by this."

"I can take it from here," Lang replied.

Patrick felt relief wash over him as he picked up his jacket and locked up the church. He made his decision there and then that Jodie and Lewis would forever be his priority and nothing would ever stand in their way. He was honest with himself when he realised that this decision should have been made straight after Ross had died. There was nothing in the world that Patrick wanted more than to protect his family from anything or anyone that could bring them potential harm. He looked down at his phone to see there was a text message from Jodie.

I'm at home whenever you're ready to talk. Lewis is excited to see his Daddy. Love you. J x

Patrick smiled as he made his way across the street.

Partick was still bustling with people and traffic and as he looked up Byres Road, he decided that he would travel home by taxi. He flagged one down and gave his address. It had become dark and the wind had picked up and as the taxi was stationed at a set of traffic light, Patrick could feel the taxi swaying in the wind.

"They say there's a storm on the way," the driver said over the intercom.

"Aye, looks like it."

The driver was quiet again as they continued their journey, which Patrick was glad of; it would give him time to think about what he was going to say to his wife. He had no idea how he would explain himself and why it had taken him so long to decide that his life with Jodie and Lewis was more important to him than the church and the dead. Before he knew it, the taxi was approaching the house.

"You want me to go up the drive, mate?"

"No thank you, I'll walk from here."

Patrick paid the driver and began walking up the drive. Lewis's bedroom was in darkness and

Patrick understood that he was most likely to be asleep. Jodie was such a good mum and he would be eternally grateful for her commitment to their family.

Patrick approached the front door and realised that it was open slightly; that wasn't like Jodie at all. "I'm home," he called out.

Jodie appeared from the living room door and she had a mixture of emotions on her face. She hugged Patrick tight as and held on to him with every bit of strength she had.

"I'm sorry for what I've put you through. I should've realised what I had to lose *well* before now. What made you come back? Is Lewis doing ok? Are you ok?" Patrick could not stop himself from talking. He was so glad to see his wife back in their home.

Jodie smiled at him. "I'm fine, Lewis is fine and I came back because we are worth fighting for, don't you think?"

Patrick nodded.

"But before we go any further, I have something to tell you." Jodie said.

"What is it?"

Jodie smiled. "Someone is here."

Patrick looked through to the kitchen. "Who?"

"Someone who used to be friends with the girl

who lived here before us, she was really upset when I answered the door so I let her come in for a bit."

Patrick's stomach flipped. "What do you mean you let her in?"

Jodie was puzzled. "She was upset, I couldn't just shut the door in her face."

Patrick let go of Jodie and searched the kitchen and living room. Jodie frowned. "What on earth is wrong with you?"

"What did she say her name was?" Patrick whispered.

"Jane; and why are you whispering?"

Patrick gritted his teeth. "Where is she?"

"She went up to the bathroom to wash her face. What the hell is the matter?"

Patrick took his phone out to phone Lang.

"There's a strong possibility that she *murdered* the girl who used to live here. She's been impersonating someone else for the last year or so, so she could form a relationship with Sam Leonard, the guy who came to me for help."

Jodie's eyes widened. "Are you being serious?"

"Yes. Stay calm, I'm phoning Jim Lang. Just keep her talking and they'll be here within the next ten minutes. And don't let her know I'm here if she doesn't already."

Jodie began to climb the stairs and Patrick went inside the living room to make the call.

"Jim; Jane Preston is here, in my house. You'd better get over here now, I think…" Patrick's voice stopped dead when he heard Jodie's screams coming from upstairs. He dropped the phone and ran upstairs. He found Jodie in Lewis's bedroom. Lewis was not in his cot. Patrick searched all of the bedrooms but found nothing. He took hold of Jodie and cradled her in his arms.

Jane Preston had taken their baby boy as he slept soundly.

CHAPTER THIRTY NINE

Lang had arrived at Henderson Manor in around ten minutes after Patrick's phone call. He had stayed on the line after he had heard Jodie screaming and understood straight away what had happened. Lang had informed Preston of what had happened but no amount of reassurance from Lang could keep him and his family away.

"It is not a good idea for you to be involved now, Paul, you know this already." Lang had said. "I promise I will sort this and everything will be ok."

Preston shook his head in disbelief.

"How could she do this to us, Jim? How could she do it to them? I mean, that poor wee baby has been taken from his bed and taken to God knows where."

Lisa Preston, along with her mum and grampa,

were sitting in the back seat of the police car outside Henderson Manor. A uniformed officer was sat in the driving seat. Lang had gone inside with four uniformed officers and taken a statement from Jodie, who was worse than distraught.

"We'll do our very best to find them Jodie, I promise you that." Lang's voice was soothing, something that Patrick had never seen in him before.

Outside the house, Lisa was trying to come to terms with what her sister was being accused of.

"I can't believe that this is happening. I mean, Jane wouldn't harm a fly. Why all of a sudden is she being accused of murder and kidnap of a baby?"

Janet Preston wept silently as she stared out of the window, up at the house. How could her own flesh and blood cause so much chaos?

A voice came through on the radio.

"We've had a call in of a possible suicide attempt on Erskine Bridge south bound.
Young child present at the scene, we request back up."

Inside the house, the radios on the officers' jackets sounded out and the words echoed around the living room.

"It's her, I know it." Jodie became hysterical.

Lang felt bile rise to his throat.

"Come on, we're going. All of us."

Jodie and Patrick followed Lang out to the cars in the drive and climbed into the one Lang was driving. Patrick wasn't surprised to see Sam in the back seat.

"Are you two ok? I heard what that officer said on the radio."

"No, I'm not fucking ok. That psycho bitch has stolen our baby boy and is hanging off the fucking Erskine Bridge with him." Jodie said

Sam stayed silent.

"I think she knows the game is up, we'll get him back baby. He'll be ok." Patrick said.

"I'm sorry." Sam replied.

"Jodie, this is Sam, the guy who I've been helping since you left. He's been fooled by Jane too. She's been living under another identity for the last year. She's suspected of murdering Sarah, the girl who lived here before us. Sarah used be Sam's girlfriend."

Jodie did not reply. She turned her head to face out of the window, refusing to let the scream escape which had risen from her throat.

Lang rushed over to the car which was holding the Preston family.

"We're going now, if you insist on following

please don't get out of the car when we arrive. It will only encourage her to jump sooner."

Janet let out a sob in the back seat.

"I'm sorry Paul, I really am." Lang jumped into his car and all of the vehicles sped down the drive and into the street; sirens screaming along the way.

Turning onto Great Western Road and heading towards the Clydebank area, Auld Tam Preston had turned green with nausea.

"Paul, I need to tell you something," he said, trying to be heard over the sirens.

Preston turned to face him.

"What is it Dad?"

"The other day, when I was at your house; the day Barbara won at the bingo?"

"Aye, what about it Dad?" Preston sounded distant. He worried that his daughter would be dead by the time they reached the bridge.

"Well, I tried tae log on to my Facebook on the computer and I found a Facebook page already logged on. It was Jane's, but it wisnae her name. It was Deborah Bell but oor Jane's face in the picture."

Lisa looked over at her grampa's face and saw that he had tears in his eyes. "It's ok Grampa, you weren't to know." Lisa reached out and held his hands.

The car zigzagged in and out of the traffic at Anniesland Cross and sped through towards Knightswood.

"Aye hen I know that, but if I'd questioned her a wee bit more then maybe that poor wee wean widnae be up on that bridge."

Paul Preston turned round and focused on the road ahead. The car past Knightswood and sped along Great Western Road, passed Drumchapel and through the roundabout at Kilbowie Road. He watched the other police cars in front of them weave in and out of the traffic and couldn't believe that this time, they were on their way to the bridge to stop the attempted suicide of his daughter; who had kidnapped a baby.

"Paul?" Janet's voice penetrated his thoughts.

Preston slid his hand behind the seat and Janet reached out to take his hand. "It's alright. She won't jump."

Lisa closed her eyes as the car flew down the boulevard, past the Ocean Field housing estate and down towards the bridge. She pictured her sister standing on the other side of the barrier, holding that baby and she let out a sob.

The police cars in front slowed slightly, lights still flashing but sirens no longer providing a deafening ring to their ears. A police barrier had been set up at the entrance to the bridge and the officers at the scene lifted the barrier to let the cars through. Lang's voice came through the radio.

"Paul, this is Jim. Do not, I repeat, do not get out of the car when we reach Jane's location. If she sees you she might do something stupid."

Preston grabbed the radio. "So what the fuck are we supposed to do?"

Lang's heart was breaking for his colleague and friend. "Let me do my job. You can trust me."

Preston knew Lang was right. He had to keep his family in the car, they could not risk Jane seeing them. It could be disastrous for everyone involved.

"We're going to let Sam talk her down. I'll be with him too."

"What about the baby?" Preston asked.

There was silence for what seemed like an eternity.

"Our priority is to get Lewis to safety."

Preston nodded and put the radio down.

Lisa and Janet were crying silent tears as Preston watched Lang's car approach Jane's position on the bridge.

Jane Preston's daughter came into Preston's line of sight and he wasn't prepared for what he saw.

Jane had strapped little Lewis onto her back and was on the other side of the barrier. She had every intention of jumping.

The Preston family froze in horror. Screams could be heard coming from the car in front.

Jodie McLaughlin watched as her son was dangled over the Clyde.

CHAPTER FORTY

I looked across Glasgow as the lights twinkled and the wind grew stronger. The wind was cold on my face and I knew that the water would be even colder. I felt the pain in my thighs as I fought against the harsh elements to keep my stance on the bridge. The view was outstanding as I watched the lights twinkle across Glasgow. The River Clyde was almost directly beneath me and I knew that this was the best place to end everything. I wanted my last vision on earth to be a good one and that is why I picked the Erskine Bridge.

My mum used to take me and my sister Lisa there in the summer just at sunset, to let us see the beauty of Glasgow. It was a hard place to grow up sometimes and she wanted to show us that not everything in life had to be difficult, that we could make our lives sparkle, just like Glasgow did up on that bridge at night. She had a way with words, our mum. And she was such a fantastic mum when we were growing up. She still was. So what the hell had happened to me? When and why had I turned into such a monster? If this is what love did to people then I didn't want it anymore. All I wanted was to be happy and to make Sam happy. But he was not mine to begin with. Had I just left things alone, everything would be fine.

Something to my left caught my eye and I realised that there were six police cars on the bridge. I saw one of the cars doors open and my Dad's colleague Jim got out of the driver side. I turned away. There was nothing he could do to stop me ending this horrific pain. I looked out at Glasgow and took a deep breath. Just as I was about to let go, I heard the sweetest sound you could ever wish to hear.

"Deborah…"

I turned to see my beautiful Sam, standing beside me, close enough that I could reach out and touch him. I almost collapsed at the sound of his voice. I looked into his eyes to see they were blurry; he had been crying.

"Sam, what are you doing here?" I asked through sharp intakes of breath.

"Don't do this, we can fix everything."

I shook my head. He can't be serious, can he?

"What do you mean we can fix everything? You know who I am and what I've done. I'm a monster and I can't deal with this right now. You need to leave."

My legs were shaking and I didn't know if it was with fear or his presence. See what his presence does to me, my heart aches at the very sight of his face, my whole body goes numb. They say love is a beautiful thing; I think love is evil.

"I am not going anywhere until you come back over that railing and into my arms."

"You don't mean that."

Sam took a step closer, "Yes I do."

He held out his hand. I wasn't sure that I could trust him, with all the police here I was certain that he would just hand me over to them.

"I can't."

My eyes stung with tears and the wind battered my face. Then I heard the sound of a baby crying. My eyes widened. I do not know how, but I had completely forgotten all about him.

"Let me take Lewis, I'll put him in the car with Lang and then you and I can go somewhere where no one can disturb us, we can talk about everything."

I shook my head. "Why would you want to talk

to me after this?"

"Because," he said as tears fell from his eyes. "You went to all those lengths to have me as your own and you love me more than anyone has ever loved me. That has to count for something."

I was wary. Did he finally understand me? "But that psychic ruined everything."

"Is that why you took the baby? Deborah, nothing is ruined. We'll be ok. I promise. But it will only be ok if you give Lewis to me."

I thought about what he had said. Was he being sincere? I hoped with all my heart that he was.

"Ok." I said.

Sam carefully lifted Lewis from the strap on my back. "I'll be back in ten seconds."

Sam ran over to Jim and handed the baby to him. I could hear the many sighs of relief as Sam handed the baby over. I turned to face out again. It was peaceful considering the circumstances, I had to admit. Perhaps giving Lewis back relaxed me a little more. I wasn't sure that I would've jumped with him strapped to me. I just wanted that psychic to feel the way I had when he threw a spanner in my works.

I felt a hand on mine again, a tight grip. I turned and was stunned to see my Dad staring straight into my face.

"Dad... I'm sorry."

Never had I ever seen my Dad cry until now. I looked over at the police cars on the bridge and could make out that the psychic and his wife were cradling their baby. She was hysterically crying and the psychic held them in his arms. Then I saw my Mum, Sister and Grampa Tam standing beside one of the cars and they were all holding onto each other. My heart banged against my chest.

"What have I done Dad?" My voice squeaked.

My Dad took a deep breath and the tears spilled over. "You're not well sweetheart. What you have done is very, very wrong darling but you're my little girl. I promise whatever happens that will not change, do you hear me?"

I nodded and looked across to Sam, who had climbed back into one of the police cars and his gaze fell low, away from my eyes. He couldn't even look at me. I looked across at Lisa, who was sobbing.

"Jane, take hold of my hand and I'll help you over. Come on."

Jane. I was torn between Jane and Deborah; my life then and my life now. My life would never be the way it was. Never.

"I love you Dad. And Lisa and Mum and Grampa Tam."

My Dad's grip tightened on my wrist as I held onto the barrier. "We know you do sweetheart. Come on, over you come."

I twisted my body so I was facing my Dad. Then I let go. My Dad didn't catch me.

As I fell, my Dad's screams penetrated the rush of air in my ears as gravity took hold of my body. I was gone.

CHAPTER FORTY ONE
(ONE YEAR LATER)

The 'for sale' sign was finally stamped with SOLD and Patrick and Jodie began packing up the rest of their things almost instantly. After Jane's death they had both decided enough was enough and Patrick passed his leadership status at the church to the next medium in line. Patrick wanted to live life to the fullest with his wife and son and he did not want to think about death until he was faced with it himself as an elderly man.

Patrick had dealt with the courts and was able to have Sarah Henderson's body moved to her planned burial plot in the grounds of the Manor.

"This house would never have been ours truly, Patrick. It would always have been Henderson Manor no matter what we did with the place. And with the burial plots outside we would never have settled here." Jodie had said.

"I know. It's a sad but nice history to the house. At least they're all together now."

Lewis was now eighteen months old and an absolute rascal. They had decided to move into the cottage at Lomond Park for a while, to get some peace and tranquility and plenty of safe space for Lewis to toddle around in. Patrick and Jodie would never regret their time as psychics and they would always cherish the memories of helping others. But now their time was to be spent bringing up their son and Jodie wanted to be calm so that nothing would happen during her second pregnancy.

"I'll carry the big boxes out to the van and you get Lewis settled." Patrick said.

Jodie strapped Lewis into his car seat and looked up at Henderson Manor as Patrick put the last of the boxes into the back of the van.

"Do you think that a house can remember things?" Jodie asked.

"So much has happened in that house that I would be surprised if it couldn't."

Patrick climbed into the driver's seat and started the van while Jodie took one last look over the Manor. She looked up at the main bedroom window and even though she was used to seeing spirits, was shocked to see the whole of the Henderson family at the large window. Jodie blinked a few times to be sure what she was seeing was truly there.

She found Patrick at her side, looking up too.

"Tell me you see that too." She said.

Patrick nodded.

The Henderson family, all of them including Sarah, smiled as Patrick and Jodie climbed into the van and drove down the gravel drive and onto the street.

Henderson Manor was finally at peace.

***

Janet Preston opened the door and welcomed Jim Lang into the house. Today was the day of Auld Tam's funeral and Lang was not sure how Preston was coping; not on top of everything else that had happened.

"How is he?" Lang asked quietly.

"He's bearing up. He'll be glad to see you though."

Lang hugged Janet and walked into the living room. Preston was in the kitchen staring into the back garden.

"You alright?" Lang asked.

"Aye, I'm not bad. How's the head?"

Lang had been diagnosed with a brain

aneurysm just after Jane had died and had been told it was inoperable. "I'm still alive, if that's what you mean."

The two had been able to joke about it but with the death of Auld Tam, Preston was now worrying that yet someone else so close could be snatched away from him too soon.

"How do you find it?" Preston asked.

"Find what?"

"Not working on the force anymore."

Lang shrugged. "It's strange, I'll give you that. But it's nice spending time at home. You never know how long you have, eh?"

Preston nodded. "That's true."

Preston had decided to leave the police force after his the discovery of Jane's secret life. His decision was set in stone once CCTV footage had revealed that Claire Prowse's murderer was in fact Jane. It had all been captured on a street camera, right beside the car park where Claire had been stabbed in the neck. Preston never ever understood why his daughter ended up the way she did. But it had changed his life and his family forever.

Janet walked into the kitchen. "The cars are here."

Preston looked at Lang. They had known each other long enough to know the meaning behind that particular look.

"I know, mate. It is going to be hard but you'll get through it. I'm here for you buddy."

Lang put his hand on Preston's shoulder and walked out to the cars with Preston's family. Lang's wife was outside waiting by their car.

"It's at times like this where you need your friends around. I'll see you at the cemetery." Lang said as Preston, Janet and Lisa got into the car.

Lang and his wife, Mary got into their car and followed the funeral cars to the cemetery.

"I don't know how much more that man can cope with Mary, I really don't. That family has been ripped apart by their own daughter. It's at times like this you want your parents' support and he is just about to cremate his Dad."

Mary held onto Lang's hand. "I know sweetheart. But that's why you're here."

"Aye, but how long have I got left."

Mary sighed.

"You've got many a year left in you I'm sure. And if that time comes; he'll be there for me, just like you've been there for him."

The women in Lang and Preston's lives were most definitely the strongest women they would ever know. Janet and Mary had been the rocks of each family. Lang had worried about everyone other than himself once he had been given his terminal diagnosis. He had had a good life and had felt like he had made, if anything, a small difference in the City of Glasgow. He just hoped that whoever took over from his and Preston's post in the force that they would continue to make a difference to the city. Their time in the force was just a memory now and Lang wondered for just how long he would be able to conjure up those memories before his tumor would no longer allow it.

***

After the service, Preston disappeared from the crematorium and made his way out to see Jane. He walked slowly as approached her gravestone and a single tear dropped from his eye.

"Why did this have to happen to my family?" Preston dropped to his knees and wept like a baby. He felt a strong hand fall upon his shoulder and Preston attempted composure.

"Come on mate, let's have a whisky in Auld Tam's honour," Lang said as he put his arm around Preston and helped his very best friend back to the car.

***

Jenny got out of bed and picked up the post from the door mat. She searched through it quickly in the hope that there was a letter from Sam. When she saw the envelope and recognised the handwriting, her heart ached. She missed her friend so dearly. After the 'Deborah' situation, Sam had not been coping and had been turning down work. He had decided to leave and go to Australia for a year. His year was almost over and even though Jenny knew it was selfish, she was excited that he would be coming home soon.

She ripped the envelope open and pulled out the letter. As she read it, tears filled her eyes.

Dear Jenny,

How are you? My time in Oz is almost over and to be honest, the thought of going back to Scotland is making me feel sick. I am still seriously messed up over everything that has happened so I have decided to go to America for a while. Some friends I have met here have offered for me to stay with friends of theirs in Washington and so I have taken them up on their offer. I would love it if you would come out to join me.

I miss you Jenny but I just can't come home. Every time I think about it, I see her face and I can't bear it. I hope that you'll understand.

Lots of love

Sam

Jenny put the letter in her house coat pocket and went into the kitchen and switched on the kettle. The flat was so empty and quiet without Sam. Jenny knew he would never come home.

The flat would be empty and quiet forever.

EPILOGUE

The whisky flowed, the wine was poured and the dinner was served. Sarah Henderson was in awe of what was happening around her. If this was death, then she didn't mind it so much.

"The roast is perfect for a family reunion," Anna Henderson said as she placed the food on the large dining table.

"Are you alright dear?" Helen Henderson asked Sarah.

Sarah could only nod.

"We've waited on you for a long time Sarah, you must understand that." George Henderson said.

Sarah looked around the dining table at her whole family, ancestors and all. Henderson Manor was filled with every Henderson she had ever known of. She turned to her left and found her mother sitting next to her, Audrey Henderson. She smiled sweetly at her daughter and couldn't believe everything that had happened in... how long had it been? She couldn't be certain but what Sarah was certain of, Patrick McLaughlin had found justice for her and that was all she had ever wanted. He had somehow managed to have her body moved to its proper resting place; with the rest of the Hendersons' at Henderson Manor. Now she found herself in spirit, sitting around the dining table with the rest of her family.

"I can't quite believe how this is actually happening but I couldn't be happier that it is. I never thought this was possible."

As the conversation continued into the small hours, Sarah excused herself from the table and made her way out to the hall where she had met her death. She remembered how she had died and tried not to allow Jane Preston's memory to flood her mind.

Audrey Henderson was by her side then, looking down at her daughter's place of death. "I would certainly assure you that I wanted more for you in life than you had. It couldn't have been nice to have had to deal with what you did. I was with you the whole time."

Sarah smiled. "I'm glad I'm here, if this is death, then it's not as scary as I thought it would be."

The happy family sounds from the kitchen made Sarah feel at peace forever.

***

The estate agent closed the door of Henderson Manor and once again felt deflated. "You're sure you don't want to think about it a little more?" He said to the family he had just shown around.

The little girl in the blonde pigtails and pink dress tugged at her mother's skirt, "I don't want to live here Mummy; the people are scary."

The woman looked down at her daughter and then to her husband. "I'm sorry, if my daughter doesn't like it, then we're not buying."

The estate agent tried not to show disappointment, even though every family who had ever viewed Henderson Manor seemed enthusiastic at first and then by the end of the viewing said that they were no longer interested. Most of those families had young children. "Ok, what about the other properties we talked about?"

They walked slowly down the gravel driveway, the sound of their voices droning in the little girl's ears as she looked up at Henderson Manor. When she saw the old woman who was stood at the window of the room which her mother said would be her bedroom, she froze. The woman waved at the little girl and smiled before she was surrounded by several more people, all of different ages. They all wore very different clothing to the types of clothes the little girl saw her parents and even her grandparents wear. The oldest woman, whom the little girl had seen sitting in a rocking chair with a ball of wool and knitting needles, was now standing at a separate window and she was also waving. The little girl had been truly terrified when she and her parents had been looking around that house, although when she had tried to tell them that they were not alone in the house, they told her to be quiet as they listened to the man in the suit talk about the house and its history.

She continued to stare up at the house as the old people faded away from window. The little girl ran after her parents down the gravel drive way and never looked back.

The house would never belong to anyone else, it would always remain as it was, as it always had been; Henderson Manor.

About The Author

Emma was born in Glasgow in 1985 and was brought up in a small village on the outskirts of the city. She has always had a love of books and writing and began penning her first novel, Beyond Evidence in 2010. Beyond Evidence came from a love of the psychic world and so she thought she would write about what she enjoyed. Henderson Manor is the second book in the Patrick McLaughlin series. Emma has begun work on her third book and has decided to step away from the paranormal world... for now.

Emma is always writing and creating new stories and characters and will be forever thankful to anyone who picks up one of her books.

Emma currently lives at home in Scotland with her partner and two lazy cats, who love to curl around her feet as she writes.

8137566R00223

Printed in Great Britain
by Amazon.co.uk, Ltd.,
Marston Gate.